Dollar Bill

Triple Crown Collection

Dollar Bill

Triple Crown Collection

Joy

www.urbanbooks.net

Urban Books, LLC
97 N18th Street
Wyandanch, NY 11798

ISBN 13: 978-1-62286-925-1
ISBN 10: 1-62286-925-7

First Mass Market Printing October 2015
First Trade Paperback Printing December 2014
Printed in the United States of America

10 9 8 7 6 5 4 3 2 1

Distributed by Kensington Publishing Corp.
Submit orders to:
Customer Service
400 Hahn Road
Westminster, MD 21157-4627
Phone: 1-800-733-3000
Fax: 1-800-659-2436

Other Books by this Author

If I Ruled the World
Mama I'm In Love With a Gangsta
Girls From Da Hood 2 ("Wanna Be")
The Root of All Evil (Joylynn M. Jossel)
When Souls Mate (Joylynn M. Jossel)
Wet (Joylynn M. Jossel)
An All Night Man (Joylynn M. Jossel)
Please Tell Me if the Grass is Greener
(Joylynn M. Jossel)
World on my Shoulders (Joylynn M. Jossel)
Me, Myself and Him (E.N. Joy)
She Who Finds a Husband
Been There, Prayed That
Love, Honor or Stray
Trying to Stay Saved
I Can Do Better All By Myself
And You Call Yourself a Christian
The Perfect Christian
The Sunday Only Christian
Ordained by the Streets

"A Woman's Revenge"
(Anthology: *Best Served Cold*)
I Ain't Me No More
More Than I Can Bear
Flower In My Hair
Even Sinners Have Souls (Edited by E.N. Joy)
Even Sinners Have Souls Too
(Edited by E.N. Joy)
Even Sinners Still Have Souls
(Edited by E.N. Joy)
The Secret Olivia Told Me (N. Joy)
Operation Get Rid of Mom's New Boyfriend
(N. Joy)
Sabella and the Castle Belonging to the Troll
(N. Joy)

This book is dedicated to my Uncle John Allen Davis
(R.I.P. 2003)

Damn, I'm missin' you!

ACKNOWLEDGMENTS

My grandparents, Mr. and Mrs. Oliver Edwards, who believed in me and supported me without question.

Daddy, what can I say? I'm daddy's little girl. Thanks for telling me how proud you are of me EVERY TIME we talk.

Vickie and the TCP family, who is responsible for my first book deal. There are no words strong enough, and a mere "thank you" would be an insult.

My PR firm, Down to Earth Public Relations (Earth Jallow). We did it! All those years of working for me on the strength of belief instead of the almighty $ finally paid off.

Nick Ross, my son and daughters: MY EVERYTHING. Thank you for allowing me to do me and get the dang on thing done! I love y'all . . . live, breathe, and would die 4 y'all.

And although you had no idea you were inspiring me, Cheryl. Just know that you have inspired at least one person in life, me, and you didn't even know it. Imagine how many others you have inspired. Keep doing you (and keep writing those raps . . . what happened?). It's never too late to get into the game . . . Look at me.

For Trini of Chi/Gary, thanks for being my road map.

Uncle Billy, thanks for your insight and terminology.

Thanks, Sissy, Angie, and Uncle Johnny for always offering me your extra ends toward those printing orders in my self-publishing days.

Thanks, Mom, for everything.

Terri Deal, my hair stylist, thanks for repairing my hair after months of my pulling it out trying to meet writing deadlines.

CHAPTER 1

Popped Cherry

Where the fuck are my boys? Dollar thought as he held Cartel and his two partners at gunpoint. The four of them, each with their own degree of fear, stood terrified in the middle of Woody's Garage. Way down under in that place called hell, Satan and his advocates were probably taking bets on whose heart was beating the fastest. Niggaz are always loyal at entertaining the devil and his advocates. This situation was no exception.

Dollar nervously handled the black semiautomatic as he aimed it at the three men. "I swear, not one of you bitches better move," Dollar said to the men. Not taking for granted whether Dollar's word was bond, the men obeyed as beads of sweat expelled from their foreheads and could be heard hitting the cement ground of the garage like water droplets from a leaky faucet in the middle of the night.

"I bet your punk ass don't even know how to fire that gun." Tone, Cartel's bigmouth, big Jay-Z lip having partner, snickered. Although scared as hell on the interior, he had to test Dollar. He had to find out if Dollar was pussy in dick's clothing.

"You can probably hardly handle your own dick when you piss, let alone a gun."

Before Tone's chuckle could completely spill from his mouth, a bullet escaped the barrel of Dollar's gun and whirled past Tone's dome. Dollar just had to fire off a warning shot to let them muthafuckas know that he meant business. The bullet soared through the air, piercing the red can of paint that was sitting on a work shelf behind where the three men were standing. The red paint from the can oozed on the floor in sync with the trail of piss that was now running down Tone's leg. Tone felt the slight breeze the bullet produced as it whizzed by him. It was as if the kiss of death had been blown at him, making him lose control of his bodily functions.

"Now what, you bitch-ass ho?" Dollar said, surprising his own self that he could handle a gun. When he packed the piece, he never had any intention on actually using it. He had never used a gun in his life. Thank God the fear of ignorance hadn't paralyzed him and kept him from popping one off when he needed to. Now he just prayed he didn't actually have to put a bullet in one of these cats. He wasn't about killing niggaz; just taking their paper. That's all he'd ever been about: making dollaz!

A smile crept across Dollar's full lips, a smile that was a cross between a grin and a pout. The right corner of his mouth would slant upward and the left slanted downward. This was his "I'm that nigga" smile.

Not wanting to get too confident, Dollar kept at a couple of arm's lengths in distance from the men. He had seen enough action movies to know that the closer he was to the prospective victims without pulling the trigger, the more chance he had in lodging the bullet in his own skull. The slightest flinch made by any of the three dead men standing ignited a reflex, causing Dollar to simultaneously point the gun at each one of them. Back and forth, from one to the next, the gun steered, Dollar willing himself to keep his hand from shaking. This was not the time to show fear.

Dollar might have been doing a fine job of controlling his emotions, but there was one of his bodily functions that he couldn't control. The steamy stream of sweat occupying Dollar's hand made it a challenge to keep a firm grip on the gun. It soon became the weight of a cannon.

Dollar was squeezing his hand so tightly around the handle that his nails punctured through the flesh of the pit of his palm. The stinging from the sweat hitting the open cuts made Dollar feel as though he was holding a fistful of bumblebees that were stinging the hell out of him.

Underneath Dollar's baggy Levi blue jeans, his long legs had a faint tremble. He had to get himself under control. He couldn't lose it. He was too damn close. Actually, he was at the point of no return.

If his victims decided to bum-rush him, Dollar knew he was a dead man. This wasn't no old Western flick where he could shoot all the men in a matter of one point two seconds. He hadn't trained for that John Wayne shit. As a matter of fact, Dollar had never even played cops and robbers. He'd never stood in the mirror as a little boy pretending his hands were a gun, declaring to his reflection, "'Make my day.'"

Dollar knew, if need be, he might be able to hit one or two of the dudes, but all three? He had to silence the voices in his head. He was starting to scare his own self with all of the negative thoughts he allowed to constipate his mind.

Dollar couldn't help but wonder if Cartel and his dudes could smell the fear rising from up out of his pores. If not smell it, he wondered if they could see it rising like the vapor from a hot apple pie fresh out of the oven. Dollar had on his game mask over top of his timid face, but he still couldn't help but wonder if they could sense that he was just a pup at this robbing niggaz shit. He stood before these unlawful tycoons a virgin to the game, like a pussy that had never been fucked.

"Where the fuck are my boys?" might as well have been tattooed on Dollar's forehead. He gazed over at the door a thousand times, hoping to see them burst through. Through Dollar's actions, Cartel and his partners expected the company of some uninvited guests real soon. Not soon enough for Dollar though.

"You expecting someone?" Cartel finally found the balls to speak through his thick mustache. He sensed that Dollar was a rookie and one false move, or word for that matter, might compel his index finger to become trigger-happy. At the same time, from past experience, Cartel felt that if he petted the young pup on his head a few times, he could find a way to gain his trust and turn the tables.

"Where are your friends when you really need them?" Cartel said in a friendly tone, twitching his nose as if it was itching.

"Shut the fuck up!" Dollar replied. He couldn't focus on the door and engage in a conversation. He wasn't able to multitask.

"Young blood," Cartel said, pushing his luck. "I been where you at now, literally. I know what it's like to want to have everything with limited options of getting anything. But, yo, you're making a mistake here. I'm not the enemy. I can help you. The little shit you might yank off of us tonight ain't nothing compared to what I can make happen for you."

Dollar appeared to be comprehending Cartel's words. The only thing better than money was more money. Cartel had Dollar's attention.

Cartel slowly eased his hands down until he had a straight shot of his freshly manicured nails. "All I wanted to do was help you get where I'm at. I still can help you. Like I said, young blood, I been there, so I can't hold this against you. I won't hold this against you. We can do this shit. We can do it together. We can make money together."

Slowly Cartel's hands dropped just below his chin. His partners prayed he could continue stroking Dollar long enough to go for his piece. All the while, Dollar wondered where his own partners could be. He surmised that maybe they couldn't find the garage. Maybe they were just bullshitting around or arguing or something. The one thing Dollar did know was that by no means had they bitched out on him.

It was very possible that Dollar's partners were lost. Woody's Garage sat way back in an alley off of Cleveland Avenue in Columbus, Ohio, near a housing project notoriously known as Windsor Terrace. The black and orange SORRY WE'RE CLOSED sign was a permanent fixture on the building's entrance door. The garage was regularly closed to unsolicited guests but always welcomed those with an appointment. Cartel, who ran a shiesty hustle out of the garage, had penned in Dollar to meet with him that night. Dollar had driven in from Indiana in order for Cartel to make good on a transaction in the matter of a stolen vehicle.

Cartel was the mastermind behind a car theft ring. Not so much a mastermind as a man who managed to induce some young and dumb thugs into doing his dirty work. For less than a 20 percent cut of the street market value, these wannabe Dons would heist whichever vehicle was Cartel's flavor of the month. The other 80 percent must have gone toward what was known as administrative fees. Little niggaz didn't care though. A quick grand for their misdeed satisfied their adolescent appetites for life's material wants. If they weren't lazy and put in work every week, a quick grand averaged out to $52,000 a year. How the fuck they never managed to make a come up out of the hood on that type of salary was beyond insane. Dollar was determined, though, to get up out of the ghetto and he planned on taking his brother and his mother with him.

Standing there with his gun aimed, Dollar knew the move he had made on Cartel was foul, but a nigga had to do what a nigga had to do. He was sick of the grimy-ass lifestyle he, his mother, and brother were living on the streets of trifling Gary, Indiana. He had to do something. He had to make this move.

Yeah, this shit that's going down right here is for my peeps, Dollar tried to convince himself. He didn't need to work with Cartel, only his ride or die crew.

As he stood there in Woody's Garage, nervous as all get out, thoughts of growing up in Gary, Indiana spun webs in his head. He didn't want to struggle financially anymore, or see his mother struggle anymore. Dollar thought about having watched his mother leave their one-bedroom apartment for work at six o'clock in the morning and not return until after ten o'clock at night. At one point or another, she had managed to work for every fast food chain in America, as well as a few hole-in-the-wall neighborhood restaurants, just to keep a leaky, cracked roof over Dollar's and his younger brother, Klein's, heads. On most occasions, she would work at two and three joints at a time. Once, she got herself fired from Burger King because she kept referring to the kid's meal as a Happy Meal.

In spite of all the long work hours, Dollar's mother made sure that she did everything she could to see to it that he and his brother did well in school. It didn't matter how late she got in at night; going over homework was a must. Seeing their mother work so hard was probably what kept the two latchkey kids out of trouble the duration of their youth. The last thing they wanted their mother to have to worry about was two bad-ass boys running the streets. She already had to tolerate the white man's franchise all day long.

When Dollar was about twelve years old, one night his mother didn't come home from work as expected. They couldn't afford a phone, so it wasn't like she could have called to give a reason behind her tardiness. Dollar was too afraid to go out and use the corner store pay phone to call the police. He feared the boys in blue might take him and his brother away and put his mother in jail for leaving them alone at night in the apartment.

It was after midnight when their mother's sister, Auntie Charlene, came knocking on the apartment door. Dollar scooted the footstool over to the door. He stood on it and looked out of the peephole to make sure that the voice was that of his auntie Charlene.

Dollar unlocked the door and his auntie Charlene barged in like Ms. Sofia from the movie The Color Purple.

"Where's my mama?" Dollar asked his auntie Charlene, almost with tears in his eyes. Like a dog can sense a bad storm coming, children can sense when something's wrong.

Auntie Charlene stared into Dollar's sad brown eyes. "Don't question me as soon as I walk in the goddamned door, boy," Auntie Charlene said. "You and your brother just get y'all's shit and let's go. And don't be cryin' and carryin' on and such either."

Auntie Charlene, since Dollar could remember, had always been a bitter, hardcore type of woman. She knew it too. "Hell, yeah I'm a mad, bitter black woman. But behind every angry black woman is a nigga who made her that way," Auntie Charlene would reason. And let the streets tell it, she'd had plenty of men in her past, all no good for one reason or the other.

Auntie Charlene ordered the boys to gather some clothes and their toothbrushes because they would be staying with her for a couple of nights. She had always been a stern, no-nonsense woman, cussing a sailor under a ship. Thing was, though, she'd never directly cussed at the boys before. Something bad had happened, something bad enough to put fear in Auntie Charlene's heart and a dirty tongue in her mouth.

Dollar would soon learn that his mother had an accident while running after the city bus and had been taken to the hospital by ambulance. Their auntie Charlene comforted the boys' worries by assuring them that it wasn't a serious injury and their mother had probably only sprained her ankle.

Apparently, Dollar's mother had been a little late leaving her first job. As she headed down the street to the bus stop to catch the bus to her second gig, with only one more block to hike, she could hear the roar of the bus trailing up behind her. While running to the bus stop, the edge of her shoe skidded on a small pebble. She skipped a step, losing her balance, and came down with all of her weight on her right leg. She could hear a crack and felt a horrendous jolt of pain. She cried out in agony while she lay on the sidewalk, unable to move. After an ambulance was called and transported her to the hospital, she learned that she had broken her ankle and busted up her kneecap.

Once his mother returned home from the hospital, as the oldest, Dollar naturally became the caregiver for both his mother and little brother. Auntie Charlene did her part, too, but she couldn't be there for them twenty-four/seven. There were occasions when Dollar even had to help his mother use the bathroom or wash up. Around twelve years old at the time, this was probably one of the reasons why Dollar never got overly excited about girls like some boys his age did. He, unfortunately, had been forced to learn the female anatomy through the caring of his mother. This took away any future thrills of trying to grab at little tender nubs and booties, and stealing peeks at bald coochies.

Dollar never once complained about all of the duties and responsibilities he was buried in as a child. He thought that it would only be temporary and that everything would be back to normal once his mother fully recovered. Neither his mother, nor Dollar himself, ever dreamed in a million years that ultimately she would end up losing her entire right leg. Initially, her toe had to be amputated, and shortly thereafter, so *did her foot. Dollar was too young to grasp all of the details but he knew it had something to do with his mother neglecting a prior diagnosis of diabetes.*

After the initial amputations, only a few months went by before Dollar's mother ended up losing her entire right leg. The government had the nerve to deny her social security two times before finally giving in to her claim. Auntie Charlene convinced Dollar's mother to hire a lawyer, who in the end would receive a third of the retroactive benefits awarded. By then, Dollar's mom could barely afford to keep toilet paper on the roll. Seeing his mother in such a helpless condition murdered Dollar's young spirit.

Because their mother had worked so hard to earn that almighty dollar, Dollar and Klein thought that money was the answer to everything. Dollar and his brother did anything they could think up in an attempt to become instant millionaires. They had yard sales that consisted of their broken toys and old clothing. They even set up a lemonade stand. There was nothing more rigorous for Dollar and his brother than setting up a lemonade stand in the projects and trying to sell lemonade to people just as broke as they were. Everybody wanted a free cup, wanted to use food stamps to pay for a cup, or didn't have any money period. Dollar's heart was always bigger than his pocket, so most of the time he ended up giving away free cups on IOUs. Perhaps if Dollar had gone down on the price of a cup of lemonade, he might have made some sales. One dollar was pretty steep for only a Dixie cup of lemonade.

Everything that Dollar and his brother attempted to sell, Dollar would price at one crispy dollar bill. Whether it was a cup of lemonade, a broken old toy, or a painted rock, Dollar would hold the item up and yell, "Dollar, dollar. It's only one dollar, y'all," which was how he got the nickname Dollar. Pretty soon, everyone in the neighborhood ceased the use of his given name, Dareese Blake, and started calling him Dollar.

As Dollar and his little brother grew older, Dollar's brother decided that he would use his mind to gain riches instead of trying to get the crackheads and bums in the neighborhood to come up off of a measly dollar. His mother had always hammered the importance of education in her boys, so Klein set his mind to acing school and earning a free college education. His dream was to become a doctor someday, enabling him a plentiful income in order to take care of his family.

To Dollar, college was four years that he didn't have time to fool around with. Completing high school had already taken up four years of his time. College meant four more years of being broke. He decided that, like his younger brother, he too would use his mind to gain wealth. He would use his mind to think up a way to get fast loot.

Growing up in the projects and watching his mother shuffle from gig to gig, Dollar learned that everybody had to have some hustle in them in order to conquer life. Be it legit or otherwise, everybody had to have a hustle. It was the only way to survive.

Dollar came to the conclusion that he would let the love of money put its mojo on mankind. He would let the bankers bank, the pimps pimp, and the teachers teach. He would let the plumbers plumb, the thieves steal, the hoes fuck, and the ballers ball. Then, he'd catch them slippin' and rob all of 'em blind. This resolution was how Dollar would find himself with a firearm aimed at Cartel and his two partners.

Dollar portrayed himself to Cartel to be this eighteen-year-old kid from Indiana who jacked cars on a regular. Dollar had never stolen a bike, let alone an automobile. He convinced Cartel that he could present him with a white

*Benz with a gold kit and honey leather seats.
He ran down his bogus resume of a life of
carjacking and won Cartel's greedy ass over.*

*Cartel couldn't wait to brand Dollar as one of
his little accomplices to the good life. He never
saw this setup coming. He'd only seen dollar
signs.*

Dollar's reminiscing thoughts of growing up
in Gary, Indiana, were interrupted by Woody's
Garage's door suddenly flinging open off of its
hinges. At the same time, this startling occur-
rence would finally bring about some relief to
Dollar. Two persons dressed in all black with
black ski masks made their way through the
doorway. It was Tommy and Ral. Dollar's backup
had finally arrived. Cartel and his partners'
hands were damn near touching the ceiling now.

Without taking his eyes off of his targets,
Dollar said through gritted teeth, "Where the
fuck y'all been? Eleven o'clock, muthafuckas.
Eleven o'clock."

"Nigga, we here now and that's all that matters," Tommy replied while pulling out a 9
mm with Ral close behind following suit. They
each stood next to Dollar like statues with their
leather glove–covered hands gripping the guns
pointed at the designated targets.

In the midst of their captor's brief spat, instead of taking their chances and attempting to gain control of the situation, Cartel and his partners decided to remain submissive. If Dollar had planned on killing them he would have done it by now. They had a better chance of staying alive if they just waited this thing out and did as they were told.

"Strip," Ral yelled to Cartel and his partners as he walked toward them. The three of them looked at each other with their hands still in the air.

"Did you hear my boy?" Tommy asked. "Strip, take your muthafuckin' clothes off. What y'all niggaz waiting on, for us to throw y'all some dollar bills or some shit?"

"Yeah, to make it rain." Ral laughed. "Take all your clothes off and put them in a pile in front of you. Start by removing those pieces y'all carrying one at time. And don't try no funny shit either."

The three men slowly removed the guns they were carrying from either their back, hip, or calf holster. *Thank God.* Dollar hadn't slipped up and given them a chance to go for their shit. Time and circumstance was on his side after all.

The men laid their guns on the ground as Ral stood behind them with his gun to their backs. "Now the clothes," Ral said.

"Oh, y'all some faggots, huh?" Tone said as the men began to peel their clothes off slowly.

"Duck that ho right there," Dollar said to Tommy. "He talks too fuckin' much. As a matter of fact, duck all three of 'em. I don't want to hear their voices anymore."

"Quack, quack," Tommy said, obediently following Dollar's orders, pulling out duct tape.

Cartel laughed. "Perhaps you should have finished school. It's duct tape, not duck."

Tommy walked in close to Cartel, not happy at all that he was trying to clown on them. "Duck, duct, whatever. It's all interchangeable." Tommy tore off a piece of tape and threw it over Cartel's mouth. "See, I just ducted this duck's beak." Tommy let out a chuckle.

After a few minutes, the three men stood buck naked displaying only their jewelry and a strip of duct tape across their mouths.

"Trick or treat, muthafuckas," Ral said as he walked in front of them carrying a brown paper bag he had removed from his jacket pocket and popped open. "Check all that shit in."

The men began to drop watches, necklaces, and rings into the bag. They removed their diamond earrings and bracelets as well. That's what they got for trying to show off. Bling blinging and ching chinging was one of the tactics Cartel used to lure his employees into his ring. He wanted to show them the things they could end up owning. The bling ching to the baby thugs was the dead, raw fish being thrown to the killer whale to calm him into doing tricks. Dollar had studied Cartel and his crew's game like it was a textbook. He knew their steelo and was prepared to get paid off of their vanity.

Tommy went through every pocket of the pile of clothes on the floor. Some contained money clips filled with one hundred dollar bills. There were loose wads of money, also. The clothes were thrown to Dollar after they had been successfully raided by Tommy.

Dollar balled the clothes up under his armpit and headed toward the exit door. Tommy scooped up anything that slipped from Dollar's clutches.

"I want all of you to count one hundred Mississippis before you even consider moving. I mean, your dicks better not even get hard and start to rise or you're dead," Ral shouted. "Start counting now!"

Dollar, Tommy, and Ral looked around making sure they hadn't overlooked anything of value. Ral spotted what looked like a couple of cell phones lying on the worktable behind the men so he fell behind to go back and retrieve them.

Ral picked up the cell phones. As he skimmed over the worktable, Cartel looked to make sure that Dollar and Tommy's backs were still toward them. They were pretty much walking out of the door at that point. Cartel knew that between him and his two dudes, they could be quick enough to overpower Ral, take his gun, and use him as a shield to escape, after getting their shit back. Cartel couldn't risk word getting out on the street that some young punks robbed him for some jewelry and chump change. That would make the real niggaz think they could test him.

It was a risk to go after Ral, but it was one Cartel was willing to take. No way was he going to have his street reputation tainted by some punks. If Cartel allowed Dollar to get this one off, every little nigga Cartel had working for him would end up tryin' him and his crew. This was the last chance Cartel saw visible to eliminate future scenarios. So in his mind he said, *fuck it!* It was worth the risk.

Cartel ran toward Ral in attack mode. His partners were right behind him. They had only gotten to twenty Mississippi, but this was their chance to beat Ral down for his gun, pump lead into Dollar and Tommy, and get their money, jewelry, clothing, and egos back.

Dollar held the door for Tommy to come through and Tommy did the same for Ral. When Tommy discovered that Ral wasn't there, Tommy looked just in time to see the three men dashing toward Ral. Not one of the parades of bullets Tommy let off hit Ral, but Cartel and his dudes dropped dead like flies. Obviously someone had studied the old Western movies and practiced in the mirror.

"Whoa wee! Hell yeah!" Ral shouted as he looked at the three bodies piled up on top of one another. "Didn't I tell y'all fools not to move until you got to one hundred Mississippi?" he said to the corpses. "Perhaps you the one who should have stayed in school." He kicked Cartel's dead body. "You would have learned how to count to one hundred, fool, and that shit would have kept your asses alive."

"Let's get the fuck out of here," Dollar shouted as he snatched the cell phones from Ral and threw them on the ground. "Who the fuck was you going to call, man? Ghostbusters?" Dollar gritted his teeth in anger. "We got bodies on our shit now and for what, some fuckin' cell phones?"

"Fuck," Tommy yelled, still in shock at the sight of the dead bodies, one suddenly grasping for one more chance at life. Tommy began to wipe down the place with a shirt collected from one of the dead men, making sure that not a single smudge of evidence was left behind.

Tommy threw Dollar the car keys and all three of them ran out of the garage to the rental car that Dollar had some chick back home cop for them. They sped off, leaving nothing but tire prints and three dead men full of bullet holes.

"That could have been my ass lying back there fuckin' 'round with you two late-ass niggaz," Dollar said as he consistently looked in his rear-view mirror for any sign of the police or someone following them. "I ought to fuck y'all up."

"Did you see that shit, man?" Ral asked from the backseat, still hype from the gunfire. "Tommy laid them sons of bitches out flat. Holy shit. I could hear those caps poppin' they asses. Pop, pop, pop!"

"Tommy Gun to the rescue," Dollar said. "But I still ought to beat the both of y'all's asses for showing up late. Ral, you need to take your own advice about staying in school. You learn how to tell time."

"You need to quit talking to me like I'm some dude," Tommy, who was sitting in the passenger seat, said, removing the baseball cap from her head and allowing her long, jailhouse braids to fall down her back.

"Aw, you know you like one of the guys, Tommy, so quit trying to play all sensitive," Dollar said, lightly punching her on her shoulder with his fist. "I consider you to be one of my boys. You've always been one of the boys, you know that."

Dollar loved teasing Tommy about being a tomboy. She tried to act like it didn't bother her, but Dollar knew it did. Nonetheless, he still teased her. The only time Tommy ever looked like a girl was when she was defending her womanhood. All that neck snappin' was a given.

"Well, I got the goods to prove I'm all woman," Tommy said, rolling her eyes and snappin' her neck out like an ostrich.

"Don't talk like that. I'm not trying to visualize you with a pussy," Ral yelled from the back seat as he and Dollar began to laugh.

"Both of you can go to hell. This pussy done saved y'all's life many a time," Tommy replied. "Besides, I'd rather be a chick than a trailer park trash lookin' white boy."

Dollar continued laughing, but Ral's laughter faded quickly.

"Why you gotta make racial comments and shit?" Ral said, getting an attitude as he ran his fingers through his orange-red hair. "That's why I hate when a muthafucka save your life a couple of times. They think you always owe them something and that they can talk to you anyway they please. They be throwing it up in your face and shit."

"Quit acting like a bitch," Dollar said. "We got over $200,000 in cash and prizes and you back there crying."

Dollar always had to break up arguments between Tommy and Ral. He was the peacemaker of the trio. Besides that, Tommy and Ral were like family to him and he didn't want to see family beefing.

"Man, I'm just saying," Ral added. "Why I gotta be trailer park trash just 'cause I'm white? I'm just saying that shit ain't cool."

"Well, don't just say shit. Tommy done had your back since she was whooping niggaz on the playground for your ass. You do owe her."

Tommy looked back at Ral and stuck her tongue out at him.

"Well," Ral said lightweight under his breath. "Just let a muthafucka die next time."

"You think I won't?" Tommy said. "Talkin' 'bout some 'count to a hundred Mississippis.' What kind of shit is that? White people, man, I swear." She shook her head in dismay.

Dollar couldn't help but laugh as the three jumped onto 70 West, the interstate that would take them from Columbus, Ohio back home to Indiana. This was their first joint robbery and it looked like it would pay off pretty well. It was the end of a life of have-nots and the beginning of a life of having it all.

All Dollar wanted to do with his share was take it home to his mother. He was the epitome of a mama's boy. He felt just as proud to be in a position to give his mom some ends as a result of the Cartel stickup as he would have been if he were turning over a hard-earned paycheck to her.

Dollar hadn't thought of the lie he would tell his mother as to where the money had come from. If she knew what her son was doing, if the lack of will to live didn't kill her, the truth surely would. She had raised her boys to never put themselves in a position to encounter any sort of brush with the law.

Dollar had promised his mother that he would keep on a straight and narrow path and not end up like some of the other boys in the hood had: in gangs, in jail, or in the grave too soon. He had tried hard to be loyal to his words. His father had been anything but loyal to her and he never wanted to cause her that kind of pain again. Dollar's loyalty to his mother was fueled by his father's disloyalty to the family. Ironically, Dollar's loyalty to providing for his mother and brother would be the force behind him doing things that were against his mother's wishes.

Tommy and Ral, on the other hand, had engaged in some criminal activity before their task with Dollar, but nothing of this caliber. Tommy had a hustle flipping bank accounts. She would get people to give her their checkbooks and ID, make spurious deposits into the accounts right before the weekend, then spend the entire weekend on a shopping spree writing one bad check after another. She would purchase jewelry, clothing, food, and electronics, and use Ral on the instances when the owner of the checks was a man.

If the owner of the checking account was light skinned, Ral could get away with it by wearing a baseball cap. But being a white dude with red hair, it was hard for Ral to pass as a brotha. Nonetheless, he and Tommy would flip and split when they could.

After all had been said and done, Tommy would pay the owner of the account up to $1,500, depending on how much dirt she got away with over the weekend. Sometimes the collaborator would have special merchandise requests and Tommy would just shop for them instead of giving them money. Come Monday morning, the collaborator was to report their checkbook missing to their financial institution. By that time, Tommy and Ral had damaged the account severely.

When Dollar came up with the idea for the three of them to start robbing people, Tommy and Ral were game. They were ready for a bigger and better hustle. The shelf life of flipping bank accounts wasn't that long, so when opportunity knocked, Tommy and Ral were quick to open the door. Dollar, on the other hand, had just gotten his criminal cherry popped with the Cartel job. He had successfully robbed three occupational criminals. It wasn't in the plan to see them dead, but circumstance always determines the outcome.

No longer a pup on that night, July 4, 1994, Dollar became a Dawg. He, Ral, and Tommy had set the stage to become career hustlers. They had no intentions of stealing petty stuff or holding up liquor stores. Their hustle would be taking advantage of and profiting from other people's hustle. They would make a life for themselves by straight-out robbin' muthafuckas and pray to God that one day they never got caught slipping and had the tables turned.

CHAPTER 2

Got Money?

The title of "Stick-up Kid" just didn't seem to fit the bill: the Dollar Bill. This eighteen-year-old kid stood six feet and four inches tall, weighing 200 pounds. Dollar appeared to be anything but a kid. He looked more like a man with an innocent baby face. His smooth, baby-soft, honeycomb complexion added to his innocent look. He never worked out, but God decided to bless him with a nice little build. He wore his hair in a low fro, of which he picked twenty-four/seven it seemed. There was a peculiar poise about Dollar, a mystery that the ladies loved and the fellas envied.

As far as haters, there were none; none who spoke their piece anyway. It would be hard to find one person in the hood to say something bad about Dollar. As far as the block was concerned, Dollar was that kid who would grow up to be something, like LeBron James or some shit. He wouldn't necessarily play ball, but everyone was sure he'd do something noteworthy.

People still pictured Dollar as that little kid in the neighborhood trying to make a dollar the honest way. He didn't fit the stereotypical, dark-skinned, nappy-headed description of a brotha that most people inconspicuously feared when walking down the street. Dollar was proof that criminals came in all shades and personalities.

Dollar's suave and honest-like appearance worked for him. It was most appealing to the ladies. Sometimes when Dollar strolled the Indiana University campus, the oncoming females prayed that Dollar's fine ass would approach them. Little did they know that once he did approach them, after only a very few kind words of flattery, Dollar was snatching off their gold chains and running off down the street with them. This shit was funny to Dollar. It wasn't intended to be a part of a major come up. He just did it because he could.

Once Dollar realized that he had gotten away with it, he would toss the chain to the ground. He never actually wanted the chain itself; he just wanted the confidence of knowing that he could get it. Dollar couldn't recall where he heard about chain snatching, but it became his way of practicing being surreptitious and flattering.

While Dollar was practicing for a life of crime, his brother was practicing for a life of lore. His love for knowledge was just as intense as Dollar's love of money. Although the two had two different means of seeking riches, Dollar supported his brother's ambitions and made sure he showed his support with his actions.

"I'll give you this twenty-five dollars I'm holding in my hand if you can tell me how many ways there are to make change for a dollar," Dollar said to his sixteen-year-old little brother, waving the money in his face.

"293 ways," Klein responded, almost without thinking, as he scooped up the money from Dollar's hand.

This was Dollar's way of making his brother earn money from him. At first, Dollar was going to deposit a lump sum of money into Klein's bank account. Their mother had seen to it that Klein started the account back when he got a paper route. But Dollar didn't ever want his brother to grow up thinking that anybody was just ever going to give him something for nothing. So instead, every couple of days Dollar quizzed Klein, after which he paid him twenty-five bucks for every correct answer.

Without fail, Klein headed to the bank with the money in hand. It was twenty-five dollars more toward his college tuition money. Up until he and Dollar started their very own ghetto rendition of *Jeopardy!* the balance of Klein's account was only $203.52. After a couple of months, his balance grew to the point that it could cover at least his first quarter at the community college.

This made Dollar feel good, and it kept Klein on his toes. He was already one of the brightest kids in his school. Dollar knew how important college was to Klein and wanted to do everything possible to see that it happened for him. Although Dollar graduated high school, he had no intentions of ever going to college. Klein still admired Dollar though, and in his eyes, his brother could do no wrong.

That's why it was important to Dollar that, other than Tommy and Ral, no one was to have knowledge of his underlying demeanor. Dollar never wanted rumors about him skimming the streets and getting back to his family. That's why Dollar wouldn't even entertain the thought of having anyone outside of Tommy and Ral in his circle.

Tommy's evil ass never spoke to anybody, so Dollar never had to worry about her running her jaws. That's what Dollar loved about Tommy most. She was a mean-ass bitch and always had been. She didn't allow new friends in her life. Even if she did, they wouldn't have been friends for long. Unless a person knew Tommy from way back when, tolerating her attitude was impossible.

Back in school, chicks, and dudes too for that matter, couldn't look at Tommy funny without getting a beat down. She grew up fighting, mostly her mother's abusive boyfriends, so she was always on the defense. She hated the world and trusted no one, with the exception of Dollar and Ral. Dollar never questioned why, of all the people in the world, she'd let him in. He didn't have to question it; he already knew why. As tough as Tommy was on the outside, she was still just a girl, and Dollar had a way with getting girls to trust him. Besides, Tommy saw that Dollar shared the same theory as she did: that no one really could be trusted. Trust definitely had to be earned. Ral had obviously earned Dollar's trust, so it was almost by default that he'd earned hers.

Ral, on the other hand, was the Gary Indiana Crusader on foot. Because he pretty much lived on the streets, which he felt was better than staying at home with his junkie mother, he knew everything that went on in the streets. It wasn't like Gary was this huge town anyway. Most of the folks there commuted to Chicago to work and play. But if an ant was fixin' to piss, Ral had already informed everyone before a drop ever hit the ground. He was good people though and not seen as a threat to anyone. Folks only paid attention to half of anything Ral said anyway. Ral was somewhat of a walking joke in Gary.

Ral, whose full name was Ralphie Kennedy, ever since grade school, tried to pass himself off as one of the members of the prestigious and infamous Kennedy family. He pretended to be one of the family member's illegitimate kid or something. It was almost believable. This fool had studied everything about the Kennedy family from the great-great-great ancestors to the young, bad-ass cousins. Whenever Ral did come into some money or material things, anyone who would listen to him boast surely thought one of his rich relatives had sent it to him.

Ral was a year and a half older than Dollar and Tommy, who were the same age. Since his early youth, Ral had been in trouble with the law; nothing serious, but enough to have done a few months in the joint over a time span. Whenever they booked Ral, the arresting officer would always say, "Make sure y'all give this kid an extra blanket; he's related to John F. Kennedy." Of course everyone would burst out laughing, but underneath the laughter, a few were still curious as to Ral's bloodline.

The last time Ral was arrested was for petty theft, he had just turned eighteen so it was his first adult criminal offense. He had to do six months in the county. He ended up getting pinched because his loose lips bragged to some skank ho how he was the one who robbed a local electronics store of five DVD players in broad daylight simply by walking out of the store with them in his arms. When the owner posted a sign offering $1,000 in reward money, the slut dropped the dime on him.

During Ral's six months in jail he was raped. He learned the hard way about acquiring bragging rights. From then on, if he found a quarter on the ground he kept it to himself. He trusted no one; no one except Dollar and Tommy. They were the only ones who ever looked out for him and protected him. His own mother didn't even visit him when he got locked up. Dollar and Tommy were there for every visit. It was Dollar who did everything from yard work to cashing in aluminum cans to make sure that Ral had money on his books and soap to wash his ass. Dollar and Tommy were the only ones who ever wrote him a single letter. They were the only ones he ever told about being assaulted.

Dollar and Tommy ended up paying a visit to the chick who had dropped the dime on Ral. No one has seen her since. It was just unspoken that the three would never again discuss the girl or Ral being raped. This was the ultimate proof of loyalty in their friendship . . . or was it?

Since Dollar was the one responsible for setting their licks up, he was the designated purse holder of the Cartel robbery and any other robbery he, Tommy, and Ral were to engage in. Right after the stickup, Dollar distributed $3,000 to each of them to tide them over until they could split the entire pot after pawning, selling, and cashing in the material items. They had to either take the valuables they got off of Cartel and his partners to the pawnshop or sell them on the street. Once all the material items had been transformed into cash, the three were to congregate, cash in, and split the remaining proceeds.

At Chase Middle School, where the three met, Dollar, Tommy, and Ral would sit in the schoolyard and dream the same dream. With their dingy, torn-up clothing and holey tennis shoes, each of them would tell tales of how they would be "thousandnaires" (a thousand bucks was a lot of money to twelve- and thirteen-year-olds). Now, six years later, after the Cartel stickup, the three were thousandnaires.

Words couldn't describe how proud it made Dollar feel to be able to pay the rent for his mom. For his mother's sake, though, Dollar pretended to be going to work every day. He lied and told her that he had some construction gig laying asphalt. He would really be hanging out over Tommy's house all day or with some chick on the block who had noticed his new sophisticated, cocky demeanor.

Dollar had to let his mother think he was out making legitimate money so that she would take the couple hundred dollars a week he gave her. He went behind her back and paid off every debt she had so that the bill collectors would let her live in peace. He paid her utility bills down including the excessive balances that were accumulating in her PIPP accounts: accounts set up for customers below poverty level, which allowed them to only pay a small portion of their utility bill. She never seemed to pay close enough attention to the billing statements to even notice their depletion. Half the time she didn't even open the bills. She pitched them straight into the garbage knowing that she couldn't afford to pay them anyhow on her small, fixed income.

Dollar wasn't worried about filling his own pockets with his profit from the Cartel robbery. He was planning out stickups in neighboring cities and states that would give birth to his own personal come up. He would get his, no doubt, but first things first. He had to look out for his family. Since Dollar had officially become the true man of the house at the ripe age of twelve years old, he felt it was his duty to take care of his family.

Dollar was only three when his father abandoned them, never to be heard from again. Word on the street was that he got into the pimpin' game and mastered it. Dollar's father treated pimpin' like it was a franchise. He supposedly let one of his partners man his hoes in Indiana while he went to Detroit, Michigan to set up shop, and eventually to Ohio. Over a period of time, every ho in the Midwest would want his name tattooed on their pussy.

The authority of having the power over another human being's body went to his head. He became one of the most crucial cats in the game. Bitches, and his so-called assistants, feared messing up his money. Stories about Dollar's father and the pimp game were eventually overshadowed by success stories of the new entrepreneurial opportunity: slingin' crack.

Dollar figured that the hustle in him was the only thing he had inherited from that sorry excuse for a man known as his father. Dollar was determined to do for his family what his father didn't do. He would hustle, but only death or jail would keep him from taking care of his family.

Tommy was the complete opposite when it came to family. She'd bought her a little house right outside the hood in order to get the hell away from her family. Her humble abode wasn't in the suburbs or anything, but it wasn't suspicious either and that's all that mattered. Tommy didn't want anybody sniffing around trying to put the pieces together of her slight come up. She had to get a little job bartending on weekends to prove she had an income in order to keep Uncle Sam out of her business. The house wasn't much, but it was better than the two-bedroom house she had been living in with her mother, her mother's boyfriend, and her pregnant sister and niece. It felt good to just be able to kick back in her own place.

"Yo, T," Dollar, who was sitting on the couch in Tommy's living room, called to Tommy, who was in the bedroom. "Let me cop another one of these sodas." Dollar took the last swallow from the Coke can in his hand, pitched it in the trash, and grabbed another one out of the fridge.

"Nigga, you ain't gon' come up over here drinking up all my shit all of the time," Tommy said, entering the room with a brown paper bag in her hand.

"Must be that time of the month," Dollar joked, popping open the Coke can.

"For real," Tommy continued. "You and Ral always coming up over here eating and drinking up my shit. Come over with some shit in hand next time. Replenish a muthafucka's kitchen."

Dollar ignored Tommy as he watched her dump out the contents of the brown paper bag. Dollar bills flooded the coffee table. "Damn, T, have you spent any of your money?"

"Only what I've needed to spend," Tommy said, licking her thumb right before she began thumbing through the money for a count. "Let me guess," Tommy said. "You done tricked yours away like Ral, huh?"

"I'll beat my shit before I trick," Dollar said. "I had to take care of family matters. I ain't spending my shit on no hoes."

"Please, it's me: Tommy. I know all your business. Shawanda, Tish, Monique: all hoes. Don't none of them fuck for free and you with one or the other every other day of the week."

"I don't be fucking them tramps. I might let them sucky sucky, but that's it."

Tommy twisted her lips up and said, "Umm hmm, yeah, right," as she continued counting her money.

"For real!" Dollar defended himself.

"So you ain't spending no money on them?" Tommy asked with an underlying self-concern.

"I mean, shit, I done bought 'em some DQ or something, but I ain't never took one of them bitches out nowhere big or nothing like that."

Tommy began to laugh and replied, "I'm just fucking with you, Dollar. Calm down."

"So Ral trickin' tuff, huh?"

"Ral is trickin' his new money with every ho who gets a whiff of it. Whatever portion of Ral's money that don't get stuck down some ho's G-string, he puts in his arm."

"Word?" Dollar asked, puzzled.

"Nigga, please. Where you been?"

"Why you ain't said nothing before now?" Dollar said, becoming serious.

"Shit, I thought you knew Ral was on that stuff. Everybody know. If you pull your nose out from under them hoodrats' asses."

Dollar stood up and began pacing across the living room floor.

"You're kidding right?" Tommy laughed. "You really didn't know about Ral?"

"I ain't had time to babysit muthafuckas. I been making sure my family is taken care of and planning our next hit and shit."

"Relax," Tommy said. "Ral is a grown-ass man. What he does is his business."

"No," Dollar snapped. "What that fool does is our business. We the same muthafucka. If he fucks up, then we fucked up. I can see his ass now wrapped up in some bomb-ass pussy running his fuckin' mouth. Damn, T, you should have hollered at me on this."

"You know Ral likes street candy. Quit acting brand new. You also know that the last thing Ral is ever gonna do is tell some trick his business, especially after what happened last time."

Dollar and Tommy sat in silence, giving each other a knowing look.

"But that fool got a pretty nice hunk of change. That ain't safe for him if he fiendin' like that."

Tommy looked at Dollar and sighed. She balled her money up and placed it back in the bag. She knew what had to be done. She went into her bedroom with the bag in hand and came back out with car keys in hand. "You ready to go save that fool from himself?" Tommy asked as she shoved her braids up into a baseball cap.

"He ain't no good to the clique strung out," Dollar replied.

"A'ight," Tommy said. "Then let's go find this fool so I can get back to counting my shit."

Dollar and Tommy exited her house, jumped in her car, and scoured the streets until they learned that Ral was over at a house party on

Twenty-sixth and Connecticut. Some cat named Chico was throwing a party at his mom's crib, which he did every time she worked graveyard shift. That's how he made his lunch money: a lunch that consisted of clothes, weed, and hoes.

"Three dollars, niggaz," the li'l Martin Lawrence lookin' dude at the door said to Dollar and Tommy as they approached the house.

"I'm just looking for somebody," Dollar said. "I don't plan on staying."

"What the fuck we look like?" the little dude at the door said. "This ain't missing persons. I said three dollars."

Tommy sucked her lips, pulled out a ten dollar bill and handed it to the dude. He took the ten and waved his hand as to give Tommy and Dollar permission to enter.

"Keep the change," Tommy said sarcastically, realizing that's what he'd intended on doing anyway.

"Thanks, my man," the dude replied to Tommy.

She was used to being mistaken for a guy so she just proceeded through the door.

The male R&B group Jodeci's "Come and Talk to Me" remix was blasting through the speakers and niggaz was blazin' herb in every corner of the room. Tommy and Dollar shifted through the crowd of mostly high-schoolers. It didn't take long for the two to find Ral. He was in the half bath in the basement sticking a needle in one arm while some chick was sucking his dick.

"This shit right here is the muthafuckin' life," Ral said as he put the needle down on the sink and allowed his head to fall back. After only a few seconds he could barely keep his eyelids open. His mouth hung open as he began to moan at the almost immediate sensation of the high and the nut that erupted down the chick's throat.

"Now give me some, baby," the girl begged. "Now give me some blow, baby."

The girl wiped her mouth of any of Ral's cum that had managed to escape and removed the rubber band like object from around Ral's arm. She then placed it on her own arm. She picked up the needle from the sink that Ral had placed there and prepared the meal for her veins.

"Kick mud, ho," Tommy said, as she and Dollar entered the cracked door.

The girl was in a trance as she flushed her veins with poison. Just then Tommy and Dollar realized that Ral was sitting on the toilet with his limp dick hanging out of his pants.

"You want some too?" the girl said to Tommy, extending the needle to her.

"Hell naw! I don't fuck wit' no drugs," Tommy replied.

"No, baby, I mean do you want some of this here?" The girl pulled up her cheetah-print mini tube dress, lifted her leg, and allowed her nicely trimmed triangle to show. "You can get up in this hole for some blow. I do whatever you want me to: 'round the world, golden shower; you can even shit on me as long as you ain't got the runs. I'll fuck your friend too. It's good. You won't be sorry. Ask Ral here."

The girl winked at Tommy as she let the needle drop on the floor. She placed herself in a straddling position on top of Ral and began to laugh as if she was watching Richard Pryor's *Live on Sunset Strip*.

Beyond the point of disgust, Tommy grabbed the girl by her hair and yanked her from off of Ral. The girl began to scream and attempt to escape Tommy's clutch.

"Look here, Little Red Riding Every Dick in the Hood. If I ever see you around my boy again, you gon' be wearing your nipples as earrings. Pass it on to your other trick-ass friends." Tommy turned the girl loose and flexed on her, daring her to try something stupid.

It wasn't that serious as far as the chick was concerned. She straightened up her dress and went on her way. She brushed by Dollar, but not without him getting a free feel of her fat ass.

"What the fuck you doing?" Dollar asked, turning his attention to Ral.

"Nothing, now that you two cock-blockers are here," Ral replied.

"I'm serious, man," Dollar said. "Is this what you doing with your loot? Is this what you call your muthafuckin' come up?"

"I was trying to get up and cum, but you two fools—" Ral attempted to joke before Dollar grabbed him by his throat.

"You think I'm playing? You think this shit is a game?" Dollar shouted as Ral began to turn blue.

"Yo, D, let him go, man," Tommy said as Ral began his attempt to peel Dollar's fingers from around his neck.

"All those years of dreaming on the play-ground. We finally get just a little bit of loot and this is what you do with it," Dollar said becoming emotional. "Man, don't you want shit out of life? Or do you wanna end up like your mother?"

Suddenly Ral found the strength to escape Dollar's clutch. He tried his damnedest to take Dollar on but his little ass was no match. They tussled until Tommy managed to pull them apart.

"Don't ever talk at me about my mama!" Ral shouted.

"Will you two fuckin' stop," Tommy said. "You supposed to be boys. This is bullshit!" Tommy's eyes welled up with tears. Her frozen spirit wouldn't allow her to cry in front of anyone. She angrily pushed Dollar and Ral and stormed out of the bathroom.

Ral and Dollar remained in the bathroom breathing heavily from the energy they had used up tussling with one another. Finally Dollar spoke. "I'm sorry I talked about your moms, man," Dollar said, holding out his hand in apology.

"It's cool," Ral said, shaking his hand.

Dollar pulled Ral toward him and hugged him. He then pulled away. "Let me know now if this is the life you want," Dollar said. "Tommy and I are putting our lives on the line to get out of the muthafuckin' projects. We don't want to have to leave you behind, man. But if this is where you want to be, just say the word. If we know to expect this shit, then it won't be as disappointing."

"I want shit, man," Ral said, getting choked up. "I want out too. I want out too."

"Then the drugs, the hoes, man, you got to give it up," Dollar said.

"It ain't that easy, Dollar, man," Ral said, putting his head down.

"Shit ain't never been easy, but we've managed to overcome it, right?"

Ral nodded his head in the affirmative.

"Come on, let's go find T," Dollar said.

Dollar and Ral found Tommy waiting outside for them in her car. Dollar got in the front seat and Ral got in the back seat. None of them spoke a single word. Dollar put his hand on Tommy's knee. She tried to ignore him, but no woman, not even Tommy, could ignore Dollar's touch.

Tommy sighed and looked up into Dollar's radiant brown eyes. Still, no words were spoken. None had to be. Their eyes said it all.

Just as easy as the money came, it was going. The three couldn't resist spoiling themselves with some name-brand fancies such as shoes, clothing, and jewels. FUBU, Gucci, Lugz, and Figaro became necessities.

Before Dollar could start working on setting up their next job, the police were beginning to link the trio to the killings in Columbus. Eyewitnesses reported seeing the rental car leaving the scene of the crime. The plates were traced back to Budget Car Rental, where the vehicle had been borrowed.

A couple of detectives made their way to Indiana to question Bubbles, the girl who rented the car from Budget for Dollar. They shook her up so bad, threatening to charge her as an accessory and put her daughter in a foster home, that she gave them everything on Dollar except his blood type.

When the detectives arrived at Dollar's mother's apartment, she told them that her son was at work. She told them that they would be wasting their time with any questions they might have had for him because her son was a good child and didn't even as much as hang out with the wrong crowd.

The detectives waited outside the apartment in an unmarked car until they spotted Dollar walking up the porch. Dollar never saw the detectives approaching him.

"Dareese," one of the detectives said to Dollar. "Are you Dareese Blake?"

"Yes, uhh, no, uhh," Dollar stuttered. His smooth, suave stance must have only worked when dealing with females.

"Are you Mr. Dareese Ramelle Blake?" the second detective asked. "Aka Dollar Bill!"

"I'm Dollar," Dollar replied.

"We need you to come with us. We'd like to ask you a few questions regarding a robbery and triple homicide."

The detectives might as well have punched Dollar in the gut. A sharp pain darted through the pit of his belly. Dollar's head began to spin. He was dizzy to the point of fainting. There had to be some mistake. No way was this shit about Cartel and his boys. What did anybody care about some low-life criminals? No, this had to be about something else, some local shit. Yeah, it had to be. He hadn't been involved in anything local. He'd made it a point not to be, so he had nothing to worry about. He just needed to stay cool and calm.

"Will you come with us, please?" the detective asked Dollar.

As Dollar's eyeballs floated about the sockets, for a split second he thought about running. Did he have the strength? Where would he run to? Where would he hide?

"Dareese, Dareese," Dollar's mother began to shout from their living room window.

Dollar turned and looked at his mother in the eyes. It was as if her worst nightmare was manifesting right in front of her eyes. Dollar refused to make it worse by attempting to run and forcing his mother to see him get shot in the back and die right before her eyes. That would be the final straw for her. That would be the death of her for sure.

By this time, one of the detectives had sensed Dollar's temptation, pulled his gun out and placed it hard against Dollar's back.

"Go for it," the detective threatened Dollar. "I dare you to try to run. Every time your mother comes outside, do you really want her to see her son's blood stains in the cement until the rain washes it away? Go for it!"

Dollar took in a deep breath and then exhaled. "It's okay, Mama," Dollar said. "It's nothing, Ma. I'll be back in time for dinner."

"Dareese, baby, what's going on? Klein, Klein," Dollar's mother began to call to Klein who had been in the bedroom studying.

"What's wrong, Mama?" Dollar could hear Klein asking. Shortly thereafter, Klein's head peeked through the window. "Dollar, Dollar," Klein shouted.

"It's okay, man," Dollar replied. "You take care of Ma. I'll be home soon."

"Dollar, Dollar!" Klein continued to shout. "What's going on, man? Where they taking you? Please, Dollar. Please don't leave us. Don't you leave us too."

Dollar could hear Klein's voice cracking. It was breaking his heart. He wanted to break down right then and there, but he had to pull himself together.

"Who does the King of Diamonds represent?" Dollar said to Klein.

"What?" Klein asked as tears ran down his face.

"In a deck of playing cards, who does the King of Diamonds represent?"

"Man, I don't know."

"Yes, you do! Yes you do," Dollar insisted. "I got twenty-five dollars for you when I get back. Who does the King of Diamonds represent?"

"Julius Caesar," Klein said as he began holding his mother to comfort her. "The King of Diamonds in a deck of playing cards represents Julius Caesar."

The detectives cuffed Dollar's hands behind his back and began to read him his rights. They pushed and shoved him over to their car. Dollar was scared, but he wasn't going to let it show. He sucked it up and allowed the detectives to throw him into the back of the car.

The engine started and Dollar wanted so badly to look back up at his mother and brother who were broken up as they watched him from their apartment window. The car rode off. Even though it could have very well been the last time Dollar ever saw his mother and little brother again, he didn't look back at them. He didn't look back.

Dollar spent a total of fourteen hours and thirteen minutes being interrogated by the detectives. They asked him the same questions over and over again, sometimes switching words around in an attempt to catch him in a lie. Dollar stuck to yes and no answers. He didn't offer anything extra, which pissed the detectives off.

In the meantime, Dollar's fingerprints were being matched to those found on the cell phones in Woody's Garage. Once the detectives informed Dollar of this major piece of evidence, it was time for Dollar to start talking.

The detective suspected that Dollar hadn't pulled off the robbery and killings solo. No way did some young punk with no street respect take Cartel and two of his dudes down alone. The detectives wanted the names of Dollar's accomplices. If Dollar didn't tell, he would go down, taking all the heat alone for a triple homicide. He would very well spend the rest of his life in jail. If Dollar did give up the name of the triggerman and any other accomplices, he would go down as an accessory and walk away with a smack on the wrist as a first-time offender; that was the deal.

Although Tommy was the one who actually pulled the trigger, Dollar still knew that Ral would go down hard as well. Unlike Dollar, Ral wasn't in a position to be making any type of deal for himself. He had several strikes on his record that would guarantee him time in the slammer.

To Dollar, it didn't make sense for all three of them to go down. Besides, he couldn't see himself snitching on his partners and he especially couldn't picture Tommy spending the rest of her life in prison. He knew, without a mustard seed of doubt, that if the shoe were on the other foot, both Tommy and Ral would do the same for him.

Dollar had learned quite a few things about hustling. No matter the nature of the hustle, every hustle has the same rules. One can only get down with people whom they have 100 percent trust in. The clique had to be willing to die for the hustle, do time for the hustle, and Dollar was willing to do just that.

CHAPTER 3

Murder Was the Case

Dollar couldn't look at his mother after initially seeing her as he entered the courtroom in his jailhouse garb. When he first set eyes on her, she smiled at him. Her smile had always been a comfort to Dollar. Like the time he had a solo in the school Thanksgiving program. Dollar was so nervous as he stood on the stage. But when he looked out into the audience and saw his mother smiling at him, he knew that everything was going to be okay. That day, Dollar had a feeling that his mother's smile wasn't going to make everything okay.

Dollar's mother's smile quickly faded as tears began to fall from her eyes. Auntie Charlene sat next to her, hugging and comforting her as she wept endlessly. Dollar could see by the harsh look his Auntie Charlene was giving him that if by chance he did get set free, she was going to tear him a new hide no matter how big he was.

Dollar had to start thinking about things like sunshine and penny candy to keep from breaking down at the sight of his heartbroken mother. He had feared this day for the past few months that he had been in custody. Being charged with a triple homicide, bail wasn't an option for Dollar, so all he had was time in his jail cell to think about this day.

Dollar had failed his mother. He could only imagine the pain it was bringing to her. It was far worse than that D he'd gotten in Spanish when he was in the ninth grade. It didn't compare to the time he drank the last two cans of soda from the fridge and swore on Grandma Davis's grave that he hadn't done it. It was the type of failure that was an entire flight of steps up from telling a mother that her early teen child was about to become a parent.

If only it was as simple as Dollar impregnating some fast-ass chick from the block. Being incarcerated is the ultimate reflection of bad parenting to any mother. Dollar knew the years of his mother working so hard, even to the point where she lost a leg, were now proven to be in vain.

Dollar's mind was instantly taken over by the vision of Tommy sitting in the front row behind the defense table. "What is she doing here?"

Dollar said under his breath. Tommy could read his mind as she quickly stole a glance at Dollar's expression and put her head down in disobedience.

Dollar made himself clear when he put the word out that Tommy and Ral were to lay low. Dollar had psyched himself up to take the fall alone. He'd feared that Tommy's female characteristics would deliver her to the Franklin County Courthouse in Columbus, Ohio on the day he was to enter his plea. Now there she sat.

Dollar stared Tommy down as he walked to his chair at the defense table. He knew she had to lift her head sooner or later, and just as soon as she did, Dollar's eyes would be pinned on her.

"Don't do it," Dollar lipped to Tommy while shaking his head in the negative. "Don't do it." He could hear his heart beating as he just thought about Tommy being all dramatic and just as they were sentencing him, she'd jump up and confess her guilt.

Just then the judge entered the courtroom.

"All rise," the bailiff ordered.

The gallery stood up.

In Dollar's eyes, the man appeared to be moving in slow motion. He was the Grim Reaper in the flesh. This robed man held Dollar's fate in the palm of his hand and on the tip of his gavel.

He would dictate the outcome of the robbery
gone bad. Dollar's life, if there was to be any
more to his life, was in the judge's hands.

As the judge began to read aloud all the spe-
cifics of the case, Dollar's body became ice cold.
The judge's lips were moving, but Dollar couldn't
hear a word he was saying. He was zoned.

"Dareese Ramelle Blake," the judge addressed
Dollar. "You have been charged with three
counts of murder in the first degree. How do you
plead?"

The courtroom filled with the sound of Dollar's
heartbeat. The floor flooded with his pouring
sweat. The time was now. If Dollar was going to
vacate his commitment to the hustle then this
would be his last chance.

"Your Honor." Dollar gulped. "I plead—"

Just then Tommy stood up. Before she could
say anything Dollar's mother began to cry out.
"My baby," Dollar's mother yelled. "I know my
baby. He couldn't kill anybody. Please have
mercy."

"Order!" the judge shouted. "Order in the
courtroom."

Dollar turned to see his auntie Charlene caressing his mother. He wanted so badly to let his
mother know that her labor was not in vain,
that her firstborn son, although was capable of
murder, was not a murderer.

"Is there a problem, young man?" the judge said to Tommy, who was still standing, mistaking her for a man. "And please remove your cap."

This was the moment of truth. If Tommy was going to save Dollar from spending the rest of his life in prison for a crime that she had committed, then she had to speak up now.

Tommy removed her ball cap, balled it up, and stuffed it into the pocket of her oversized White Sox jacket. She and Dollar stared down one another like cowboys at a high noon shootout. In this case, though, no matter who let off the first round and no matter who was left standing, there would be no victor.

Tommy took a deep breath and spoke, "No, Your Honor. There's no problem."

Tommy quickly walked down the aisle way to the exit door. The door closed slowly on its hinges until she could feel it hit her back. As Tommy stood there while her eyes welled with tears, she heard Dollar's voice speak the words, "Guilty, Your Honor." Dollar confirmed, "I plead guilty."

"Yo, Dollar Bill," Ed, the coolest CO in the joint, shouted to Dollar. "She's back, man. What to do?"

"You know what to do," Dollar replied as he kept his face buried into this novel being passed around the joint titled *Gangsta* by this kid named K'wan. "I'm refusing the visit."

It had been five years since Dollar was sentenced to prison. It had been five years of his mother making attempts to visit him. Every month, Auntie Charlene, against her better judgment, drove her to Ohio, where Dollar was doing his bid, in hopes that Dollar would change his mind and join her in the visiting room. Dollar wouldn't pour salt into her wound by allowing his mother to ever see him caged.

Dollar had written his mother a ten-page letter apologizing and explaining why he couldn't bear to see her. Dollar wrote to his mother that if anyone asked about her eldest boy that she was to say he was dead. The same message was passed along to his brother. Life in prison, he might as well be dead.

Klein stopped trying to visit Dollar in jail a long time ago. He knew Dollar better than anybody did. When Dollar had made up his mind, there was no changing it.

Dollar wanted his mother and brother to continue life without the worry of him. He assured them that he could take care of himself and that they were to forget that he ever existed. There was nothing they could do for him while he was behind bars, so they need not waste time.

Although not having his big brother around hurt, Klein didn't sacrifice his education, something he had worked so hard toward. He continued schooling; as a matter of fact, he graduated high school a year early. Klein missed the hell out of Dollar, but now he was all their mother had. He had to be strong and move on, just like when their father left them.

Being sentenced to prison forever, forever ever, forever ever, was hard for Dollar too. He couldn't conceive trying to go on, especially knowing the hurt that he was causing his loved ones. The day the gate that separated him from freedom closed behind him was the day he considered both his mother and brother dead. That was easiest for him.

For some people locked up, it was their loved ones on the outside who kept them going, but not Dollar. He programmed himself to erase them from every seed of his soul. He had even gone as far as returning every single letter that anyone, including his mother and brother, had written him. Dollar waited for the month his mother would obey his wishes and cease her attempts to visit him.

Dollar hadn't communicated with his mother in years. Years, decades, or even centuries, though, could not have dissolved the deep-seated love and bond Dollar had with his mother.

"So, you plan on living the rest of your life not seeing your mama?" Ed asked.

"This ain't living, man," Dollar replied with his back against the cell bars as his eyes scrolled the lines of *Gangsta*.

"I guess you got me on that one," Ed said, walking away, allowing Dollar to continue reading his book.

Just like every other cat who gets jail time, Dollar spent his days pushing weights and reading. He didn't get into the Muslim loop, but sat in on a couple of Jumans just to kill some time.

A religious man in prison, Dollar thought. *Yeah, right. What I look like following the holy words of a criminal now claiming to be a changed man?*

Dollar kept to himself. He didn't ride with any crew. He was the respected prison lone wolf. He didn't fuck with inmates and they didn't fuck with him. He didn't look their way and they didn't look his. This was how Dollar planned on serving his time.

In the beginning, though, Dollar wasn't nothin' but an eighteen-year-old fresh piece of meat, especially to the old heads. Niggaz placed bets on who was gonna get in his ass first and make him their bitch.

Wojo was the prison roughneck back then, before he was released. He was feared by most and challenged by few. Wojo was one of them pretty muthafuckas, half white, half black, good curly hair, and gray eyes. He had tattoos all over him, everywhere from his neck to his hands. Wojo loved boasting about all the pussy that fell onto his doorstep before he got locked up. He enjoyed mostly bragging about the two bitches who sliced each other up over him. Wojo had a nice-sized crew. Plenty of cats had his back, but his best friend was his dick. With Wojo portraying himself as such a ladies' man, Dollar was shocked and caught off guard when Wojo and his crew set up shop in the showers to rape him.

Right before entering the showers that evening, Dollar had an ache deep in the pit of his stomach. Dollar had only been locked up a little under nine months. No one had tried him to date, but on this particular occasion, Dollar could sense some foul shit was up in the air and about to come down on him.

When Dollar entered the showers, Wojo gave a look to the other inmates that immediately caused them to disburse. Before Dollar knew it, it was just Wojo, three of his crewmembers, and him in the showers.

Wojo watched Dollar shower as he stood across from him with a devilish look in his eyes. He lathered his private area and began to stroke his suds-covered penis.

Dollar became uncomfortable and sick to his stomach at the sight of a grown man stiffening up over him. "Who da fuck you looking at, yo?" Dollar shouted. He thought about what his words would mean, but it was too late; they had already made their way through his lips. *Fuck it,* Dollar thought. *These niggaz was gonna try me sooner or later. I might as well stand my ground now.*

"I'm looking at you, bitch," Wojo replied as he and his crew began to walk up on Dollar.

Dollar had to think quickly. He couldn't run. There was no way he could have gotten around the four buff men. The only choice he had was to fight.

"You want a piece of me, little nigga?" Wojo asked Dollar.

"Man, I think he do," one of Wojo's homies instigated. "If he didn't, his dick wouldn't be hard."

"My dick is hard because I'm thinking about how good it felt fucking your moms before I came here," was Dollar's comeback.

Dollar knew the mama insult would get whatever it was that was about to happen to him started and over with. He braced himself as the four men rushed him hard. Blows punctured every part of Dollar's body. He fought back as best he could. The men had to have punched him over a hundred times before his naked, lifeless body slid down the shower wall and onto the floor. He watched his blood be carried downstream through the drain by the falling water.

Like a new gang member, he had been initiated into the system with his first beat down. Wojo and his crew stood over Dollar, asking him if he'd had enough. When Dollar finally decided to nod in the positive, Wojo reached his hand out to help Dollar up.

Before Dollar could even balance himself, he was spun around and slammed against the shower wall. He felt Wojo's penis against his buttocks as the crewmembers each grabbed his limbs and nailed him to the shower wall. He stood there pinned against the wall like Jesus on the cross.

Dollar was helpless. He couldn't move. He couldn't scream. He had no idea what he was supposed to do in that situation.

"I'm 'bout to shoot these nuts up off in that ass," Wojo whispered into Dollar's ear as he positioned his penis to enter Dollar's anus. "When I get out of here, this is what I'm gonna do to your mama, you bitch-ass nigga."

"I'll kill you, muthafucka," Dollar shouted to Wojo. "I swear to God, if you stick your dick in me you gonna lose it. You gonna have to sleep with one eye open the rest of your bid. I swear, if it's the last thing I do, I'll cut your fucking dick off, chop it up in little pieces, and eat it over rice like fucking stir fry."

Before Dollar knew it, he had broken free of the men. With his eyes closed, he stayed pressed against the wall. Eventually, he heard the men's feet pounding the puddles of the shower floor growing farther and farther away.

After a few moments, Dollar turned around to confirm that the men had in fact exited the showers. There was no one in sight, only a silhouette through the steam that Dollar couldn't make out. Dollar stood erect and mustered up enough strength to battle some more if he had to. Just as he positioned his dukes, the image vanished and Dollar was alone in the showers.

Dollar knew that God must have been watching over him. Why else was he still standing, alive?

Ever since Dollar stood up to Wojo, he had appeared to have lightweight gained some true respect in the joint. If by chance his eyes did meet with another inmate's, they didn't mean mug him. They gave him the "what's up?" nod and went on about their business.

Dollar might have had to exchange a few words with some new cat trying to be hard, but other than that, prison life for Dollar consisted of minimum drama. Now, after five years of being locked up, Dollar couldn't understand why anyone would want to fuck with him. But, lo and behold, maybe because he felt intimidated by Dollar's solemn youth, some Old G had recently started eyeballing Dollar big time. Dollar knew it was only a matter of time before some shit would go down.

CHAPTER 4

Keep Your Enemy Close

"So, little nigga," a deep, Barry White–like voice clouded over top of Dollar's head. "I hear you got three bodies on you."

"And?" Dollar said as he sat against the bars of his cell reading the last page of *Gangsta*.

"Oh, so it's true?" the voice said. "I thought for sure your little punk ass was in here for stealing cigarettes or something."

"Ah ha," Dollar said. "The old man got jokes. Let me guess. You're in here because you pick-pocketed the guests while you were working as a Walmart greeter."

Before Dollar could get his cackle out, a thick, muscular hand collected his throat through the cell bars. Dollar dropped the book and held his breath. He didn't fight or try to get away. He held his breath hoping his lungs were stronger than the Barry White impersonator's hand.

What seemed like forever passed before the hand released Dollar's throat. Dollar sat on the floor coughing and taking deep breaths, trying to get his breathing rhythm back.

"Don't you wonder why all these years you been sitting with your back against these bars and ain't nobody cut your fucking throat yet, boy?"

Dollar didn't respond. He was so mad he could have spit bullets. All he wanted to do was kick that muthafucka's ass. By the time Dollar stood up to face the assaulter, he was gone. All Dollar could see was the silhouette of his body clearing the hall corner.

Dollar, even without seeing his face, knew it was the Old G, the old man known in the clank as Romeo. Dollar had never even looked Romeo's way and now all of a sudden he had beef.

What the fuck was his problem?

As Dollar made his way to his grubbin' spot in the jail slop house he could feel a pair of eyes burning him. The old man was back on his trail. "What is it with that old geezer?" Dollar mumbled under his breath.

Dollar could barely enjoy his tasteless chow that consisted of meatloaf, peas, and mashed potatoes. He chewed the same bite of meatloaf for five minutes as he watched Romeo out of the corner of his eye. Dollar reached for his milk, with his eyes still glued on Romeo, and knocked it over.

"Fuck!" Dollar shouted as he scrambled to clean up the mess with napkins. He sopped up the milk and proceeded to continue eating. He took a bite of his mashed potatoes and prepared to stand watch against Romeo again. When he looked up, Romeo was no longer sitting at the table he had been dining at. Dollar gulped down the bite of mashed potatoes and felt a presence behind him.

"You ain't scared that you might scoop up a razor blade in them mashed potatoes?" Romeo asked.

Dollar closed his eyes. He knew he had fucked up. He knew he had been caught slipping. But like with Wojo, he was ready to stand his ground.

"Look, old man," Dollar said without looking away from his tray. "What's your beef? I ain't done shit to you, but if you want to throw them thangs, then let's do it and get it over with. It ain't gon' hurt my heart none to beat down an old man."

One could have heard a pin drop. Silence filled the air and Dollar braced himself for the first blow. Surprisingly, there was no blow. Dollar whirled his body around to face Romeo, but just as quickly as Romeo had appeared, he had disappeared.

By this point Dollar was a basket case. He was watching his back tougher than ever. He even discussed hiring some of Wojo's old crew to have his back. Dollar started asking around to find out what Romeo's story was or if there was word on why he was out to get him. All the inmates he tried to get at were acting like hoes. Nobody, supposedly, knew anything. Just the mentioning of Romeo's name made half of them piss on themselves. The most information Dollar could dig up was that Romeo was in for life. He had nothing to lose.

For the next couple of months, Dollar slept with one eye open. He saw everyone up in the joint as his enemy. Dollar lay on his cot while he started on his next book, *Please Tell Me if the Grass is Greener*. No longer was his back against the bars.

Dollar molested every food item on his tray before sticking it into his mouth for fear a razor blade or any other deadly object might be embedded in it. He was always one of the first in and out of the showers. There was no way he was going to let the old man sneak on him. It was only a matter of time before the ultimate confrontation between Dollar and Romeo would erupt, and Dollar could hear the clock ticking loud and clear.

One afternoon while Dollar was lifting weights, Romeo entered the weight room. Dollar continued lifting as if everything was everything. Like zombies, dudes started surrounding Dollar. Romeo was no longer in his view as the inmates smothered Dollar with their shadows. Dollar continued lifting as if they weren't there. All the while he was scared shitless, nonetheless prepared to knock somebody upside the head with them weights if he had to.

"Boy," Romeo said, "when you see trouble coming your way, why do you remain in its path?"

Dollar placed the dumbbells on the rack and stood erect. Romeo looked at his fellow inmates and they immediately disbursed. Before Dollar knew it, it was just Romeo and himself alone in the room.

"How is it you've managed to survive in this piece for almost six years without getting laid to rest with that cocky ass attitude of yours, like you rule the motherfucking world?" Romeo asked. "Why do you think that's so?"

"'Cause I mind my own business," Dollar replied.

"Shit." Romeo laughed. "There's plenty of cats up in here minding they own business. That don't mean shit to these killaz up in here."

"I've got a question for you. How is it I've managed to survive in this piece for almost six years without anybody constantly fucking with me, and then along comes you?" Dollar smartly replied.

He looked Dollar up and down, nodded his head, and said, "My point exactly," then walked away.

Romeo actually had Dollar spooked. This was the first time since his incident with Wojo he was feeling the wrath of the prison walls. If someone was out for you in the joint, it was far different than when someone was out for you in the streets. It wasn't about no laying low. There was nowhere to hide.

Dollar knew that since Romeo was a lifer he didn't have shit to lose. This was what worried Dollar the most. For the first time Dollar knew what it felt like to have genuine fear in his heart and that was some scary shit. It was like being in a pitch-black room with a lion. You could hear his roar as he could hear your every maneuver. It was like walking a mile-long tight rope for the first time in your life without a net to catch your fall.

Dollar would soon realize that prison life exists six feet under hell.

CHAPTER 5

Sweet Dreams

A couple months later, right before lights out, Dollar was reading one of Donald Goines's old joints when Romeo appeared outside of his cell. Dollar closed the book and sat silently on his cot as he waited to see what fly-ass shit came out of Romeo's mouth this time.

Romeo stood quietly as he stared down at the ground. He eventually looked up at Dollar and sighed. "Truce," Romeo said.

"What?" Dollar asked, just to make sure he was actually hearing what he was hearing.

"You heard me, little nigga," Romeo replied. "I'm done fuckin' wit' your punk ass. It ain't even fun no more. Truce."

Dollar paused for a moment, stared at Romeo's hand, and then replied, "Truce."

Their mouths had said it, but had their hearts?

The next morning the beads of water from the shower spigot beat against Dollar's well-cut physique. Too bad those hoes from the block couldn't reap the benefit from his custom-designed body. What was good about Dollar going to prison so young was that he had only been laid a few times. He had let bitches make him sandwiches and suck his dick on an occasion or two, but he wasn't laying pipe to the chickenheads who roamed his block.

Dollar hadn't gotten a taste of the various flavors that pussy came in so the lack of pussy didn't affect him all that much. The few times Dollar had gotten him some it was always from the same couple girls.

One of the girls was this chick named Pam, who had lived next door to his Auntie Charlene. Pam let him run up in her for the very first time on his sixteenth birthday. Pam was a couple years older than Dollar and had been putting out since she was twelve years old. Her own stepbrother had popped her cherry. As a matter of fact, he was the one who hooked up her and Dollar. It was his birthday present to Dollar.

Dollar was nervous as hell when it all went down, but he managed to get through it long enough to bust his first nut. Pam and Dollar did it right up against the side of Auntie Charlene's house. After that, when it came to Pam, Dollar was like a dog in heat. Whenever his mother would take him and his brother to visit his Auntie Charlene, he would hang out on the porch waiting to catch Pam coming or going. He could smell her coming before he saw her. A squirt of Chanel No. 5 that Pam would sneak and use from her mother's dresser always gave her away.

If the timing was right, Dollar knew if Pam's mama wasn't home that Pam would lead him straight to her mother's bed. The bunk bed she shared with her sister wouldn't suffice. The sound of Pam's mother's king-sized wooden headboard banging up against the wall intensified Dollar shoving his penis into Pam.

They never worried about getting caught because pussy was brand new to Dollar. He never lasted more than two minutes tops, three minutes if he couldn't find the hole right off the bat.

Because Pam lived in Chicago and Dollar lived in Gary, getting between her legs on a regular was difficult. Dollar soon familiarized himself with the technique of jacking off. It became an everyday thing almost. This newfound skill would pay off during Dollar's years in prison.

Dollar closed his eyes and allowed the shower water to rinse him of his sudsy lather. This was the first time he had rested both eyes in what seemed like an eternity. Now that Romeo had declared a truce, Dollar was more at ease.

Dollar aided the water with his hands as he stroked his now 230-pound cut physique. After making sure his skin was squeaky clean, Dollar reached for the shower knobs in order to turn the water off. Just then, a striking pain streaked through Dollar's back. It was as if someone had taken a cement block and slammed it into his back with all of their might. The pain was unbearable. Dollar lost all strength as he fell face down onto the tiled shower floor. In and out of consciousness, he could see inmates standing over him. Among the inmates, and before losing complete consciousness, he caught view of that all too familiar silhouette.

Damn, Dollar thought as the entire scene faded to black. *Dat nigga caught me slip* . . . And he slipped in and out of consciousness.

Dollar didn't know what Romeo had hit him with, but he knew for certain Romeo had done it. Both angry and in pain, Dollar was torn between wanting to die to escape the pain and wanting revenge.

In the infirmary, Dollar woke up to a blond white girl standing over him. It was Crissy. She was one step up from being like the prison hospital candy striper.

"Hey now," Crissy said with a smile as Dollar's eyes slowly opened.

Crissy's face was the most pleasant sight Dollar had seen in years. Dollar didn't know if it was because he had been locked up so long, but he never saw a more beautiful white girl in his life. A white chick had never even turned his head before. The only white girls he had ever looked at were the ones on the porno tapes and *Playboy* magazines he used to jack off to. Crissy was nothing like them. She wasn't trashy looking. She could have been an angel as far as Dollar was concerned.

"Am I dead?" Dollar asked Crissy.

"What?" Crissy smiled.

"Am I dead?" Dollar repeated.

"No, silly," Crissy said. "Someone busted up your back pretty bad though. I don't know who did it or what they did it with, but they sure got you good. But fortunately, you're not dead."

"Then you shouldn't scare people like that," Dollar said, attempting to sit up but prohibited by the pain. "I opened my eyes and saw you, an angel, and thought I was in heaven."

"Good one." Crissy laughed. "But do you really think a man in prison for a triple murder is going to wake up in heaven?"

"You got me on that one." Dollar snickered. "Ouch."

"Oh, you're in pain," Crissy said as she grabbed a hypodermic needle that was lying on the tray next to Dollar's bed. "I was just getting ready to give you something for that. You're bruised up pretty bad. You must be in severe pain. That's why we've been keeping you out of it. Let me help you try to turn over so I can take care of your discomfort."

Dollar looked at Crissy as if she was crazy as she flicked and plucked at the giant-sized needle in her hand.

"Oh, you were right," Dollar said. "I am in hell."

"Come on now," Crissy said. "Be a big boy. Roll it over."

"Oh hell no! You gon' stick that in my ass? You are out of your mind. Ouch!" Dollar screamed as the slightest movement sent volts of pain through his body.

"Okay, have it your way," Crissy said, laying the needle down and walking away. "I can think of far worse things to get stuck in your ass while in prison."

"Okay, okay," Dollar said, hailing her back. "Do what you got to do. Just make the pain go away."

Crissy walked back over to Dollar in an "I told you so" demeanor. She picked up the needle and eyeballed Dollar to turn over so that she could stick him in his banana pudding dipped ass. Embarrassed that Crissy was about to see his bare bottom, Dollar hesitated.

"I've given you a sponge bath for Pete's sake," Crissy said. "I've seen everything you've got already."

Dollar rolled over very slowly, with Crissy's help, and braced himself as Crissy inserted the needle into his right butt cheek. It was almost instant gratification. Crissy helped Dollar turn back over and get comfortable as his eyes began to prepare themselves for more rest.

"Now that wasn't so bad, was it?" Crissy asked as she ran her hand across Dollar's forehead.

Dollar smiled as false illusions of Crissy in a little white nurse getup danced throughout his mind. He had a vision in his mind that he was still unable to move, lying in the infirmary bed as Crissy began to tear her clothing off piece by piece.

Before Dollar knew it, she was straddled on top of him with nothing but a white lacy garter belt with a matching corset and some white four-inch, ice pick heels.

Crissy's tongue brushed across her cherry red gloss-covered lips as she placed her hands behind her back and began to unzip the corset. All the while she was grinding her warm pussy on Dollar's dude. As Crissy threw the corset to the floor, she took her fingers and pushed her laced thong to the side as she began to tease Dollar with the masturbation of her pink pussy lips. She twisted her clit with her forefinger and thumb and moaned softly. The candy apple red polish on the tip of her nails plunged in and out of her cunt as she began to breathe heavily.

Dollar just lay in the hospital bed unable to move; unable to contribute his own fingers in and out of her as his hands were pinned down with Crissy's knees. Crissy began to moan intensely. Dollar knew this was a sign that she was about to cum. Crissy quickly climbed higher up onto Dollar until her pink, sticky pussy lips met Dollar's mouth.

"Taste it," Crissy said. *"Get drunk off of my cognac."*

Dollar had never eaten pussy in his life. But he had a feeling that if he ate that pussy right, Crissy would handle his dick proper like. Niggaz in jail told him that they stole plenty of niggaz' hoes because their man didn't go down on them right. That bitch, Pam, Dollar thought.

That trick, who had been fucking and sucking dick since she was twelve, never once instructed him as to how to eat a woman out.

Dollar's dream of getting laid was now a nightmare. Pussy was literally in his face to do what he wanted to do with it and he was dumbfounded.

"Eat it," Crissy demanded again, becoming impatient. "Eat it, Dareese. Dareese, do you hear me? Dareese!"

"Yeah, yeah, what?" Dollar said, exiting his dream and reentering reality.

"Would you like to try to eat, Dareese?" Crissy asked.

"Word." Dollar smiled. No one had called him by his given name in years. Hearing Crissy call him Dareese sounded strange.

"You haven't been able to eat," Crissy said.

"Yeah, I know," Dollar said.

"We've been feeding you intravenously since yesterday when you came in. Would you like to try to eat something?"

Slightly disappointed that Crissy was referring to real food and not her private part that she had been referring to in his vision, Dollar nodded his head. "Yeah, that's cool," Dollar replied.

"Don't sound so depressed," Crissy said. "How about we skip this jailhouse food and I give you the sandwich from my lunch? It's salami on rye, decked with lettuce, tomato, and onion."

"Yeah, that would be nice," Dollar moaned with a smile on his face.

"Okay, you try to stay awake and I'll be right back," Crissy said, heading out the door. "Oh, and Dareese, I was just kidding about that heaven thing. God forgives us all."

CHAPTER 6

Rules of the Game

It was a few days before Dollar returned to general population. He hated that every time an inmate walked by him they hissed and laughed at the back brace he sported.

"Damn, Dollar," this faggot-ass dude named Shawny said as he brushed by Dollar with his little T-shirt tied into a knot at his belly button. "If I had known you put your back into it like that, I would have tattooed your name on my ass years ago."

The inmates within ear distance laughed as if they were watching *Def Comedy Jam*. Dollar just brushed that shit off and went on about his business.

He passed a table where a game of chess between Romeo and some other inmate was taking place. As Romeo began to make his move, he spotted Dollar walking by. A grim grin took over the bottom portion of his face as he declared checkmate against his opponent without taking his eyes off of Dollar.

Dollar stared him down all the same. *Fuck it!* Dollar looked at it this way: both them niggaz was going to die in jail anyway. They might as well go out gangsta. Although Dollar was in no position to battle, he wasn't going to bow down to no man. The look he gave Romeo confirmed such.

Ironically, Dollar's life always seemed to come full circle. Like déjà vu, one night, right before lights out, Romeo appeared outside of Dollar's cell. Dollar was ready for the old man this time though. Earlier that day, while Dollar was shaving, he removed the blade and placed it under his tongue. When he returned to his cell, he inserted it into the bristles of his toothbrush and secured it with tape. Fuck buying a dozen cans of soda pop and loading his pillowcase with them to blast Romeo with. Dollar was going for the jugular. The old man had brought out something in Dollar that he had managed to bury deep inside his soul: the killer in him.

"I bet you think that was me who busted up your back in the shower," Romeo said, tooting on a cancer stick.

"Look, old man," Dollar said, raisin' up off of his bed. "Fuck you and the mind games you playin'. If you got beef, then come on wit' it. Like I said before, let's do the damn thang."

Romeo couldn't help but burst out laughing. "You little niggaz kill me. What is it y'all call yourselves? Hard? Ain't nothin' hard about you hoes except for your dicks when you wake up in the morning. Put the Old Gs back on the street and we'll show y'all dumb bitches how the game is played."

"Well from the looks of all the Old Gs occupying these prison cells, y'all lost the muthafuckin' game."

"Yeah, but that's when the teachin' comes in," Romeo said, exhaling two synchronized streams of smoke from his nostrils. "When you lose, you have time to sit back and think of where you fucked up along the way. Mentally, you can correct that shit. Of course you can't go back in time and change things, but you can school the next muthafucker tryin' to come up in the game. Take you, for instance. You sat with your back against the world. What kind of shit is that? The world is your enemy and you turn your back to it. You assumed because you Dolla Dolla Bill that shit is tight for you. Son, even Jesus was crucified. You grubbed on your slop thinking there wasn't one nigga up in here wishing you dead."

Romeo shook his head and then continued. "You never forked through your food for foreign objects; you just sat down and ate like it was the last muthafucking supper. Do you really think that if I don't fuck with nobody they ain't gonna fuck with me bullshit works? Jealous-ass niggaz want you dead 'cause they think your dick is bigger than theirs, but a nigga scream 'truce' and throw up deuces and you think everything is all good. Just because a muthafucker say they cool with you doesn't mean they cool with you. Just because a muthafucker wanna roll with you don't mean they down for you. Half these niggaz trying to be up in your corner don't wanna be down for you. They only want to be you, recognize."

"So what the fuck, old man?" Dollar said, becoming agitated as if he was attempting to put a Rubik's Cube in order. "Why you telling me all this shit? I've survived in this piece this long. I'm doing something right."

Romeo laughed again. His laugh was beginning to infuriate Dollar.

"Back in the day, that Wojo shit," Romeo recollected. "Do you really think them niggaz didn't draw blood out of your asshole because you shouted out a threat or two? When it was all said and done and your asshole was still as tight as a virgin's pussy, didn't you think that God must have been watching over you?"

Dollar thought back at the close calls he had and could have had. He thought back at how he knew God must have been on his side. He looked up at Romeo speechless, not willing to give him the gratification of being right.

"Well, little nigga," Romeo said as he put the lit cigarette out with his index finger and thumb. "I'm God."

One would have never known Dollar and Romeo had ever had beef. Nowadays, they were joined at the hip. Although Romeo had a twisted way of doing it, he taught Dollar how to survive. He taught Dollar how to constantly watch his back and never, under any circumstance, trust anyone; not even himself.

Even though Dollar might not have 100 percent trusted Romeo, he trusted the words he was schooling him with. Besides, finding out Romeo's respect behind the bars had been part of the reason for Dollar's survival, Dollar at least owed him a listening ear, never once questioning why, why him? Why had Romeo chosen to take Dollar up under his wing? But then again, Dollar had always had a way of gaining his own level of respect as well.

Romeo spent hours crowning Dollar with all of the street knowledge he had in him. This was shocking to other inmates. No one knew too much about Romeo personally, not even his given name. He was never one to brag and boast about his dirt. He never put his business in the yard. But for some reason he had found something in Dollar that made him vocal.

Dollar spent endless hours listening to Romeo's "old school" tales. Romeo did everything from snatching gold chains off of college girl's necks, to mackin' hoes, to robbing banks. Romeo broke down all the things he would have done differently to keep from catching a case, like keeping his eye on the prize instead of getting greedy. He even schooled Dollar on other inmate's fuck-ups: how they had picked the wrong crowd to roll with; how they should have detected that, in the end, backstabbing muthafuckas wouldn't be down for them.

"Loyalty and betrayal are muthafuckers," Romeo said to Dollar as they sat in the yard rapping. "There are times in life when your head gets all fucked up trying to figure out who you need to be loyal to and who the fuck you just might have to cross. It's even harder trying to figure out who is actually loyal to you and who just might cross you. Eventually you'll have to

play both roles. You gotta be that backstabbin'
nigga to one muthafucker in order to stay loyal
to the next. But you gotta be careful because if
you get it twisted, one or the other, loyalty or
betrayal, might destroy you . . . sometimes both."

Dollar would spend his nights dissecting
Romeo's words. Romeo had so much he wanted
to hammer into Dollar's brain. The main lesson
Romeo tried to teach Dollar was to be low-key.
The less people who knew him and the less
people knew about him, the less people to be
jealous of him and the less people to try to put
salt in his game.

"Take the game of basketball for instance,"
Romeo said to Dollar. "Half them niggaz ain't
about the team. They about showboating,
making a tight play that's going to bring about
recognition in the game. They want ESPN play
of the week and shit. Them same muthafuckers
be the first ones in the spotlight when shit ain't
right: rape charges, failing drug tests, shootin'
they babies' mamas and shit. Now take that
cat who just gets out there and does what he's
supposed to do, sticks his man, passes the ball,
and shoots only when he knows he has a sure
shot. We hardly know that cat's name. His house

is just as big as the next baller's. His wrist is just as iced, yet we wouldn't even recognize his ass walking down the street. That's the muthafucker you want to be."

Now that Dollar had been let in on the medley of hustles that existed, he wanted to stick his spoon into every pot of hustle there was on the streets and scoop up a taste. Unfortunately, that was no longer an option for Dollar.

Still, that didn't keep Romeo from spoon-feeding Dollar knowledge, making him fiend for the streets, making him want to give his left nut to be back on the streets again.

"So how did you finally get caught?" Dollar asked Romeo while they sat at the chessboard.

"Fuckin' round with other muthafuckers," Romeo said. "They was some iffy cats. I should have known to just do the damn thing without them. Whenever a cat gets iffy on you, like they wanna bitch out, cut 'em the fuck off. They useless."

"So why didn't you take your own advice and cut 'em off?" Dollar asked.

"Because I didn't know then what I know now, li'l nigga," Romeo answered sternly. "I robbed plenty of spots by myself. I don't know what in the hell made me think I needed to pull them niggaz in on that hit."

Dollar continued to listen to Romeo as he went on about how his nervous-ass partners botched what would have been the biggest lick in Romeo's criminal career.

Dollar could tell by the way Romeo spoke with such passion that he, too, wished that he could be back on the streets to do shit all over again. He could tell by the intensity in Romeo's tone every time they talked. Dollar and Romeo found that they were so much alike. Hell, they even started to look alike.

"Damn," Dollar said one day while attempting to be taught the game of chess by Romeo. "With all the shit I know now, if I was on the them damn streets today, I'd be a Don."

"Fuck that!" Romeo said, becoming angry. "You'd be your own man, not a made man. You little niggaz watch too many Al Pacino movies. You think them Mafia muthafuckers running around talkin' 'bout they wanna be a nigga? Hell no, but you niggaz always want to be them. All y'all worry about is being fly and making sure everybody knows who y'all is. Well, that's where y'all fuck up. The bling-bling brings too much attention from the wrong people. Why a hustler would want everybody to know who they are and what they do is beyond me. It's a stupid, egotistical mistake. You don't wanna do too much in

the game. The less you stand out, the longer your
chances are of remaining a player. Get in the
game, do what you came to do, and get the fuck
out! Take your championship ring and retire."

"You right," Dollar agreed. "I'd be my own
man. Fuck trying to show off to these wankstas.
It's all about me."

Dollar dazed off, envisioning what he used to
know as freedom. Romeo could see the look of
desperation in Dollar's eyes. It was as if Romeo was
living the street life once again through the dream
in Dollar's eyes. Romeo knew that the time had
finally come. His work was done . . . well almost.

"What if I was to tell you there was a way for
me to put you back on the streets?" Romeo said,
pausing from the chess game.

"I'd say, damn, you really are God." Dollar
laughed.

"Seriously," Romeo said with deepest sincerity.

"I'd say do that shit." Dollar turned serious.

Romeo bowed his head and ran his hand
down his face. He took a deep sigh and looked up
at Dollar. "I got something that the state wants.
If you give it to them, you're a free man."

"But that don't make sense," Dollar said. "If
you have something that could make me a free

man, then why wouldn't you just use it to free yourself?"

Romeo smiled a huge grin. He patted Dollar on the shoulder, who was clearly confused at this point. "You finally analyzing shit," Romeo said. "See what a game of chess will teach you?"

"Come on, I'm serious," Dollar continued.

"All right, calm down," Romeo said. "Because what I have that the state wants is me," Romeo replied.

"The state already got your black ass, old man," Dollar said.

"They got the Romeo who shot and killed a guard and two tellers during a bank robbery," Romeo said. "They ain't got Romeo aka the Midwest Serial Killer."

Dollar's mouth dropped. He had heard of those killings from years and years ago. Dead bodies of young white females were being found throughout the Midwest. There were a couple of Latino and black chicks, too, but the FBI didn't want to taint the Caucasian killings with the minority ones. Each victim's case had similarities. Profilers couldn't piece together a suspect because nothing corresponded with their typical serial killings.

"That's you, man?" Dollar shouted.

"Shhh," Romeo ordered.

"Damn, old man," Dollar said. "All this time we been kickin' it, you never found the need to tell me that you were a notorious, coldblooded murderer?"

"Shit, I figured you were one also so what would it matter?" Romeo said sarcastically.

"I done told you, man. I didn't kill nobody!" Dollar stood up and shouted in his defense. "Besides, poppin' a couple of niggaz ain't shit compared to torturing and murdering bitches."

"All right. I hear you. Sit your happy ass down," Romeo said. "It wasn't even like that. Them hoes asked for that shit. Look, little nigga, this is a 'get out of jail for free' card. Do you want it or not?"

Dollar slowly seating himself back down was sign enough that he wanted the card. "I just can't see you doing no sick-ass shit like that, old man," Dollar said.

"It ain't even like that, young blood," Romeo argued. "I didn't just go out stalking and killing girls. It was part of the game. But never you mind the reasoning behind the slayings. You wanna reap from them, right?"

"I'm in for a body. How am I gonna get out on a body?" Dollar replied.

"Your bodies are some thugs, criminal niggaz who deserved to be dead anyway as far as

the man is concerned. You did them a favor.
My bodies: white girls. Over the years, these
unsolved murders prevented the reelection of
two mayors and a governor, and the resignation
of a police chief. There's a million dollar reward
for the arrest and conviction of the Midwest
Serial Killer. To make the deal mo' better, you
decline the reward money. You do the math,"
Romeo said.

Dollar listened intensely as he nodded his
head. As always, Romeo was making sense.

"So do you want the card or not?" Romeo
asked Dollar.

"Hell yeah," Dollar replied.

"Good, then listen up."

For the next few weeks, Romeo gave Dollar
explicit details of the crimes such as weapons
of choice, material used to bound and gag the
women, what the women were wearing, et cetera.
He even informed Dollar of a couple of bodies
that had not yet been discovered.

Last but not least, Dollar and Romeo would
have to stage a falling out. The prison would need
to see that Dollar and Romeo were no longer on
the same team in order for Dollar dropping the
dime to be taken seriously.

Once Romeo was comfortable that Dollar
had everything down to the T, the two of them

acted out a fight in the prison yard. Blood was drawn and Dollar even ended up with a month in the hole. This action would validate Dollar's decision to snitch on Romeo and would be sure to guarantee him life on the outside.

"I got something the state wants," Dollar said to the district attorney as his lawyer and the prison warden each sat beside him.

Dollar, after a thousand attempts, managed to retain the skills of a public pretender, also known as a public defender. He needed him to initiate and mediate the game of tit for tat between him and the State of Ohio.

The PD recorded Dollar's statement in relation to the Midwest Serial Killer and researched the facts of the crimes. Sure enough, Dollar's story about the crimes panned out. There were facts of the case that Dollar would have only known if the killer told him or if he was the killer himself; they determined the latter wasn't a possibility.

The PD contacted the district attorney's office, and after some major convincing, got him to agree upon a meeting with Dollar in the prison warden's office.

"I'm listening," the DA said to Dollar as he tilted his chair back onto its two hind legs. "Get to talking. Time is money. It's not every day I allot my time to some two-bit killer convict."

"My client has the key to unlock a case that has had law enforcement's heads spinning for some time," Dollar's attorney pronounced. "Do you remember those five unsolved homicides here in Ohio, and the seven others throughout the Midwest? You know, those nice little Caucasian princesses?"

"The Midwest Serial Killer? Okay, you've got my attention," the DA said, positioning all four legs of his chair onto the floor.

"Do you want them closed after all of these years?" Dollar's attorney asked.

"Don't play games with me," the DA said. "You know goddamn well the public and the media were all over our asses on that one. Whenever one of those girls' parents decides to talk to *Dateline* or Court TV or Oprah or some shit, the shit hits the fan all over again."

"Then I'm sure you'll be willing to sweep the lives of three dead African American thugs under the rug in exchange for the lives of five beautiful, hell, twelve, give or take a few, would-be doctors and lawyers, white females," Dollar's lawyer said.

"It's hard telling, sometimes, the difference between when someone's jerking my dick and when someone actually has me by the balls," the DA said. "I want the killer on a platter. No hints, tips, or premonitions. I'll settle for nothing less than being the one to shoot the needle into the son of a bitch's veins."

"It's hard telling, sometimes, if I'm being made love to or if I'm being fucked," Dollar said. "If I give you the name of your man, I'm screwed. I'm deemed a snitch and risk getting my tongue cut the fuck out. I'm not waiting around for no conviction, trial, or any bullshit like that. I turn snitch for the state then the state frees me. I'll give you a minute or two to check shit out, but that's it."

"Look, nigger," the DA said. "Oh, pardon me, how do you people like to say it these days, 'nigga'? Anyway, if you can give me the Midwest Serial Killer, then you're a free man, no halfway house, no probation officer, nothing. In the words of your former, great African American leader, you'll be 'free at last, free at last, God almighty, you'll be free at last.'"

Dollar knew the DA was being a bigot-ass prick, but what could he do? He wasn't free yet; not free enough to tie the DA's testicles in a knot for using Dr. King's quote as if it were some lame-ass cliché.

"You're already in on three bodies," the DA started to ponder. "This could be tough. I mean, hell, how can I convince the state to let a killer out for turning in another killer? It just doesn't add up," the DA said.

"Well, I didn't see the family of those three dead men on television threatening the skills and abilities of the judicial system," Dollar's attorney said. "And just think, the person who finally breaks this case is going to be a saint in the community, and I'm sure that $1 million reward money that my client is willing to waive will find a nice home."

A crooked smile swept over the DA's face. The things he could do with a million dollars. He could figure out some way to bank the million dollar reward money himself. He would probably have to pull a few strings and pay off a couple of folks with a portion of the reward money, but he just might be able to find a way to make the deal work. He was a politician; of course he could find a way.

"I think we can work this out somehow. I mean, perhaps there were some technicalities that were overlooked in your client's case," the DA said with a devilish grin. "But if your client is bullshitting me, then you'll have him to thank for your new position," the DA said to Dollar's lawyer.

"What new position?" Dollar's lawyer asked.

"The one you'll have mopping up floors in the prison toilets, you dumb fuck."

CHAPTER 7

The Deliberate Stranger

Dollar couldn't believe this day was coming to pass. It was the day he was going to be a free man again. The State of Ohio was throwing him back onto the streets: the streets Dollar would have to get reacquainted with. He knew so much shit had changed over eight years that he would have to perform foreplay on the streets before running up in them again.

Dollar had big plans. He learned so much from Romeo that the sky was the limit. As he packed up the little bit of shit he owned, all he could think about was all of the tax-free money in the streets that had his name written all over it. No way was he going to fuck up this time around. This was his second chance to redeem himself to the game. Sure he could go back out in the streets vowing to live an honest life so that he'd never end up in jail again. But what were those chances? No matter what good deed the state thought he'd done, to society he was still a convicted felon, which meant no voting and no good jobs. He had better odds at winning the lottery, so he'd bet and take his chances on the streets.

"I'm a big-ass nigga," Dollar said to himself as he buttoned up his blue dress shirt that was compliments of the prison. He flexed his muscles and thought about all the pussy his new build would gain him. There was no doubt in his mind that once he showed up on the block honeys would be all on his jock.

He entered prison looking like LL Cool J from *Krush Groove,* but came out looking like the new, buffed-up LL. He had picked up an extra forty pounds of muscle. Yep, yep, pussy and money was all that was on Dollar's mind but not necessarily in that order.

Dollar brushed his hair, then ran his tongue across his perfectly straight white teeth.

"Who would have thought it?" Ed said as he came to escort Dollar out of the prison. "Dollar Bill back on the streets. Where you gon' go, man?"

"I'm copping a cot at the YMCA back in Indiana," Dollar answered. "When I leave this bitch I get a bus pass and one hundred dollars."

"Then what?" Ed asked.

"Shit, man," Dollar said. "I don't know. I don't give a fuck. All I know is that I'm kissing this place good-bye."

"I'm sure you'll be just fine," Ed said, reaching into his pocket. "But, hey, I got some peoples you might want to contact. They can hook you up with some ol' simple-ass shit. You know, just something to get you by like cleaning, painting, construction, working at a gas station, or what-not."

"Good looking out," Dollar said, taking the piece of paper Ed had retrieved from his pocket.

"Well, I guess it's that time, partna," Ed said.

"Let's do this," Dollar said, grabbing his bag and following Ed's lead.

A crescendo of whistling followed Dollar throughout the prison as Ed escorted him to freedom. He gave dap and pound to some of the inmates. Most of them couldn't care less about Dollar being freed; they were just caught up in the idea of freedom alone. Underneath the whistling there was some hissing, like the sound of a snake. That's one thing Dollar had to mentally prepare himself for: being thought of as a snitch. He had planned on spending the rest of his life having people think he was a murderer and he really wasn't, so what the fuck if they thought he was a snitch?

Dollar obeyed the street code. He hadn't snitched on his partners. This situation with Romeo was different. He couldn't help it if a "get out of jail free" card had been placed in the palm of his hands. Only a fool would have declined it.

"Yo, Ed," Dollar said. "Where's Romeo?"

"Come on, Dollar, man," Ed said. "Don't even think about it. You on your way out of here. Don't start no shit now."

"No, it's cool," Dollar assured him. "Just take me to him."

Ed thought for a minute. "Man, I don't know." Dollar pleaded silently with his eyes. Ed exhaled. "Shit, man, come on." He took Dollar to solitary where Romeo was moved to while he awaited trial for the murders.

"Five minutes, man," Ed said noided. "Five minutes and don't start no shit, Dollar, or I swear to God."

Ed left Dollar outside of Romeo's solitary cell as he stood at the corner conversing with another CO and keeping watch for any of the big dawgs who could have his job if he was found out.

"Oh Romeo, oh Romeo, wherefore art thou, Romeo?" Dollar whispered outside of the steel door.

"You out, man?" Romeo asked through the slot.

"I'm out," Dollar replied as silence fell upon them. "Any last words of advice?"

"You know everything I know now," Romeo said. "Be good, Dollar, and be good at it."

"I hate to leave you in solitary like this, man," Dollar said.

"I'm going to have to buy all new shit," Romeo said. "You know them niggaz done had a field day raidin' my shit."

"Why, old man?" Dollar couldn't help but ask.

Romeo ignored Dollar's inquiry as he pressed his head against the door holding back his tears. One of the hardest cats in the system, for the first time since he could remember, Romeo felt like he was about to break. "Do me a favor," Romeo said to Dollar.

"Anything, man," Dollar replied.

"Make sure the first thing you do is go see your family," Romeo replied.

"No doubt," Dollar said. "That goes unsaid."

"You take care of yourself," Romeo said.

"Peace out, old man," Dollar replied as he prepared to walk away. "Yo, Romeo," Dollar said, "what's your real name, at least?"

"Don't matter now," Romeo said.

"Come on, man," Dollar begged.

"I said it doesn't matter!" Romeo spat.

"Damn, all right," Dollar said, leaving the situation alone. Hell, he could read it in the papers. "Anyway, take it easy old man." As Dollar walked away, heading over to where Ed was, Romeo called out.

"Blake," Romeo said. "Ramelle Blake."

Dollar immediately stopped in his tracks. A sudden chill took over Dollar's body. His blood boiled throughout his body and he could hear his heart beating as loud as thunder. Dollar hadn't heard that name since he was three years old. The last time he heard it was when his mother was begging and pleading for his father not to leave her.

"Ramelle Daren Blake," his mother cried. "Don't you dare walk out of that door. Do you think I don't know what people are saying about you out there in them streets? You think I don't know how you come about the money you bring into this house? It ain't from working down at Junie's club like you say it is."

"That money feeds this family don't it?" Dollar's father replied. "So what's it matter where it came from?"

"So, are you saying it's true? Is it true what people are saying? Do you have women out there on the streets for you, Ramelle?"

"Don't you question me, woman. Who in the fuck do you think you are?"

Dollar never heard his father swear at his mother before. He rarely heard them argue in *his few years. The disrespect Dollar's father was showing his mother was the first sign that the streets were taking over him . . . or he was taking over the streets.*

Dollar's mother felt as though her husband had just spit in her face. He had never talked to her that way and now he was scolding her like one of his hoes. "You know what?" Dollar's mother replied. "You go. You get out of here. I don't want my boys growing up around you. They might mistake you for a man."

"Fuck you, bitch," Dollar's father said to his mother as he exited the apartment, leaving him, his mother, and his screaming ten-month-old baby brother for dead.

He never even came back for a change of clothes. Dollar's mother never threw out one thing of his, hoping that one day he might return. He never did. Dollar felt it in his little soul that he'd never see his father again. He was wrong.

Dollar couldn't move as he stood in the prison corridor. The man he had spent almost his entire life hating, the man who gave him life, was now, once again, giving him life. Dollar wanted to rip Romeo's fucking heart out, though. He wanted to spit on him. He wanted to stomp him for each year his mother spent working in fast food restaurants. He wanted to stomp him for each year him and his brother went without a daddy. In Dollar's head, he was envisioning him shankin' Romeo until every ounce of life oozed out of his body. But in reality, he was stiff.

"I know you can't speak," Romeo said. "And even if you could, no telling how cruel your words might be even in spite of the situation at hand. And I wouldn't blame you one bit. Believe me, any hate you've had for me over the years, I've hated myself ten times as much."

Dollar was still cold speechless. He couldn't even blink for fear a tear of anger might drop.

"You asked me why, why I'm doing this for you," Romeo spoke. "When you were born, I remember watching you sleep in the hospital. I never took my eyes off of you. When you opened your eyes for the first time I wanted to be there. My mother, your Grandma Stevie, told me that you can see your soul through the eyes of your child.

"When I looked into your eyes I saw everything that I knew I had to be. I didn't see the person I was, but the person I needed to be. Sooner than later, the streets started calling me. I wanted so much for you and your mama. I wanted to give y'all the world. But then your little brother was born and the world was on my shoulders.

I couldn't luck up on a decent job and couldn't hold on to a halfway decent one. Instead of pushing myself and being strong I answered the call. I answered the calling of the streets. Hell, I don't need to tell you. There was tax-free ends to be made out there, but your mama wasn't with that. No way was she going to be a hustler's wife. That's why I told you what I told you back when I first started kickin' knowledge to you. If you find a good woman and you love her, then you have to choose. You have to choose either the streets or her. If you really love her then you fo' sure don't want to bring her into the life. You have to choose. Don't ever make her choose. You won't win."

Dollar listened intensely as Romeo continued.

"Anyway, the first time I looked into your eyes I promised your mama I would always be there for you. I told your mama I'd trade in my life for you. I made a lot of promises to her. So far this one, trading in my life for you, has been the only promise I've been able to keep. Go out there, son. Take everything I've given you and rule them streets. The world is your playground, remember that."

Dollar swallowed and stuck his chest out. He regained his composure and looked straight ahead at Ed to signal him that he was ready to walk. He felt as though he had to say something to Romeo. This was his only opportunity to have words with the man he now knew to be his father.

As Dollar proceeded to exit the jail, he said to Romeo, "Don't you ever call me son."

Back in the day when Dollar first went to jail, Jodeci was the male group dominating the charts. Now in 2003, these young cats named B2K was ripping up the airwaves. Dollar bounced his head as one of their songs played on the radio through the walkman he had copped off of an inmate a few years ago.

The Greyhound bus ride from Ohio to Indiana was like a luxurious limousine ride. Dollar could have ridden on that bus forever. Anything but the jail cell was like paradise.

Dollar knew that the bus ticket and one hundred dollars wasn't going to get him far, but it would get him as far away from that jail as possible. He was free and clear of his debt to society. He didn't owe the State of Ohio, or any other state for that matter, a thing. He knew he was going to have to stay at the YMCA until he could blueprint some shit out, but he was cool with that. He needed time to think. He needed to clear his mind of what he had experienced for the last eight years and put into action all that he had learned.

Dollar knew that there were three kinds of smarts in the world: street smart, book smart, and prison smart. Dollar now possessed each. Once he put things in perspective and learned what was presently going on in the streets, he would be invincible.

When Dollar's bus finally arrived in Indiana, he exited the bus and took in a whiff of the smell of the streets. Damn, he had missed that scent; the scent of cruddy sewers and cigarette smoke with just a hint of beer that some cat had poured onto the ground for his homie who no longer walked the earth. City life: there's nothing like it in the world.

After taxiing over to the Y, Dollar was down to $88.21. The taxi fare was only $7.80, but he purchased an Extra Value Meal from McDonald's at one of the rest stops the bus made. Dollar knew he was going to have to start setting up a hustle, but it was going to be impossible to do it without a crew. With only $88.21 to his name, time was of the essence.

As Dollar had learned in prison, everyone around him was his enemy. No way could he trust these new age gangstas. These cool-ass muthafuckas wasn't about nothin' but the bling-bling and screwing each other's hoes. He knew that much from the young bucks who were starting to fill the prison. It was time to drop in on Tommy and Ral. Hustling ran in their veins. No matter what they were up to these days, Dollar knew in his heart they would be down for a hustle. Besides, they owed him. The way Dollar saw it, them niggaz owed him the trouble of getting his life on track, for it was his life that spared their own.

First thing was first; he had to look up his family. The guilt of betraying them by being loyal to Tommy put Dollar in between a rock and a hard place. The choice he made meant having to abandon his mother and brother.

How in the hell was he going to explain things to his mother and Klein? He hoped they would forgive him and understand his reasoning for not wanting to stay in contact with them while in prison.

When he showed up on their doorstep, would they believe their eyes? Would they believe him when he told them that he was no longer dead as far as they were concerned, but that he had been resurrected back onto the streets by God?

CHAPTER 8

Puttin' In Work

"This funky-ass place is worse than the joint," Dollar said as he brushed away an oversized cockroach that made its way up his arm. As it flew in the air, he followed it with his eyes. Upon its landing, he stomped it dead with his foot. Dollar scraped the cockroach off of the bottom of his flip-flop. Looking at the flip-flop reminded Dollar of the joint.

"I gotsta get me some real house shoes," Dollar said out loud. Soon enough Dollar would catch back up with the latest fashions. It was now 2003 and things had changed plenty since 1994. Dollar would be back on top of his game in no time with the right planning. Dollar spent most of his days sketching out different types of stickups he could work. He was fiendin' for dem streets. Part of him understood how his father was drawn away by the call of the streets. But the other part of him kept saying, *fuck that! He had a wife and two kids. Something should have eventually brought his ass back home. Now look at him.* Ramelle Blake, aka Romeo, B.K.A. Midwest Serial Killer, had been sucked up by the streets. He set out to own the streets and the streets ended up owning him.

Yeah, Dollar was glad his father was able to rebirth him, but years of hate for this stranger overpowered a few months of liking him. He was glad that man would be sentenced to a slow death. After all, that was the sentence he'd given his family when he walked out of that door twenty-three years ago. Dollar swore he would never abandon his wife and kids like that, and to ensure such, he decided that he would never have his own family. Good conversation and pussy was all any role a woman would play in his life, but a wifey, hell no! He would father no children to abandon and would husband no woman.

So many cats in the prison had gone down because of their so-called wifey. Hoes start ratting those fools out when they knew and had access to what Store-N-Lock facility the Expedition and $600,000 in cash was located. Dollar wouldn't make that mistake. He wouldn't be one of those cats who spent years risking their life in the game to feed kids who weren't even his because a bitch done fucked one of his partners and got pregnant and didn't know who the damn daddy was. Talk shows and the news brought to light and aided in Dollar's list of do's and don'ts.

Speaking of family, Dollar had already been in Gary a week without looking up his mother and little brother. It was time to start the preparations for getting his life back. He needed to come at them with more than, "I'm out of jail and I'm just hanging out at the Y not doing shit with my life." Dollar had to stop staring at the ceiling and make a move.

Dollar went into the communal bathhouse at the Y and got himself cleaned up. He spent $33.54 on some clothing items he picked up from a local thrift store. He pieced together an "I'm looking for a job" ensemble that consisted of a tan pair of khakis and a white three-button Henley. He roped a husky brown belt around his waist that was the same shade of brown as his boots. Dollar armed himself with the $54.67 he had left and the list of job contacts Ed had given him, and copped a ride on the city bus to the first address on the list.

Dollar hit the buzzer for the driver to stop the bus and let him off at the next stop. He walked a couple of blocks down Oak Street before he came to the address he was in search of.

"I'm looking for Redd," Dollar said to the group of men hanging outside, in the cold, of the worn down–looking building that had a hand-painted sign that read WORK FOR A DAY.

The men pointed Dollar toward a double glass door. As he walked through the doors he could see, through the reflection, a few of the men screwing up their mugs at him. No one said it aloud, but those whom he managed to make contact with during his inquiry gave him that "yeah, that nigga just got out the joint" look. People saw a buff dude and automatically assumed he been locked up. Although Dollar looked as though he had been in the World Gym training for the Schwarzenegger Classic, the men were correct in their unspoken assumptions.

"Are you Redd?" Dollar asked the biker type–lookin' redneck sitting behind one of the two cluttered desks that were in the office.

"I am," the man answered. "You come for work?"

"Yes, sir," Dollar said.

The man laughed and replied, "No need for that 'sir' shit. This ain't IBM or nothing like that. Next thing I know you'll be handing me a resume."

Redd immediately handed Dollar a stack of papers to fill out. He informed Dollar that it was just some general liability waivers and whatnot. Redd gave Dollar a clipboard and a pen and invited him to have a seat.

"Can you read?" Redd asked Dollar.

"Excuse me?" Dollar said.

"Can you read?"

"What the fuck kind of question is that?" Dollar said, taking offense. "A black man walk up in here for a job and you think he can't read?"

"Whoa!" Red exclaimed. "Slow down, brotha. Homeless men and white men with a first-grade education come up in here for jobs and can't read, or write for that matter. They get embarrassed and they run out of here and miss out on making money that could have afforded them their next meal. I hired Kera to help out those types. She reads and completes the paperwork for them. That's all I'm saying."

Dollar, feeling a little salty, apologized to Redd. "That's good looking on helping out cats on the streets and those fresh out of the joint." Dollar proceeded to complete the paperwork one sheet after another. As he completed the final page, which was more so biographical information, a soft aroma filled the air. Redd's Benson and Hedges menthol light smoke odor had been superseded by JLo's Glow, which was similar in scent to the Night Queen oil Dollar's mother would always wear.

Dollar looked up at the sweet young thing who was walking over to the second cluttered desk that sat behind Redd's. Ma had it going on. She was a soft, yellow-toned, petite flower. She wore her hair in a natural, curly bob that could have very well been a wet and wavy weave. She had a medium-sized frame with a chunky bootie. Dollar could see her panties because her jeans were gapping around her waist. Obviously she had to purchase larger-sized pants to get over her big ass.

"Filet fish with extra tarter, large fry, and large Sprite," the girl said, handing Redd his lunch.

"That's my little girl," Redd said.

"Oh, Daddy," she replied.

Hell no, Dollar thought. He couldn't believe Redd was sticking his finger into the chocolate pot. If this was Redd's baby girl, she had to be by a black woman. The first fine sista he saw and she's the boss's daughter. There went Dollar's vision of tagging dat ass.

"All finished, sir," Dollar said, handing Redd the paperwork. "I mean, Redd."

"Oh, just give them to Kera," Redd said, pointing to the girl. "Kera, this is . . . I didn't catch your name. I guess I got off track thinking you were going to try to beat my ass after that statement about not being able to read."

"Oh, come on now," Dollar joked. "Let's squash that already."

"I'm just joshing you," Redd said.

"It's Dareese. Dareese Blake. But you can call me Dollar. That's my nickname. Everyone called me that as a kid."

"Kera, Dollar. Dollar, Kera," Redd said.

"Nice to meet you, Dolla," Kera said seductively as she slowly slid the papers from Dollar's hand.

"Same here." Dollar smiled.

Dollar knew that pussy was his if he wanted it. Compared to them raggedy dudes who were standing out front, Dollar was probably the finest muthafucka Kera had seen up in there. Dollar knew he was making an impression as Kera took the papers from him, not taking her eyes off of him once. No way was he going to run up in the boss's daughter. That would keep Dollar out of work for real. Love 'em and leave 'em was the game plan. He could see her now crying to Daddy. Dollar had to shake this one off. He couldn't go getting caught up with no chick. He had to focus on getting that paper.

"So, what can you do?" Redd interrupted Dollar's thoughts. Dollar looked puzzled. "What type of work can you do? What was your last job?"

"Oh, uhh . . . I can, uhh . . . It was, uhh . . ."

"Fresh out the clink, huh?" Redd embarrassed Dollar by asking him that in front of Kera.

Dollar didn't respond verbally. He answered Redd with his eyes.

"Thought so," Redd said.

The fact that Dollar was a former jailbird seemed to attract Kera to him even more. Her eyes lit up for this beefed-up bad boy. Dollar knew right then and there that she was young, eighteen tops. She had that look in her eyes that little girls get when they get a whiff of a dangerous man: a man who ain't afraid of the streets, a man who would break another man's muthafuckin' neck for her ass.

"It's cool," Redd assured Dollar. "Not everybody who comes through those doors have always been on the up and up. People need a break. Hell, I did a dime for the Feds."

Redd looked as though he had done a decade that consisted of ten unrelenting years. This explained his hard look.

"Look, Ed sent me. I don't even know how this type of gig works. I just know I need some cash."

"Ed." Redd laughed. "That's a blast from the past. What's he been up to?"

"Same ol', same ol'," Dollar answered. "He's still a CO over in Chillicothe, Ohio."

Redd almost choked on his French fries as he started laughing. "He's a CO? He never told me that. Ed used to terrorize the neighborhood. I always pictured him on the other side of the law."

"You know I told you Uncle Ed was working as a CO," Kera added. "That one time I went to visit Mommy in Ohio, I told you about Uncle Ed being a CO. He's only been a CO forever and a day."

"Did you?" Redd said. "I don't remember."

"That's why you need to lay off of that stuff, Dad."

Redd gave Kera an evil look. He couldn't believe she was putting his business out there like that.

Sensing her father's anger, Kera got prissy. "It's not like he's deep cover. He just got out of jail, for Christ's sake."

"You Ed's niece, huh?" Dollar asked.

"He's my ex's brother, Kera's mom's brother," Redd answered for Kera. "Ed's cool. His sister's a bitch, but I don't hold that against him."

"That's my moms you talking about," Kera snapped.

"'Bitch' is a compliment," Redd tried to make Kera believe. "You're only seventeen. You'll know what I'm talking about in a few years."

Damn, Dollar thought. *She's only seventeen. I ain't going out like R. Kelly, people running around thinking I'm robbin' cradles and shit.* Not only was Kera the boss's daughter, but she hadn't even grown hair on her coochie yet.

Dollar's hard dick he had been concealing went limp. He wouldn't be putting it to use anytime soon on Kera. He didn't care if her eighteenth birthday was next week; underage was underage.

"Not for long," Kera replied. "I'll be eighteen in a couple of weeks.

It was almost as if Kera noticed Dollar's loss in interest in her and was aiming her comment more so toward him than her father.

"Oh yeah," Dollar said with his eyes. On second thought, maybe he could hold off for a couple of weeks. By then that hot little pussy would really be ripe for the pickin'.

"Anyway, how this here thing works is that you can come hang out here every day and wait for some work to come through. It can be anything from cleaning offices to building a deck," Redd said to Dollar. "With your size, I'm sure you'll be the first pick on the kickball team. Where you staying? Over at the Y, a halfway house?"

"The Y," Dollar answered.

"Well, when you get yourself a phone I can call you up for work. Like I said, with your size, folks will be requesting you by name."

"So, should I come back tomorrow?" Dollar asked.

"Yeah, if you don't want any work today," Redd replied sarcastically.

"So, that's what the men outside are doing, waiting on work?" Dollar asked.

"Yeah, the folks who need workers, sometimes just for a day or sometimes for a full project, come through and scoop up workers," Redd said, looking at his watch. "Yeah, it's still early enough. Somebody might come through looking for some workers. A few of my men have gotten on permanently at some gigs."

It was all making sense to Dollar. Redd basically pimped out workers. Probably got a bonus when one got hired on permanently. But he had papers on them and paid taxes, which made it all legit.

Dollar knew he needed some change for his pocket so he decided to go hang out with the other dudes. He felt like a hooker waiting on a trick. After a couple of hours, some man pulled up in a pickup and went inside the building.

"That's Marlon," one of the guys said. "Whenever he's down a man or two, he comes by here to find replacements."

"What's the job?" Dollar asked.

"Construction," the guy answered. "He frames houses and shit. Do you know anything about that?"

"If it's paying money I do."

"That's what I'm saying." The dude laughed. "I'm Jay."

"Dollar," Dollar said, shaking Jay's hand.

"You straight out the joint?" Jay asked.

"Damn. Is that shit written across my forehead or something?" Dollar joked.

"You know how it is out here on the streets," Jay said. "You either homeless, a crackhead, or freshly released from that gated community. You don't look like a crackhead, and you don't smell homeless."

"Right, right." Dollar nodded.

Just then Marlon and Redd came out of the office. "Any of you men know anything about tarring and cementing?" Marlon asked.

Of course all the men proclaimed of having such knowledge. Marlon knew some were lying.

"You, you, and you," Marlon said, pointing at Jay, Dollar, and some crackhead-looking dude. "Redd, I need 'em on the set the rest of the week. Write it up for me, okay?"

"You got it!" Redd replied as the four men piled into the pickup and drove off.

Dollar had never worked so hard in his entire life. Four days straight, he laid hot tar, axed cement, lifted cement blocks, and spread new cement. He was not trying to spend the rest of his life working this hard. He had to set something up, and fast.

The good thing about it was, when the job was completed, Marlon drove the men back to Redd's and settled the pay. Redd received 30 percent of what the job paid and the men received the other 70 percent tax free. It was the men's responsibility to file taxes at the end of the year as independent contractors. Redd merely served as an agent, a consultant: the middleman. The workers at Work for a Day were considered self-employed, independent contractors. What was even better was that sometimes the men were paid in straight-out cash, but Redd had paperwork and receipts on each man and each job that they did through his company just in case there were any questions from the IRS.

Dollar's bank account was now looking at around $470. It made him feel good. Although it wasn't much, it was enough for him to feel as though he could stand before his mother and little brother. He could tell them he was working and it would be the truth this time.

With a bed at the Y, a couple of outfits, and a job, it was time for Dollar to face his family. Dollar didn't know where to start. He was hoping his mother was still living in the same apartment, and if not, that a neighbor would be able to point him in the right direction.

Saturday morning after Friday payday, Dollar took the bus to his old neighborhood. When he got off the bus, he walked the strip as if he had never abandoned it for eight years. The block hadn't changed. As he approached his old apartment building, he stopped at the steps. He recalled the last time he had stepped foot on them. It was when he had been escorted by the Columbus detectives to a downtown interrogation room. Dollar shook off the negative memory and proceeded to walk inside the building.

"Dollar Bill," a voice called before he could make it completely through the main entrance door. "Dollar, Dollar Bill, y'all. I know that ain't you."

Dollar turned around to find a frail old man approaching him. He was wearing some dirty jeans with holes worn in both knees. The man had on a navy blue fishing jacket with the hood pulled over his head. Dollar didn't recognize the man from back in the day and the expression on his face stated such.

"You don't recognize me, man?" the strange looking guy said. "It's me, Stephan."

As the man walked closer up on him, Dollar recognized him. It wasn't an old man at all. It was his old classmate, Stephan Crouse. He was one of the smartest kids in school. He was voted the most outstanding leader of the senior class. It was visible that the streets had eaten him alive.

"Stephan Crouse." Dollar smiled. Ordinarily, Dollar probably would have showed him street love with a masculine hug and some dap, but the odor that reaped from Stephan's body prevented him from doing so.

"I thought I was seeing a ghost," Stephan said. "I thought you was supposed to grow old and die in the joint."

"Yeah, well," Dollar said, shrugging.

"What you doing back in the old neighborhood, anyway? You ain't no escapee, are you?" Stephan laughed as he stroked his index finger underneath his nose and sniffed. "'Cause you know if there is a reward for your capture, a brotha got to turn ya in." He laughed and play hit Dollar in the arm.

Dollar looked down at his arm and then back at Stephan as if to say, "Don't do that."

Stephan cleared his throat. "I, uh, just saw your little brother about a month ago over at the clinic."

"The clinic?" Dollar said. He wondered if his brother was sick or something.

"Yeah. He's doing some internship or something over at the free clinic."

Dollar was relieved to hear that.

"He been there for a while now," Stephan said, realizing that Dollar obviously hadn't contacted his brother.

"Well, I guess I need to go check out little bro," Dollar said. "Does my moms still live up in here?"

"Nah. She ain't lived here in some time. I don't even know where she staying at, man. I meant to ask your brother 'bout ol' Mrs. Blake."

"Well, it was good hollering at you, my man," Dollar said as he headed for the clinic, which was only a couple miles away.

Dollar saw a few familiar faces as he strolled the block. He saw girls who had once been the finest on the block now looking like crackhead hoodrats. He spotted some of the old hangouts like Mudbone's candy store. Every city had a candy store ran by some fat dude named Mudbone. The candy was always a front for the dope he sold. Mudbone's lazy ass always hated counting out penny candy for the kids.

Dollar couldn't believe his eyes when he saw that Fat's BBQ was still in business. That was the joint when he was a kid. At least once a month some customer at one of the neighborhood restaurants his mother worked for would give her a nice tip. On her way home from the bus stop she would stop by Fat's and surprise the kids with it. Dollar couldn't resist stopping in for a quarter chicken meal with baked beans, greens, and a corn muffin. It brought back some good memories; memories that would soon have a dark overcast.

CHAPTER 9

Is There a Doctor in the House?

"Is there a doctor in the house?" Dollar asked the brown skin, Blair Underwood–looking guy behind the sign-in desk at the clinic. People used to always ask Dollar and Klein if they had the same daddy because Dollar had the majority of his mother's features and Klein had more of their father's features.

"You need to sign in," the man replied as he flipped through a file. "Have you ever been seen here before?" As the man looked up at Dollar, he lost his words. He never expected in a million years to look up and find his big brother standing before him.

"What's up, Doc?" Dollar said.

Dollar's little brother still couldn't respond. He wondered if he was dreaming, if he was just imagining his big brother standing before him. When Dollar spoke again as he reached across the counter and put his hand on his shoulder, Klein knew he wasn't dreaming.

"Can I call you Doc? Long time no see, Doc. I know you're speechless right now. Wasn't expecting to see me today, huh, or any other day for that matter?"

"What are you doing out?" Klein said, finally able to find his words. "You got life." He raised an eyebrow and said, "You didn't—"

"No, man, I didn't break out if that's what you were about to say," Dollar said. "It's a long story, but I'm out legit. I got a job and everything."

The two just stood there, one not knowing exactly what else to say to the other.

"What time do you get off?" Dollar asked. "You ate yet? Look, I got you something." Dollar handed his brother the foam-sealed meal he had gotten him from Fat's BBQ.

"Fat's," Klein said nostalgically as a huge grin took over his face. He then looked up at Dollar and the grin vanished.

"Can we go somewhere and talk?" Dollar asked.

"Uhh, yeah," his brother replied. "Give me a minute."

As Klein walked away to inform the staff that he would be stepping away for a moment, Dollar observed the patients in the waiting room. There was a pregnant fourteen-year-old girl in every other chair. There were a couple of whites but blacks and Latinos represented.

"This way," Klein said, nodding his head toward the exit doors.

"You look good," Dollar said, scrambling for conversation. He didn't know what to say. His brother wasn't the least bit excited to see him. If anything, he acted as if he resented Dollar for reappearing back into his life. How dare he declare himself dead and then resurface as if nothing had happened?

Dollar could see that it was going to take way more than a smile and a BBQ meal to break the ice between him and his brother. Dollar knew it was going to take time so he had to just take things slow for now. Something inside of Dollar wanted to just stop and hug his little brother and tell him how much he had missed him, how sorry he was for the way he handled being incarcerated. But Dollar could sense the hostility in his brother's demeanor and knew such actions would be rejected.

"Yeah," his brother said as they took a few more steps accompanied by silence. "So, you out for good, huh? How'd that happen?"

The two continued walking outside as Dollar vaguely briefed him on his happenings of getting out of jail. He intentionally left out the part about Romeo being their father, the man who had abandoned them as children. Within months a needle would be sending him to his grave anyway. So why bother?

"I'm just glad to be out," Dollar said. "This is a true blessing."

"Yep, 'a true blessing,'" his brother said sarcastically.

With every stale remark his brother made, Dollar was closer and closer to just saying, "Fuck it", walking away, and not trying to make amends with his brother. It was obvious his brother was holding on to that grudge for dear life. But first Dollar needed some information from him.

"I stopped by the old apartment to visit Ma," Dollar said. "Stephan Crouse was walking by and told me that she didn't stay there anymore. He's the one who told me where to find you."

Doc paused as if he had run into a brick wall. He recouped himself and then proceeded to walk. "Stephan Crouse," Doc said. "He was up in the clinic not too long ago."

"Yeah, that's what he told me. Anyway, where's Ma?" Dollar asked. "Can you take me to see her?"

His brother stopped walking and looked at Dollar with cold eyes. Dollar sensed this and put both hands on his brother's shoulders. "Look, man," Dollar said. "I know how much my being in prison hurt her. I knew it hurt her even more when I forced her to swear me off as dead. I know you don't understand, but I couldn't allow her to see her eldest son in a place she wore herself ragged trying to keep me out of. But now I plan to make it all up to her, and you. I'm going to do whatever it takes to make you two understand where I was coming from. I'm sorry, Doc."

"It was one thing for you to ask us to forget you ever existed, but for you to do the same to us, sending our letters back and shit," his brother said, attempting to catch the cuss word he had just spoken.

"I know, Doc, but I thought I was dead. I felt like death," Dollar pleaded. "Prison takes a muthafucka's breath, mind, soul, and heart. It can break your spirit down to nothing. Without that shit, you are dead. I had no idea I would ever walk these city streets again, ever!"

Doc began walking again and Dollar followed his lead.

"Where you staying at?" Doc asked.

"Over at the Y."

"I tell you what, I'll pick you up in the morning at around ten o'clock. I'll take you to see Ma," Klein said. "I gotta get back to work right now, though."

"It's good to see you, Doc," Dollar said. "It's good to see that you did just what you said you'd do. My little brother a doctor," Dollar said, grinning a proud grin.

"Almost a doctor," his brother replied. "I went to school summers and everything to get this far. I'm working at the clinic as kind of like an internship under the supervision of an MD. We almost lost the clinic, but I did a little grant writing and we got some assistance."

"Damn, Doc," Dollar said. "You the man."

"Just giving back to my community in a sense," Doc said.

"Well, I guess I'll see you tomorrow. And, oh yeah, why don't you stop and get Ma some flowers? She'll like that."

The next morning, as promised, Klein picked Dollar up from the Y and they drove to go see their mother.

"Damn, Doc," Dollar said after driving about twenty-five minutes in his brother's Jeep Cherokee. "How far did Ma move away?"

"It's not much farther now," Doc replied as he busted a left off of the freeway exit.

"I can't believe I'm cruisin' the city streets," Dollar gasped as he took in the lovely view. Doc simply looked straight ahead and drove steadily. "You're pretty quiet."

"Still in shock, I guess," Doc replied.

"Yeah, I know. It's hard for me to believe it myself," Dollar said. "For the first few days I kept looking over my shoulder waiting for the man to snatch me up by my collar and drag me back to the joint."

"How long you been out?" Doc asked.

"Not too long," Dollar said. "I didn't come at you and Ma right away because I had to get myself together, you know, before I let you and Ma know I was out. I didn't want to be like all these other cats getting out of jail moving into somebody's basement rent free," Dollar said. "Plus, I couldn't just show up on y'all's doorstep. I knew I had to explain a lot to you guys. I just hope Ma understands."

"Umm hmm," Klein said.

"What, man?" Dollar asked. "What's on your mind? I can tell something is eating at you. You wanna cuss me out, punch me? I don't blame you, man. From your point of view I know I was wrong, but you've never had your life ripped from up underneath you."

"Oh, yeah," Klein said snidely.

"Yeah," Dollar replied as Klein turned into Evergreen Cemetery. "What's going on man?"

Klein ignored Dollar as he maneuvered through the trails of the cemetery roads.

"What's going on?" Dollar repeated.

"You said you wanted to see Ma, didn't you?" Klein answered as he parked the car. "Come on then. Let's go!"

Klein got out of the car and walked over to a gray marbled headstone that stood upright. It had a vase attached to it and it read MRS. SADIE BLAKE 1958–2000. Dollar got out of the Jeep and stood at the hood for a moment. He slowly walked over to the graveside and fell to his knees upon reading the headstone. He choked and lost his breath. Once he was able to clear his breathing passage, he roared out in pain. Klein watched his older brother break down and cry just as he had done three years ago when their mother had passed.

"Go ahead, Dareese," Klein said. "Give Ma her flowers."

"Why?" Dollar cried. "Why didn't anyone tell me?"

"You were dead, remember? We were dead. As far as you were concerned, that is, we were already dead. It didn't matter to call you. You didn't want anybody coming to visit you, seeing you in your prison fits. I figured you sure wouldn't want to show up at your mother's funeral in chains."

"Damn, Doc." Dollar continued to bawl. "When? What happened? I mean, oh my God, my mama!"

"Car accident," Doc said.

Dollar turned his head to wipe his eyes that had been flooded with tears. His eyes caught the tombstone right next to his mother's that read CHARLENE DAVIS. Davis was his mother's maiden name. He knew the grave belonged to his Auntie Charlene.

"Ma and Auntie Charlene both," Doc continued. "On their way to see you, or try to see you, rather. Didn't you wonder why the visits stopped?"

"Oh, Doc. Oh, man," Dollar cried. "Ma, she's gone."

"She said only death could keep her from trying to see her boy," Klein said. "She wanted you to know, she wanted to tell you face to face that she was still proud of you and that she still loved you; that you were her son. She said God told her you were no killer and she'd never believe that you were. She loved you."

"I can't believe no one told me." Dollar snorted.

"I didn't even contact the prison," Klein said. "I didn't write you or try to visit, either. I was just abiding by your request. You'll be pleased to know that I didn't even include your name in the obituary."

Dollar looked up at his baby brother with discontent. It was as if it was pleasing Klein to see him kneeled in grief at their mother's grave. Before Klein knew it, Dollar had charged at him. The two siblings punched and rolled on the ground, on their mother's grave.

Dollar managed to pin Klein down and got a clear shot to punch him dead in the face. Doc saw Dollar's fist clench and prepare to tag him, so he closed his eyes and waited to receive the blow. Dollar held his fist in midair as if he was fighting with an evil entity to keep from bringing it down on his brother's face. Dollar knew in his heart he would have killed his brother. He would have beaten him senseless. Dollar stood up over Klein, looked to the sky, beat his hands on his chest, and roared.

The sound of Dollar's pain echoed throughout the cemetery as Doc stood watching him. Eventually the two drove off together without saying a single word to one another the entire drive.

Hearing bad news while locked up, for Dollar, there was nothing like it in the world. The prison walls closed in on him. He could see them coming to smash in his mind, body and soul and there wasn't anything he could do about it.

Hearing Aaliyah's plane went down, taking the life of the young R&B princess, while in the joint was emotional. Hearing all those lives were lost and destroyed on September eleventh while in the joint was beyond putting into words. But Dollar finding out his mother had passed away was the ultimate. He might as well have still been behind bars because his mind was caving in.

Finding out his mother had passed was hell whether he was locked up or not. It takes people a long time to realize that even God's love is greater than their own mother's. That's the pedestal mothers are placed on, like angels in heaven.

Maybe it was better for Dollar to find out this way. Plenty of times while in the joint Dollar witnessed inmates receive word that the chaplain needed to see them. Most of the time, unless an inmate had requested to see the chaplain, that only meant one thing; someone had passed.

During the long walk to the chaplain's office, the inmate had too much time to wonder about who had died, and out of all their loved ones, who they hoped it wasn't, but if they had to choose, who they hoped it was. Dollar wouldn't have been any better prepared for the walk to the chaplain's office than for the very moment at hand.

Although Dollar rarely spoke with God, on this occasion, he had many words. He had words of anger. Dollar had the worst attitude a young black man on the streets could have. He had that "fuck the world" attitude. He was now dangerous to the world and to himself.

After Klein, what it seemed as though he took pleasure in, told Dollar of the death of their mother and watching him crumble to the ground, he then supplied Dollar with what Dollar saw as the appetizer to his meal ticket. It was his portion of the life insurance policy of which he and his brother were named as beneficiaries.

Auntie Charlene had taken out a policy for both herself and her sister and had the premiums deducted straight from her own checking account. Auntie Charlene's policy was just enough to cover her funeral expenses. Auntie Charlene always used to say, "I ain't no rich woman while I'm alive, so I sure don't want to make anyone rich off of my death." Plus, it wasn't like she had any kids to leave money to.

Knowing Doc was aiming to become a doctor, Auntie Charlene felt that a $100,000 policy for their mother was called for. It was like pulling hen's teeth for Auntie Charlene to get her sister to sign off on the paperwork to put the policy in effect. She didn't want to think about death. It was the one-year anniversary of the date the policy was signed when the car accident occurred.

Dollar's mother had, in print, named Klein as the sole beneficiary. She spoke words to him instructing him that 50 percent was to go to Dollar in spite of what the policy stated. With Dollar being incarcerated for life, she didn't know what would become of his percentage if she was to list him on the policy. So instead, she left the distribution into the hands of her baby boy. He was to keep Dollar's books full, which he failed to do. Klein refused to allow Dollar to profit in prison off of the death of their mother. He had no idea what he would do, if anything, with the money, but he knew he wasn't going to document those funds on prison record. So he put away Dollar's portion, not knowing that Dollar would someday actually be able to benefit from it after all.

$46,000 was left for Dollar after funeral expenses. Dollar saw the money not as a new start, but as a foundation to get started, to get started on his bigger picture. The $46,000 was more like the outline that needed filled in.

Dollar needed to get him a quaint little pad. He needed stability and what he referred to as "Uncle Sam hush money:" legitimately earned money to validate his purchases. He needed some new threads. He had to be able to play the role once he hit the streets again. But most importantly, he needed his old running partners. He needed Tommy and Ral.

CHAPTER 10

Reunited

When Dollar knocked on the locked screen door of the tiny Cape Cod home, a woman's silhouette appeared on the other side of the screen. The big door was only cracked, but Dollar could see that she was fine. Her banging curves were a beautiful sight, and not just because Dollar had been locked up for eight years. As she neared the doorway, her long, wavy locks that she, in sequence, pushed behind each of her ears with her slender fingers, became visible. Her fingernails were smothered by a fresh set of acrylic nails with a funky watercolor design. Her large gold hoop earrings, four inches in diameter, dangled from her soft lobes, slightly brushing her rouge-powdered cheeks here and there.

"Yes, I was looking for an old friend of mine, Tommy," Dollar said in awe as he tried to view every inch of the woman through the black metal bars that secured the screen door. Dollar looked down at the piece of paper he'd printed off at the library and compared the address on it to that above the mailbox on the house. His public records search had shown that Tommy owned this property.

"Ha ha, very funny. I see the jailhouse didn't affect your sense of humor," she responded as she unlocked and pushed the screen door open, allowing the daylight to shine upon her soft brown skin.

"Tommy," Dollar shouted, recognizing Tommy only by her voice, not her stunning features. "Thomasena McRoy!"

"In the flesh," Tommy said.

"Hell no." Dollar bent over laughing.

Tommy, though both excited and shocked to see her old stomping partner on her doorstep, was becoming angered by Dollar's howling laugh.

"You're a woman now," Dollar said as his laughter faded out.

"No shit," Tommy said, now full-blown pissed and unable to enjoy the coming home of Dollar. "I've always been a woman."

"Oh, my bad," Dollar said, coughing his laughter to a complete stop. "But, damn, girl. You was my boy. Now look at you. You clean up real good."

Tommy opened the screen wider and then stepped to the side for Dollar to enter.

"Your place looks nice," Dollar complimented her as he peeped out her humble abode.

"How'd you really get out?" Tommy asked suspiciously, cutting right to the chase. Before Dollar could prove her suspicions wrong, she continued. "I heard a rumor or two, but I know you, D. There's got to be more to the story." She looked him up and down. "So what brings you to my doorstep?"

Coming to her own conclusions, all types of wicked thoughts started going through Tommy's head. Maybe Dollar really was a snitch and maybe him turning her over was part of the deal. This could be a setup as far as she was concerned.

"Hold on right there," Tommy said as she suddenly walked away from Dollar. She walked down a hallway and entered a room. Just a few seconds later she returned with a brown paper bag in hand. "Here you go." She handed Dollar the bag.

Dollar looked inside to find seven rolls of money held in place by rubber bands. He looked up at Tommy curiously.

"Take this," Tommy said. "There's about seven grand in there. It ought to get you by for a while. Keep in touch and I can hook you up with more. There's more where that came from. It just might take me a minute to get that much again though."

Dollar began to laugh.

"What? What's so damn funny?" Tommy said with a twisted mug. "Is it not enough? Look, I said I can get more. Just give me some time."

"I can't believe this, T," Dollar said, looking down at the bag of money. "You ain't changed a bit. You still think everyone is out to get you or out to get something from you, huh? You would have looked good puttin' this shit on my books over the last eight years."

"You wouldn't accept my letters so I figured you wouldn't accept my money either," Tommy said as if her feelings had been hurt by Dollar rejecting her letters. "Look, Dollar, I appreciate everything you done for me back then, you know. And I know I owe you. But I got a life now. A lot of shit has changed."

"Maybe you have changed," Dollar said disappointed. "Do you think I would actually bring you that kind of drama to your doorstep?"

"Well, I have changed. I'm not her anymore. I'm not the Tommy you knew back in the day," Tommy spoke. "Things have changed. You're right; I've changed."

"So I see," Dollar said. "Street life got you noided, huh? But don't even worry. It ain't even like that. I'm out, legit. I'm free, baby. I didn't have to climb over the gate. They opened it up for me. Now how about you opening up yours for me so I can give you the real on my release?" Dollar held his hands out. "Come on; let your guard down a little."

Tommy eyeballed Dollar for a minute. She brushed by him and locked the screen door while looking left to right to make sure no one else was out there.

"Damn, Tommy, what kind of shit you into?" Dollar entered her house.

"You wouldn't believe the jealous hoes I have to deal with working at the Chocolate Factory," Tommy said. "The niggaz who be up in the bar and they bitches be trippin'. I done had my windows busted out and my car spray painted. I even got jumped coming in the house one night. But I got somethin' for they asses the next time they wanna jump out of a bush at three o'clock in the morning and rob a bitch of her tips."

"Damn," Dollar said. "Tommy Gun still keeps the Glock cocked, huh? Shit, who would have guessed the life of a bartender would be so dangerous?" Dollar pretended to have chills and wiggled his body while hugging himself.

"You's a silly mafucka," Tommy said, heading into the kitchen. "I don't bartend at the Chocolate Factory. You want a Coke?"

"Yeah," Dollar responded. "I'm a little parched."

"Oh, 'parched,'" Tommy said. "Did you learn that word in jail? You got a jailhouse degree that you can't do shit with on the outside and couldn't do shit with on the inside, either?"

"Naw," Dollar answered, laughing. "I didn't get down with getting fifteen degrees. I mean, what the fuck a felon gon' do with a master's?" Both Dollar and Tommy laughed. "So what do you do at the Chocolate Factory? You a bouncer? Them chicks be hooking you up like that with tips just for walking them to their car and shit?"

"Do I look like a bouncer to you, Dollar?" Tommy said, putting her hands on her hips. She sucked her teeth and then opened the fridge and grabbed two cans of Coke. "Besides, what do you know about a bouncer's role in a strip club? It's more than just walking chicks to their car. They're like our own personal bodyguards."

"Oh, hell no," Dollar said. "You ain't shakin' it up in there, are you?" The look on Tommy's face said it all, with her downcast eyes. "You, Tommy Gun, is a dancer now? I knew I must have been dreaming. I ain't really out of jail, am I? Satan playing some fucked-up practical joke on me, ain't he? I mean, the next thing you gon' tell me is that you got kids."

Before Dollar could even finish his sentence, a little girl, who looked to be around seven or eight years old, came out of one of the back bedrooms. She was wiping her half-asleep eyes with the backs of her hands.

"I can't believe this," Dollar said in amazement. "You really are a woman."

"Auntie Sena," the small child said to Tommy.

"Yes, Heaven," Tommy said as she approached her niece, handing Dollar his Coke along the way.

Dollar went and sat on the couch after cracking open his can of soda and taking a sip.

"I had a dream. We were at a party but nobody was singing 'Happy Birthday' or nothing. Everybody was sad."

"Well maybe the person whose birthday it was was turning fifty," Tommy joked, but her niece failed to see the humor in Tommy's comment.

"My nap is done. Can I watch 'toons now and have some Blue's Clues?" Heaven said, referring to her Blue's Clues fruit snacks.

"Sure, baby," Tommy said. She grabbed a package of fruit snacks from off the top of the refrigerator and handed them to Heaven. Heaven went back into the bedroom, not once inquiring about the stranger on the couch.

"You babysitting?" Dollar asked Tommy.

"No, they stay with me," Tommy replied as she went over and sat down on the couch. She cracked open her can and took a swig.

"'They'?" Dollar inquired.

"My sister's kids, my two nieces." Tyra must still be asleep.

"Oh, what's up with that?"

Tommy paused before replying. "My sister's dead so I took the girls in so that they wouldn't have to get dumped into the system. She was murdered."

"Damn, T," Dollar said. "I'm sorry to hear that shit. How did she die?"

"She was raped and beat to death a few years ago. Her and her boyfriend, the girls' daddy, was staying up over at the Hills. The girls were asleep right in the next room when it all happened," Tommy said as she subconsciously began to crunch the Coke can in the palm of her hands. Dollar watched as soda leaked from the can down Tommy's hands.

"So, the girls been with you ever since?" Dollar asked.

"Yeah. The state put me through all kinds of shit about getting custody, but I refused to let them be put in foster care. That's why I had to start dancing. I had to keep dropping change into the lawyer like he was a fucking parking meter." Tommy licked the liquid from off her fingers.

"How come the girls didn't just live with their father?"

"He's the one who raped and killed their mother," Tommy replied. "The girls was so used to them fighting and carrying on all the time that that particular night didn't seem any different than all the other nights they had fought. I tried to get my sister to leave his ass. She couldn't let go. Even after I shot his ass, she stayed with him."

"You shot him?" Dollar said, surprised.

"Man, my sister's face was fucked up. He beat her because when he came home he saw the man who lived next to them leaving out of their apartment. UPS had left a package with the guy next door because my sister wasn't home when they came to deliver it. He accused her of cheating with the man. He beat her and put her out the house buck naked and told the girls he'd kill them if they let her in. Keelah called me . . . Remember Keelah from South High School?"

"Yeah, ol' Keelah," Dollar answered.

"She called me and told me that she had looked out her window when she heard screaming and saw my sister beating on the door without any of her clothes on. She said she took my sister a blanket and tried to convince her to come to her house and call the police, but she wouldn't do it. She was afraid he'd do something to her girls in retaliation," Tommy said, trying to contain her emotions in order to get the story out clearly to Dollar.

"I headed straight over there," Tommy continued. "That twenty-minute drive turned into a two-minute drive. When I arrived, I told my sister to wait in my car. I went and busted that muthafuckin' living room window out, climbed through that bitch, and sent the girls outside to the car too. That punk-ass nigga gon' see my Mag and go lock himself in the bedroom like a ho. So I'm banging on that bitch yelling for him to come kick my ass, to come fight me. The longer I stood banging on that door the more pissed off I got, but I knew that punk nigga wasn't coming out.

"So I left and went out to the car. It was dark when I got there so I hadn't got a good look at my sister's face. When I turned on the interior light in the car and saw my sister's face," Tommy said as she began to get emotional, "I had to do that nigga, Dollar. I went back up in that house and just start firing at the door. I let all fifteen Mags off through that bedroom door. Do you know only one hit that muthafucka? And in the hand at that, his damn pinkie finger. I blew that muthafucka off, though. I got back in the car and drove my sister and the kids to my house. Two days later, they were back with him. One month later, she was dead."

"Did you do any time for shooting him?" Dollar asked.

"That nigga knew better than to report my ass. He told the police some dudes broke in through the living room window and tried to rob his house."

"Damn, T." Dollar sighed. "I'm sorry all that shit had to go down."

"Shit happens," Tommy said. "And you still live."

"Things can't be that bad," Dollar said. "You got Gs sitting up in here like everything is gravy. All you doing is dancing, ain't it?" Dollar raised his eyebrows at Tommy.

"You know I would never get down like that," Tommy said. "I ain't selling pussy. I sell them niggaz a little weed, but they ain't getting the cat."

"For real," Dollar said. "That's your hustle, weed?" He was pleased to see that she hadn't gone 100 percent legit.

"I don't like that look you giving me," Tommy said. "Talk to me, Dollar Bill. What's on your mind?"

Dollar took a sip from his soda and let out a loud belch. He then looked up at Tommy and proceeded to tell her how he, once again, needed her services.

"You talking about robbin' muthafuckas again?" Tommy asked. Dollar nodded in the affirmative. "Ain't you learned shit? We fucked up the first time and the last time. You don't know these streets now. These cats are ruthless. Nigga's backup got backup now."

"Introduce me to the streets again," Dollar said to Tommy, taking her hand. "All I need is an introduction and I can take it from there. Back in the day, I was a virgin to the game, but now it's a different story." Dollar told Tommy about the old head, Romeo, he had met in prison and how he schooled Dollar on the game before turning over the wild card to him.

"So you see, it's all good now. I just need you to reacquaint me to the streets. Allow me to get to know them better," Dollar's said as his words tranquilized Tommy. "You working at the Chocolate Factory, T. I know you know everything that happens in the streets before it happens. The first thing these out-of-state ballers want to do is go stick they face in pussy when they come to town. I know they be up in there telling y'all hoes their business."

"Excuse me?" Tommy said, taking offense.

"Not you," Dollar cleaned it up. "Them other hoes."

"Look, Dollar, I'm content with what I got going on. It pays the bills," Tommy said.

"But that's all it does," Dollar enforced. "In all these years, all you got saved up is seven grand? So you gon' die here, huh? You just gon' keep paying these same ol' bills? So, you're like these other wannabe hustlers? You content with some ol' two-bedroom minimum shit; and there's three of y'all living up in here, too? Is this your for life, T?"

Tommy hated to admit that it was.

"This ain't you, baby. I know you. You're like me. We cut from the same cloth. You got caviar dreams." He looked around. "This is fish sticks."

Tommy looked around her spot. Before Dollar had shown up, she loved her casa. All of a sudden it was a shack. It was nothing. It was four fucking walls closing in on her. It wasn't what she ultimately wanted, and Dollar was there to remind her of just that.

"I got these kids now," Tommy said. "I can't give the county no reason to come scooping them up. I can't, Dollar."

"I ain't talkin' 'bout making no career out of the shit," Dollar said in a convincing tone. "I mean, yeah, we gon' have to make a couple li'l hits to get our feet wet again, but I'm looking for that big hit that's gonna allow a nigga to retire from the streets."

"I don't know, Dollar," Tommy said, shaking her head.

"I need you, Tommy. I need you to make this happen," Dollar said, rubbing her face. "You know when it comes down to it I got your back. I ain't gonna never let nothing happen to you. Haven't I proven that? I can't just go out on the streets and find a crew to run with. I got out of the joint by dropping the dime, Tommy. A snitch is a snitch; muthafuckas don't care about the DNA of it. Who's gonna trust me enough to have my back? Who?"

Tommy could feel all of Dollar's weight on her shoulders. She knew she owed him. Yeah, she knew the streets like the back of her hand. The streets were her lover. They had gotten her where she was thus far. The streets had not yet let Tommy down, and with Dollar by her side, she couldn't go wrong. Tommy looked around her house and stared at a picture of her nieces, whom she breathed for and wanted everything in the world for. She had to admit that she wanted more. Not just more for herself, but more for them as well.

"So you in?" Dollar asked, giving Tommy a puppy dog face.

"If I do decide to get down, it ain't gon' be no career move or no shit like that. Just a few times, Dollar. Just enough to make some shit happen, you know? Then you're on your own," Tommy said, trying to convince herself more so than Dollar.

"So is that a yes?" Dollar asked.

"I'm in," Tommy mumbled under her breath.

"What was that?" Dollar asked.

"I'm in, damn it." Tommy rolled her eyes.

"My nigga," Dollar said, picking Tommy up and spinning her in the air. "Now alls we need is our third leg."

The grin that had been on Tommy's face vanished. "Who?" She twisted her neck back.

"Ral, of course," Dollar replied.

"Oh, we can't fuck with Ral. He's through. The monkey got him," Tommy said, shooing her hand.

"Heroin?" Dollar asked.

"That and anything else he can get his hands on to feel good," Tommy said. "I'm surprised he's not dead yet."

Tommy could see the hurt on Dollar's face as she shared Ral's current state. Dollar felt as though he had left Ral for dead by going to jail. If he had been on the streets, he would have never let Ral get that bad; bad enough to where he wasn't to be fucked with, where he was of no use. Listening to Tommy's words, Dollar thought that maybe Ral would have been better off serving time because, according to Tommy, time was serving him.

"You okay, Dollar?" Tommy asked, pulling Dollar out of his thoughts.

"Yeah," Dollar responded. "I'm cool."

The two sat in silence momentarily. It was as if one was waiting on the other to say the word. Dollar could be a dirty muthafucka and just roll with Tommy or he could be a loyal nigga and go take care of his boy.

"Well, what do you wanna do?" Tommy asked Dollar.

Dollar gulped down the remainder of his Coke, set it down on the table, and said, "As always, let's go save Ral."

On that note, Tommy had the teen girl next door come sit with her nieces and then she led Dollar to the spot Ral was known to hang out at. It was an olive green double-family home on a street that hosted dozens in various colors just like it. As they approached the front door they could hear some laughter and commotion going on. Before Tommy knocked on the door,

Dollar clutched her fist and told her to hold up. They walked around to the side of the house and peeked through the side window. What they saw made their stomachs turn. They saw Ral kneeled down on his knees in front of a guy sporting an Outkast velour sweat suit. There were a couple of dames in the living room smoking on a pipe and two dudes cutting lines at the kitchen table. The guy standing in front of Ral was waving a tiny glass valve halfway filled with liquid and yanking at his dick with the other hand.

"Com'n man," one of the guys who was sitting at the kitchen table said. "You ain't gonna get him to suck your dick. Ral will knock an old lady upside the head to get high, but I ain't never known him to suck no dick."

"Shiiiitt," the guy standing before Ral said. "I got that ho, Charise, to fuck a pit bull last week for some blow. We took pictures of that shit and everything. We had that bitch moaning as that pit bull pumped his little shit in and out of her. If I can get that pretty-ass bitch to fuck a dog, I know I can get this piece of trailer park trash to lick the lollipop."

The guy continued to taunt Ral as the onlookers laughed.

"Com'n, you know you want to get high," the guy addressed Ral.

He then waved the heroin in front of Ral and started smackin' his dick around Ral's face. Ral turned his head away, trying to avoid contact, but the guy made sure he kept up with him.

Ral needed that blow. He needed to get high. He didn't even have lint in his pockets. He was too geeked to go out and attempt to steal something; besides, he didn't have the patience to try to sell it for cash or negotiate for a hit. Opportunity to get high was right there in his face, literally.

Dollar and Tommy watched in disgust.

"What you wanna do?" Dollar asked Tommy.

Tommy pulled a baseball cap out of her back pocket, tucked her long locks up in it, and then once again reiterated, "Save Ral."

"All right. You got my back?"

"I got you." Tommy nodded.

Dollar and Tommy crept around to the back door. He looked at Tommy. "You ready?" Upon Tommy nodding, using all of his weight, Dollar caved in the door.

Tommy, dressed for the occasion wearing some green camouflage pants, a green fishing jacket, and a baseball cap, was right behind Dollar with gun in hand, something she never left home without since getting jumped. It was cocked at attention.

Their intrusion was totally unexpected. They heard one of the girls yell, "Undercover," but before anyone could move, Tommy fired a warning shot. The shot shattered the ceiling fan that was already missing a blade.

Dollar kept his eyes on the occupants. Young and dumb; not much of a threat at all, especially with Tommy Gun and Tommy's gun having his back.

"Y'all cat's trying to rob us and shit?" one of the young guys said.

"Shut the fuck up. Ain't nobody interested in y'all's bullshit-ass hustle. We don't want nothing that belongs to y'all. We just want what belongs to us."

"Ral, get the fuck up," Tommy scolded, gripping her weapon.

Hardly recognizing her, or even aware of what was taking place around him, Ral maintained his position.

Dollar went over and snatched Ral to his feet. The expression on Ral's face was as if God Himself had reached a hand down from the heavens to save him.

"That piece of trailer park trash shit is what y'all want?" The young dude laughed.

"Laugh your ass onto the ground face down," Tommy snapped. "All of you muthafuckas. Get face down onto the floor."

It was now evident to everyone in the room that the intruders were no police officers. They had no handbook of regulations to follow. They could shoot each and every one of them in the back. Without a fight, everyone did as they were told.

Tommy looked to Dollar as a question of what to do next.

"Look, man," the guy who had been trying to get Ral to give him some head said. "I was just fucking with dude. This ain't that serious. Besides, look at him. He ain't nothing but a dope fiend. I wasn't really going to let him suck my dick. I ain't gay."

Ral dropped his head as his eyes began to roll to the back of his head.

Dollar had already told these little niggaz to shut up. His initial intention was just to go get Ral, but now he had to teach these young'uns a lesson. "You holdin'?" Dollar asked the guy.

"Com'n, man," the guy responded. "I work for Ducie. He'll kill me, man. Muthafuckas in wheelchairs for doing that song and dance about getting robbed. Com'n, man."

"Stop crying, you bitch-ass faggot," Dollar said, becoming irritated.

"Come on, D," Tommy said. "You said we was just coming to save Ral."

Dollar gave Tommy the "shut the fuck up, bitch" look.

Tommy snapped her neck and turned her lips up at Dollar.

"Take your pants off," Dollar said to the guy.

"What?" the guy responded.

"Did I stutter, muthafucka? Take 'em off. You already got 'em unzipped and had your dick hanging out. Now take the pants off. You like showing your dick. Let's see it."

The guy, still on his face, slowly removed his pants and kicked them to the side.

Dollar picked up the pants and went through each pocket and took ownership of what was around $6,000.

"This all you holdin'?" Dollar asked. "Oh, you's a tennis shoe dope boy. What do you get out of this, about a grand?"

"Com'n, man," the guy begged. "You see for yourself it ain't much. Ducie gon kill me, man."

Dollar looked the guy up and down and began laughing. "What they call you?" Dollar asked.

"Tyrone," the guy responded.

"Figures," Dollar said, throwing out a snicker. "Well, I'll tell you what, Tyrone, you ain't getting this money back."

Tyrone began to cry actual tears and repeat, "Com'n, man" over and over.

"You s'posed to be hardcore, ain't you? You sitting here crying like a bitch. I can see why you like getting your dick sucked by men. You a ho." Dollar bent down and continued addressing the young thug. "See, you caused my boy here a lot of pain and suffering." He looked to Tommy. "T, if we were in a court of law, how much do you think a judge would give our friend Ral here for pain and suffering?"

"I don't know," Tommy said, shrugging. "About six thousand dollars."

Dollar looked upward. "Yeah, that sounds about right," Dollar replied, then looked back down to Tyrone, Tommy alternating the aim of her gun from one person to the next. "So, you see here, Tyrone. I'm gonna be the judge in this case and award my friend here this six thousand dollars for pain and suffering." Dollar put the money in his pocket and looked at Tommy as if giving her a cue.

"Oh," Tommy said, catching on. "There's always court costs and attorney fees. I suppose your friends here won't mind helping you out with that."

Tommy and Dollar proceeded to strip the occupants of their cash and any jewelry. These were some old sorry-ass dope boys paying some bitch's rent to let them hustle out of her place.

Their jewelry pieces combined weren't worth more than $3,000. Dollar and Tommy took it all the same, along with $4,000 more collected from the other occupants.

As Dollar and Tommy carried Ral out of the house, they could hear the cries of Tyrone. "Ducie gon' kill me," Tyrone said. "Ducie gon' kill me."

"Where we gon' take him?" Tommy asked Dollar as they threw Ral in the back seat of Tommy's Plymouth Sundance.

"We gotta take him to your house to clean him up," Dollar replied.

"I can't take him to my house with the girls there," Tommy quickly said. "You think I want this shit around them? You acting like this fool is drunk, and once he throws up he'll feel better. Dollar, he's addicted to heroin, crack, and anything else his ass can probably get his hands on. You think putting on your cape to rescue him from a dope house is going to make him quit, but he don't want to quit."

Dollar sighed. "You right," Dollar said, taking a moment to think. "This is going to take time. I gotta think. Let me think." Unfortunately neither had thought this whole thing through before portraying Batman and Robin, saving Ral's day.

Seeing Ral like this tore Dollar to pieces. Back in the day he got high, but he'd never seen him this bad off. He didn't understand how Ral could allow himself to even let drugs take over his life like this. He had a million questions and no answers.

"Where you staying?" Tommy asked.

"I'm at the Y for now, but not for long."

"Well, you definitely can't take him there with you." Tommy thought for a moment. "I got it!" She snapped her finger. "We can take him to Short Stay Motel on Pike Road."

With no other options, Tommy drove ten minutes to Short Stay where she went into the lobby and got a room for Ral.

Short Stay was a cash only, no ID, no questions asked kind of spot. Most of the girls from the titty bars took their tricks there. Some of the girls even lived there as roommates.

On Tommy's way back to the car with the key to the room, she ran into two chicks she stopped briefly to converse with. At first, Tommy felt a little uncomfortable as she thought the girls might assume she was there with a john. Tommy knew these two chicks were full-time hoes their own selves so ultimately it didn't matter what they thought about her.

Tommy hurried back to the car and helped Dollar carry Ral into his temporary dwelling, room 112. Ral smelled like a baby's diaper that had been sitting in a corner for a week. Smelling as if he hadn't bathed in weeks, the wrenching odor that erupted from his pores confirmed this fact. His teeth were rotted and his hair was an oily pit of dirt.

Dollar lightweight had an attitude with Tommy. How had she allowed her boy to get to this point? Why hadn't they stuck together and looked out for one another? Maybe they weren't the loyal road dawgz he thought them to be back in the day.

Ral never spoke a word to either Dollar or Tommy. He moaned and scratched at himself like a dog with fleas. Tommy suggested Dollar put Ral in the shower while she ran to Walmart to grab him some clothes. Dollar gave Tommy $500 of the money he had taken from Tyrone and she headed to the store.

Tommy came back with several Fruit of the Loom sweat suits, some generic brand sneakers, a couple of packages of briefs and socks, as well as some personal hygiene items. She also stopped and picked up a pizza. She knew nobody was going to deliver to the area the motel was in.

"Damn," Tommy said as she watched Ral's twitching body soaked in sweat lay across the double bed. "He's real fucked up. I told you."

"How long he been getting down like this?" Dollar asked.

"You know Ral always had a thing for street candy."

"Yeah, well, if I had been here, there's no fucking way I'd let my boy get like this."

"So, what the fuck you trying to say?" Tommy said. "You trying to say this shit is my fault?"

"Look at him, T," Dollar said. "This is your boy. He supposed to be your boy for life."

"He's a muthafuckin' grown-ass man," Tommy said. "I'm raising two kids, sliding down fishy-ass smellin' poles, bruising my thighs just to feed them. You don't know what it's like out here. Just trying to take care of my own self is hard. My nieces are my responsibility, not Ral, and not you, so fuck you, Dollar. I don't need this shit. I'm saving my money to get out of this hell-hole lifestyle for good. I don't care how long it takes me. Fuck this shit. I don't even know how I almost let you talk me into this ghetto-ass shit."

With tears in her eyes and a dose of the truth hurts, Tommy scrambled for her keys and headed for the door.

"So it's like that?" Dollar said. "You just gon' leave us hangin'?"

Tommy looked into Dollar's eyes and discovered his attempt to remind her of her debt to him. He wanted her to remember that she had shot three men dead and he accepted the punishment alone. Tommy knew she owed Dollar her life. By the same token, she had to be loyal to her nieces. She promised them she would provide them a good life. She promised that someday they would pick up and move to Cali or something, a good part. They would have a nice house, nice clothes, and breed dogs or something. They would be so well off that she wouldn't have to work so hard. She would be there for them when they woke up in the middle of the night instead of being in some bar giving a dude a lap dance.

On the other hand, if it hadn't been for Dollar, she might not even have the girls. They might be dead by now, buried next to their mother. She wouldn't have been there to save them, but in jail instead. She would be there for Dollar. Once again, she would commit herself. Just as soon as they made a big hit, though, she was gone and would never look back. On that final thought, Tommy dropped her keys and retrieved some cold, wet washcloths from the bathroom to cover Ral with.

Tommy and Dollar nursed Ral. They kept cold rags on him and made him take a few bites of pizza. He kept vomiting and moaning, though.

"He can't do this," Tommy said. "He needs help, Dollar."

"I seen cats in the joint go through this same thing," Dollar said. "If he can just get through this first twenty-four hours he'll be fine."

Ral's eyes began to roll in the back of his head. This episode scared Tommy. Dollar remained calm, insisting that Ral could get through his withdrawal.

"Dollar, can't you see he needs a doctor? He's sweating bullets, but he is as cold as a corpse," Tommy said. "He needs a doctor."

Dollar looked at Tommy who had a frantic look on her face. Maybe she was right, Dollar thought. Dollar's main reason for not wanting to take Ral to the hospital was because he had no idea what kind of shit Ral had been in and how many brushes with the law he had managed to accumulate. What if he had warrants? The hospital was sure to know he was a drug addict. Taking Ral to the hospital might have been like checking him into jail. Dollar could see that Ral was slowly but surely deteriorating. Getting through this first twenty-four hours didn't look so promising.

Tommy was right; Ral needed a doctor. This could ruin everything Dollar had planned for the three. He wanted Ral, but more so, he needed Ral alive and healthy.

Ral began to wheeze and vomit. He was near convulsions. Tommy grabbed the toothbrush she had purchased for Ral at Walmart and used the handle to hold his tongue flat so that he would not choke on it.

"Dollar," Tommy screamed. "Please! He needs a doctor."

Tommy took Ral's head and held it in her arms. Was this her fault? Maybe she could have done something. Dollar wouldn't have allowed Ral to get to this point. Ral used to be Tommy's number one running partner, and now look at him. Tommy began to tremble as she rocked Ral.

"Come on, Ral," Tommy said. "I ain't save your life all those times just so you could turn around and kill yourself. Come on, big baby, you can get through this."

Tommy kissed Ral on his forehead and proceeded to give him pep talks. Dollar had never seen Tommy like this. He had never seen an emotional, nurturing side to Tommy. The scene before him reassured Dollar that he could, in fact, count on Tommy. He watched her interact with Ral a little while longer before giving the order.

"Come on," Dollar said. "We're taking him to see a doctor."

CHAPTER 11

White Boy Wasted

"It's four o'clock in the morning. Who in the hell can that be?" Klein said as the repeated beating on his front door woke him. Buck naked, as he always slept, he slipped on some boxers and a T-shirt and headed down the spiral staircase. He separated the blind with his hand and peeked out of the picture window beside the front door to view the side profile of Dollar.

Klein dropped his hands and stood there as Dollar continued to knock. As Klein headed back up the spiral staircase, Dollar's knock became harder and more desperate.

"Yo, Doc," Dollar called. "Come on, man. It's me, your big brother. Please open up."

Dollar had driven out near the suburb of Munster, where his brother lived. He'd looked up his address in the phone book. He was surprised to find it there because most black people didn't list their information, but with Klein being in the medical profession, he was sure enough in the book. Usually folks in the legal and medical profession listed their information in the directory.

Hesitantly, Klein reconsidered. He came back down the steps and opened the door. There stood Dollar with Ral limp in his arms. Tommy had Dollar drop her off at her house with the girls and gave him permission to use her car to go get Ral help. When Klein saw Ral, he knew that he needed immediate medical attention.

"What happened to him?" Klein said, helping Dollar carry him in. "Is he hit?"

"No, man," Dollar replied. "He's fiendin'. I don't know what to do."

Klein quickly retrieved his medical bag and began to take Ral's vital statistics. Dollar anxiously paced back and forth.

"Can't we give him something like chocolate or something?" Dollar asked.

"How long has it been since he had a hit?" Klein asked.

"I don't know, Doc," Dollar replied. "He hasn't really been able to communicate with me. This is my first time seeing him since I been out. Found him like this at a dope house."

"Why didn't you take him to the ER?"

Dollar's expression answered his brother's question.

"You ain't getting me caught up in no bullshit, are you?" Klein inquired.

"You know I wouldn't do that to you, bro."

"Help me carry him upstairs to the tub," Klein instructed Dollar. "I'll do all that I can do for him, but you're the one who is going to have to stay up and keep an eye on him."

Dollar and Klein carried Ral to the tub and filled it with lukewarm water. Klein insisted that Ral's temperature needed to be regulated. He instructed Dollar to drain the water as it chilled and refill the tub. He showed Dollar how to take and read Ral's blood pressure, and how to take and read his temperature. He told Dollar to force Ral to drink fruit juice and to secure his tongue if he went into convulsions. And if this did occur, he didn't care what Dollar said, he was having Ral transported to the hospital.

All night Dollar nursed Ral like a wounded, stray puppy that had followed him home. It seemed like hours passed by before there was a sign of life in Ral.

"Yo, Dollar," Ral said, waking up half out of it, still soaking in the tub. "What am I in for?"

Ral's voice woke Dollar from his catnap. "Huh?" Dollar replied, wiping his eyes.

"What am I in the joint for? It was my moms, huh? I told that old bitch I was gonna bring her television set back to her." Ral began to twitch

and gag. Dollar grabbed him and positioned him
in a headlock to try to gain some control over his
twitching and jerking body.

"Don't talk," Dollar said. "Just relax. You're
not in the joint, Ral."

Ral was able to relax some. "Is we in heaven
or hell?"

"Stop fucking around, man. You're sick,"
Dollar said, releasing him from the headlock.
"You ain't dead yet, fool. You still in sorry-ass
G-Town. I got out the joint, man. I'm back."

"Word!" Ral said. "My N word."

"You's a silly muthafucka, you know that?"
Dollar said.

Ral looked down at himself fully clothed
in a tub of water. Dollar reached for a can of
Hawaiian Punch to give to Ral. "Is this some type
of ghetto baptism?" Ral asked.

Klein, hearing voices, entered the bathroom
to check on things. He gave Ral some towels and
clothing to throw on and moved him into his
guestroom. Next he checked Ral's vitals, which
were pretty good for the condition he was in.
He let Dollar know that Ral would most likely
go through withdrawal for a few days. He also
instructed Ral to pay him a visit at the clinic, and
provided them with information on some rehab

facilities where he could go to get help with kicking his addiction, if that was something he really wanted to do.

"I appreciate all this, man," Dollar said to Klein as Ral's arm hung around Dollar's left shoulder as he assisted him with walking. "I really do."

"That's my job," Klein said short and with an attitude. "Let me help you get him out to the car."

The two brothers got Ral into the passenger seat of the car. Dollar laid the seat back as far as it would go, strapped Ral in, and closed the door.

As soon as the car door closed, Klein went off. "Nigga, don't you ever come to my domain with your ghetto-ass bullshit," Klein said. "What the fuck you hanging around trash like that for anyway? Ain't that the same piece of shit you used to run with before you went in the joint?"

Dollar stood there, thrown off by Klein's rampage.

"Look, take that money from Ma's death, get you a nice little place, get you some schooling, a steady job, and fuck these streets, man. Damn, didn't you learn nothing while you were locked up?"

"As a matter of fact, I did," Dollar said, opening the door to leave. "As a matter of fact, I did."

Dollar made his way to the car. As Dollar drove Ral back to Short Stay to get him situated in the room, he told Ral all the details surrounding his release from prison. Dollar left out the part about Romeo being his father, as he did with everyone else he relayed the story to. Ral was barely comprehending Dollar's words, but Dollar rambled on in spite of that.

Dollar stopped at a convenience store so that he could stock the motel room with enough snacks to tide Ral over for a few days. He bought a foam cooler and filled it with ice and beverages.

Dollar ordered Ral to stay put while he handled a few things, and promised that he would come back to check on him the next day. Dollar soon learned that a fiend don't stay put when he went to the bathroom and came out to find the hotel door open and Ral gone.

Ral hadn't gotten too far down the road before Dollar caught up with him and took him back to the hotel room. It was evident that Dollar was going to have to do some babysitting for the next few days.

"Good looking out last night," Dollar said, as he drove Tommy to work in her car. "Ral would probably be lying up dead in that motel room if it weren't for you insisting we get him to a doctor."

"Either that or he'd be somewhere sucking dick," Tommy said as she looked in the back seat at Ral who was taking a snooze. "One of the two."

Dollar, not finding humor in Tommy's joke, simply gave her a dry look.

"Anyway," Tommy continued, "Shay ain't gon' give a fuck about me saving somebody's life. All she's going to care about is why my black ass wasn't at work last night."

"Shay your boss?" Dollar asked. "Shay from View Point?"

"She manages the joint," Tommy replied. "Her dude owns it. Well, he bought it, anyway. It's in her name. You know how these dope boys do it once they get big time. They graduate from buying they bitches tennis bracelets to buying them titty bars, beauty shops, day care centers and shit."

"Then why haven't you snagged up one of them ballers?" Dollar asked. "I know you done bumped into all kind of ballers in the club."

"I can't have that shit around the girls," Tommy quickly replied. "These muthafuckas are ruthless. They don't give a fuck who they shoot up trying to get to a rival nigga or a cat that owe them some money. I can see the girls and me now sitting on the couch watching *My Wife & Kids* and bullets raining through the window.

Hell no. It's a known fact; wherever trouble goes, trouble follows. I can't bring it to where I lay my head."

"Yeah, being a hustler's wifey is just as crucial as being the hustler himself," Dollar said.

"If it was just me, hell, I'd probably roll with a baller until I got tired of his ass," Tommy said. "Until I got my bookstore anyway."

"What bookstore?" Dollar asked.

"I've been thinking about shit, about what I really want to do. And I want to own my own bookstore. I want to name it after my sister, something to leave for the girls so that they never have to do some of the shit women have to do to survive nowadays."

"A bookstore, huh?" Dollar said, turning into the parking lot of the Chocolate Factory.

"Yeah, with all kinds of books." Tommy's face lit up. "Maybe a little café section, too, with a stage for some open mic. Yeah, that's what I'm gonna do someday." Snapping out of her daydream, Tommy grabbed her duffel bag from out of the back seat and said to Dollar, "Pick me up at three a.m. Don't be late, Dollar. I ain't trying to be like some of these bitches in here waiting around for their dudes to come pick them up in their own car."

"T, you know I wouldn't play you like that," Dollar said. "Thanks for letting me borrow your wheels."

"Three a.m.," Tommy reiterated. "Oh yeah, and, Dollar . . . welcome home."

CHAPTER 12

A Shot of Henney

"I love these streets," Dollar said aloud as he walked through the city's downtown on his way from the Bureau of Motor Vehicles. He had just seen a clean, fully loaded, two-year-old black Honda Accord at a Buy Here Pay Here car lot. He had to have it. It was calling his name. He had the cash, but he didn't have a driver's license. He hadn't gotten around to getting his driver's license so that was the reason for his visit to the BMV.

Dollar's plan was to own a nice set of wheels. He needed transportation first and foremost so that he could maneuver the city easier. It would also make apartment hunting that much easier. That public transportation and walking, while trying to handle his business, was for the birds.

Dollar would be rolling in that Honda soon enough. This would be the first item he could check off of his "shit to do and shit to get" list he had written up. Next he needed to get him a crib, Dollar thought as he stood at the stoplight waiting for the walk signal.

"Excuse me, sir. Do you have the time?" a woman asked Dollar as she fiddled with the watch on her wrist. "Mine stopped."

Honey was the shit, to say the least. She stood about five feet six inches tall. She was playing a money green miniskirt suit with a white blouse under it and a matching tie. Her gator pumps were the exact shade of her suit. Her coffee brown tights complemented her toned, scar-free legs. Her shiny lips, which wore only colorless lip gloss, looked like cherries dripping with melted chocolate waiting to be licked.

As the woman stood there plucking at her watch, Dollar took in a whiff of her freshly styled hair. He didn't recognize the smell as the aftermath of the perm chemical underneath a tangerine-scented spritz. Her long brown hair had the Farrah Fawcett thing going on. Each strand was feathered in place. If a tornado had suddenly rolled through, nine times out of ten, still, not a hair would be blown out of place.

"Uhh, the time?" Dollar said, stunned. He was like a deer caught in headlights. The subtle beauty of the owner of the soft voice blinded him. He looked down at the shiny gold watch he had swiped from Tyrone's wrist. Instead of numbers it had small diamond chips. Dollar began counting the stones as the lady stood impatient.

"Don't tell me you're one of those guys who spends $25,000 on a watch and can't even tell time on the thing," she said. "Never mind." She rolled her eyes.

"Damn," Dollar said as the woman whisked away like Cinderella at the stroke of midnight. Her sassiness/classiness was intriguing to Dollar.

"That shit turns me on!" Dollar said to himself. "Hold up, Miss Lady. Don't be so mean." He began walking, trying to keep up with her.

"Is that the only thing men can think of to say when y'all get shot down by a woman?" the lady said. "I'm not mean. I just don't want to be bothered. I wanted something and you couldn't give it to me. No harm done. Now you go your way and I'll go mine."

Dollar continued following her with a huge grin on his face. Her fly-ass mouth, which she probably used on a regular to fight off men, wasn't working with Dollar. Like most men, he was up for the challenge of getting something he liked.

"Why do I feel like the girl in Michael Jackson's 'The Way You Make Me Feel' video?" she said, stopping in her tracks.

Dollar couldn't help but laugh as she stood there dead serious. Eventually Dollar's laughter became contagious.

"I'm sorry for being so rude." The lady laughed after relaxing her shoulders. "It's just been one of those days."

"That's okay," Dollar said. "I recently had a few of those years."

"Pardon me?" she said, confused by Dollar's comment.

"Never you mind," Dollar said, holding out his hand. "Dollar. I'm Dollar."

"Dollar, huh?" She showed disappointment that Dollar had given her a nickname, which she thought was most likely his street name given to him by his peer of thugs. "Pleased to meet you. Anyway, Dollar, you take care of yourself."

"Don't you believe in reciprocity?" Dollar asked.

The use of the word "reciprocity," which Lauren Hill made common and sexy in her song "Ex-Factor," made the lady smile.

"Hennessey," she said as she walked away. "Hennessey Monroe."

Dollar watched her walk away until she was out of sight. But she damned sure wasn't out of mind.

Dollar hadn't been to work in four days due to his keeping tabs on Ral. Ral seemed to be through the worst part of the withdrawal period and out of the woods. Dollar had to fight him and constrain him a couple of times, but he was willing to do whatever he needed to do to get Ral through this ordeal. A rehab facility watching over him would have made Dollar's life much easier, but Ral refused to voluntarily go.

Dollar needed to get back to work. Until he got a chance to start putting the wheels in motion of the bigger ride, he had to stay on his regular routine. He knew that $46,000 was a lot of money to some people, but on the other hand, million dollar lottery winners have filed bankruptcy only a couple of years after their winning. Besides that, he had already spent a chunk of it on the Honda Accord. Dollar wanted to be sitting on so much loot that he would be able to go to Vegas and lose $46,000 playing blackjack and not even have it put a dent in his finances. All that time he did in the joint was not going to be in vain. It was now time to put everything he learned about surviving and ruling the streets into effect.

Dollar eventually had to have Tommy sit with Ral while he went to Redd's and handled a few other business matters. He then returned a few hours later.

"Get to packing up yo' shit," Dollar said to Ral as he entered his motel room. "You relocating to Delaney."

Dollar threw a bag of clothes at Ral that had a Fubu hookup inside of it, right down to a pair of Fubu shoes.

"Fubu," Ral said, looking inside the bag. "Am I allowed to wear this?"

"Am I allowed to wear Tommy Hilfiger?" Dollar replied. "Come on and get dressed so we can head on over to Delaney."

"Who stay there?" Ral asked.

"You do, nigga, now throw on them rags I just threw at you, get your little bit of shit, and let's ride. I gotta go to work."

"Whose name is the place in?" Ral asked as he started to gather his things.

"What's it matter? You trying to stay here or something? Let's go!" Dollar demanded.

"Where we going?" Tommy said, coming out of the bathroom, wiping her wet hands down her pants.

"Home," both Dollar and Ral replied in unison.

Tommy went back to her place to get ready for work while Dollar took Ral to his new pad. It wasn't much, but he now had a place to call his own. Dollar figured that maybe if Ral possessed a little bit of stuff, then he would start getting hungry for bigger stuff and want to do some things. Ral wasn't going to be any good to him as a junkie, though. Dollar had to show him that he could enjoy life much more being clean and sober . . . and rich!

Dollar arranged for some inexpensive Value City Furniture stuff to be delivered to Ral's apartment. There wasn't any use buying some expensive stuff to put in an apartment in the projects. Folk will buy a leather sectional in a heartbeat to put up in their low-income housing unit. They be having $1,000 cherry wood sleigh beds and shit. They didn't realize that, no matter what they laced their crib with, it's still in the hood.

Dollar had given Tommy some money to grocery shop for Ral's place so that he would have the bare necessities, enough to get by. Dollar even bought Ral a $2,200 cross between a get-about and a hooptie to get back and forth from seeing his rehab counselor.

Dollar didn't even have a place for himself and yet he was making sure Ral was straight. The rest of the world may have looked at it as Dollar taking a chance on a junkie, but to Dollar he was taking care of a friend. That's just how Dollar was. He knew that his crew's shit had to be on point before he could feel confident about his game. Now Dollar understood why, for all those years, his granny always ate after everybody else had even eaten seconds. She wouldn't have been able to enjoy one morsel wondering if somebody else was still hungry and she had eaten the last bite.

"How'd you do all this shit for me?" Ral asked as he cased his new pad.

"I used your money," Dollar said.

"What money?"

"Let's just say it was restitution."

"Yo, Dollar," Ral said. "Thanks, man. I mean, it's gonna be hard, but I'm going to try to do right. I owe you, man. I don't know what happened to me. I used to feel like I could control the shit. But after you got locked up, the shit start controlling me."

"Must be that Kennedy curse." Dollar winked.

Ral walked over to a corner in the living room where a large box with a television in it was sitting. He and Dollar lifted the television out and set it up.

"This television ain't gon' work without cable," Ral said.

"Damn, I knew I was forgetting something," Dollar responded. "I forgot to call Comcast."

Ral played with the television until he got a basic channel that the morning news was on.

"Damn, that's Tyrone," Ral said, pointing at the television. He and Dollar watched closely as the newscaster reported Tyrone's homicide. He had been found dead. He was murdered execution style. It was reportedly drug related.

Kera didn't even look up from the book that her nose was buried in as Dollar entered the office. Dollar cleared his throat to gain her attention.

"Oh, hi," Kera said, looking up at Dollar. "I didn't hear you come in."

"Maybe y'all ought to get a bell put on that door," Dollar replied. "You all into that book. It must be good."

"It's very good," Kera said, rolling her tongue across her teeth.

"What's it called?"

"*A Hustler's Wife,*" Kera answered.

"*A Hustler's Wife,* huh?" Dollar said. "I think I've heard of that one. What's it about?"

"It's about a young girl who knows what she wants," Kera answered in a rousing tone. "And she sets out to get it."

"Oh yeah? Tell me more."

Kera was happy to oblige. "She meets this guy who's older than her and she falls in love with him. He's not all about the right thing, but he loves her strong." Kera licked her lips and proceeded to give Dollar the synopsis. "People think that because she's young she doesn't know what she wants or what's good for her."

"Not everything we want is good for us," Dollar interrupted, referring to himself.

"She followed her heart and her head and let them lead her in the right direction."

"And what do you follow?" Dollar asked. "Your head or your heart?"

"It depends," Kera said, rising up from the desk to show off her skintight jeans with that sexy-ass gap between her inner thighs.

"It depends on what?" Dollar asked.

"On what the final destination is, on where I'm trying to go, and who's taking me there."

Bitches sure have changed, Dollar thought. It seemed as though the chicks nowadays had much more game than the ones he grew up with. Hoes in the new millennium were bold.

"So tell me," Kera said, "what do you follow?" She put up her index finger. "Wait a minute. Let me guess." Kera walked around her desk to Dollar and looked him up and down. "Your head," she said with her eyes glued on Dollar's bulge. "Yeah, you look like the type of man who follows his head."

Dollar laughed as he took a couple of steps backward, away from Kera. "Slow down, little mama."

Dollar was willing to bet the tenderoni standing before him tasted as good as she looked. He realized that he had been subconsciously grabbing his nuts. What the fuck was he thinking, knowing Kera wasn't nothin' but a baby? He was a grown, big-ass nigga. He didn't have time for the games and obsession that came along with fucking a young broad. He would put a hurting on that tight-ass little pussy of hers. Besides, he had to stay focused and get his shit together. Tommy was already on the up and up and he had gotten Ral settled in. Handling his own business was going to be a piece of cake, especially with those few Gs he was already sitting on.

He had looked into a nice spot to live. He didn't want just anything, like what he had set Ral up in. He wanted a nice crib with nice things. He put in an application at a couple of spots and was waiting to hear back from them. Until he got that call on his prepaid minutes cell phone he had recently bought, he was going to stay put at the Y. He probably could have crashed at

Tommy's, and he definitely could have chilled at Ral's, but he didn't want to be able to be associated with Tommy or Ral's spot.

Dollar hated the hours he had to waste with a nine to five. He could've been spending that time casing the streets, seeing what was what and who was who. He had enough confidence in Tommy though to get the job done, and she was in just the right spot to do it. Next to a beauty or barbershop, a skin house was the perfect pair of ears and lips. One heard all and told all up in those types of spots. As tempted as Dollar was to just say, "Fuck Redd," he knew he had to be on point with his game. One small hole could cause a leak great enough to sink the entire ship. Kera could be that hole.

"Dollar," Redd said, entering the office from the restroom. "I thought that was you out here. What's happening?"

"Oh, I can't call it," Dollar said, giving Redd a five and a snap. "What's things looking like today?"

"For the rest of those saps, who knows? But you know you the number one gem around here. Everybody after Dollar Bill." Redd laughed. "I should just get you a desk set up in here."

"Yeah," Kera concurred. "Everybody's after Dollar Bill."

Before a moment of uncomfortable silence and awkwardness could set in, Dollar quickly spoke, "Well, I'm gonna head out and shoot the breeze with some of these cats and wait on some work," Dollar said as he turned to the exit. "And, Kera, you're gonna have to let me know how that book turns out."

"I'll give you a blow by blow," Kera said, rounding her lips at Dollar, then looking to make sure her father was none the wiser of her innuendo.

"A'ight then, little mama." Dollar smiled at Kera and exited the office. When he got outside, Mr. Owens had pulled up in his Lincoln Navigator that all the cats admired. They admired his whip and his habit of paying cash to Redd for the men's services, who, in turn, then paid the men in cash. Seeing cash switch hands for their services made some of the men feel like hoes being pimped, but what the fuck? Half of them bastards didn't have a bank to cash no check at and the others desperately needed that twenty dollar check cashing fee the check cashing place would rape them of.

Mr. Owens only needed three men that day and had picked them already when Dollar came out of the building. One of the three men knew he was about to get the boot and be replaced with

Dollar just as soon as Mr. Owens noticed him. Dollar was a strong, hard worker. He managed to do the work of two men.

Just as suspected, when Mr. Owens spotted Dollar, he gave the third guy, who was fixin' to hop into the Navigator, a "beat it" stare. The guy mean-mugged Dollar as he walked back over with the other unchosen.

"Nigga, what?" Dollar said. "You got something to say then say that shit."

The man twisted his lips up at Dollar and sucked his teeth as he proceeded to walk on. "Man, I ain't even on that bullshit you screamin'," the guy threw over his shoulder.

"You don't want none of this," Dollar said, getting in the last word before closing the door.

Where was all this cockiness coming from? Dollar had only envisioned his master plan. He hadn't put shit into play and already he was starting to act like the muthafuckin' man. As far as Dollar was concerned, he had a win-win bulletproof plan. He was going to make sure everything was airtight this time around. As they rode off, Dollar thought about the long hours and hard work he was about to put in and this only motivated him more.

"I gotta stop off at my house first, fellas," Mr. Owens said. "I left my keys to the property we gotta work on."

Dollar nodded in the affirmative as if he was giving Mr. Owens permission to make a detour. He then continued deep in thought.

Dollar thought about how once he, Tommy, and Ral successfully completed their first hit for that paper, Dollar's pockets would be cool enough to show up at Redd's every other day or so. Once they really put in work, he was only gonna fuck with Redd on the weekends. But for now, he had to pay homage to one of his strongest traits of which spending time in the joint forced upon him: patience.

Dollar had nothing but time. Haste makes waste. This was his second opportunity, his golden opportunity, to redeem himself to the streets by proving that he wasn't some young thug who couldn't even pull off a simple stickup. No, this time he would do everything by the book. When all was said and done the streets would belong to him.

Dollar thought as he rolled down the window, *the streets are already mine.*

CHAPTER 13

Chocolate: Melts in Your Mouth and Your Hands

Dollar always wanted to know what the inside of the Chocolate Factory looked like. As a kid, he'd heard stories about what went on up in that spot. He witnessed a lot of men's clothing flying out of apartment windows because of those stories. Their wives must have heard them too.

The Chocolate Factory was a pretty cool-looking joint. From the outside, it looked like just another hole in the wall, like one of those raggedy titty bars on Bourbon Street in New Orleans. But on the inside, it looked like some Vegas-type shit was jumping off. Disco globes hung about the ceiling that whirled around and around, giving a hypnotic effect. There was a live DJ instead of some jukebox. He spun the beats the dancers shook their asses to from a sky box. Some smoke still filled the air where you could assume the last dancer must have wriggled her body through. Dollar was sure things had changed since back in the day, but if this was the type of entertainment the old playas fell victim to, he could almost see why them niggaz left home and never came back.

"These bitches is tizight," Dollar said to himself, grinning from ear to ear. He copped a seat at the stage and looked around for a barmaid. Fine women were in every corner of the room talking shit to niggaz. Dollar felt like he was a wishing well filled with dimes. That's exactly what the broads up in that piece were, dimes: perfect asses, perfect breasts, stomachs, and teeth. They didn't have any stretch marks, their weaves looked believable, and their cosmetics were flawless. Whoever hired these hoes must have worked at Baskin-Robbins at one point because every flavor was represented.

While Dollar was turned to his left signaling the barmaid, on his right a dancer sat down next to him. With skin the tone of a vanilla wafer, her Alicia Keys braids flowed down her back like a waterfall. Her Janet Jackson baby hair gave her a look of innocence, while her Aaliyah smile had already earned her three fifty dollar drinks that night. This black mixed with Indian looking young miss was on point.

Dollar looked her up and down. She looked like she had just stepped out of a Frederick's of Hollywood catalog. Peeking through her long hot pink sheer cover up was a hot pink little two-piece liquid leather number. Her five-inch ice pick heels were the narrator to the story her body would soon tell.

Dollar tried to find a flaw on her, but it was an uphill battle. She was perfect, right down to her edible toes that hung slightly over her shoes, in a sexy way, for them foot fetish muthafuckas. She was whole thangin' it, no doubt.

"Sup, poppa?" She smiled.

"You, ma," Dollar said as the barmaid approached him. *This broad think she got perfect timing,* Dollar thought, referring to the barmaid.

"What can I get you?" the barmaid asked Dollar.

"I'll take a shot of Hennessy, straight, no ice," Dollar requested.

"And for the lady," the barmaid said, looking dead at Dollar. Out of the corner of his eye, he could see the dancer giving the barmaid a "good lookin' out" wink.

"Ah huh huh huh," Dollar laughed. "Get ma a twenty dollar spot of whatever she's drinking."

"Thank you. I'll have my regular," the dancer said as the barmaid nodded and walked away.

"No problem," Dollar said, gazing into the dancer's eyes. "Don't I know you from somewhere?"

The dancer laughed at Dollar's use of the most abused and corny-ass line in the book. "I ain't never seen you before so I know you ain't never seen me. Although I could be that girl you been dreaming about all of your life."

"That's cute," Dollar said.

"So are you." The dancer smiled.

"What's your name?" Dollar asked. "Wait a minute, let me guess. Is it Lexus? Is it Mercedes, or is it Delicious?

"Storm," she replied.

"So, why they call you that, Storm?"

"I come across soft, like a light rain or a summer's mist," Storm explained, as she put her hand on Dollar's knee. "But I cum like a storm, a drowning rain or a roaring wave on a Cancun beach."

Just as Storm's hand began to make its way up Dollar's leg, the barmaid's arm cut between them as she proceeded to place their drinks in front of them. Dollar paid for the cost of the drinks plus a three dollar tip for the barmaid. He took a sip of his drink as the DJ introduced the next dancer.

"Like her name, she's intoxicating," the DJ said. "Fellas, fuck dem dolla bills. Y'all better pull out them tens and twenties because our next dancer, repin' the chicks in da club, is the one, and only, Wine."

As the stage went black, a figure could be seen taking its place on the stage. The dancer strutted like she was modeling for the new Victoria's Secret line. As the theme song to her act began to play, the fellas in the club got hype and drew all their attention to the main act.

"'Hoes in da club show love . . .'" the male patrons sang along.

As the lights pulled up slowly, the crowd was in awe. Before them stood a bad-ass bitch in spiked red thigh-high boots. Her red hot pants covered only the top portion of her ass, allowing for her chestnut ass cheeks to hang out. The matching bandeau squeezed her pretty brown browns tightly. As she stretched her arms high to grab the pole on each side of her, the fellas were hoping them coconuts would pop out. But she had so much grace it was as if she was rising from the ground like magic. Once she reached the ceiling with poles in hand, the lights came completely up. She swung her legs up so that both her ankles grasped one pole and saw to it that both her hands secured the other. Slowly she slid down, piercing Dollar with her eyes the entire way down.

"Son of a bitch," Dollar said once he realized the dancer was Tommy. He couldn't believe his eyes. For one minute, he imagined the trick on the pole sliding right down onto his dick. Come to find it was Tommy, someone who was like one of the boys as far as he was concerned. On that note, Dollar gulped down his drink and raised his glass to the barmaid for another.

Dollar couldn't wait for Tommy to dance her two songs and get off the stage. Shit only got worse though. On the second song, the hot pants came off and all of Tommy's ass was revealed, compliments of the matching G-string.

As "It Seems Like You're Ready" by R. Kelly played, Tommy maneuvered her body in unimaginable positions. Niggaz was filling those boots and G-string with bills. They swarmed the stage like vultures. The hoes was even showing Tommy love with all the "work it, girl" and "do that shit" shout outs. Tommy was putting her heart into that little show. She was working it like she had never worked it before.

Dollar tried to occupy his time by slamming down shots of Hennessy. Thanks to Tommy's rump-shaking ass, he had spent sixty dollars on Storm's drinks.

"You know her or something?" Storm asked Dollar. "Is she who you want? You wanna buy her drinks? You wanna fuck her?" Clearly Storm was jealous of Dollar's reaction to Tommy.

"Slow down, baby," Dollar said. "You my girl or something? Bitch, I bought you a drink, not a fucking wedding ring," Dollar said with attitude.

"I'm sorry, poppa," Storm said, realizing Dollar wasn't the kind to get off on the jealous-type acting girls. She quickly changed her role. "It's just that I get so jealous. I mean, you so fine and all. But I'm over it. I'm good. You make me better."

"You got game, ma." Dollar laughed. "It's cool. You do your thang. I respect that."

"So we cool?" Storm said, running her hand down the back of Dollar's neck.

"We cool," Dollar replied.

"Let me dance for you," Storm said, getting out of her seat and pressing her pussy up against Dollar's knee.

As Dollar licked his lips he couldn't help but be slightly turned on. "The game is crazy," Dollar said. "You wanna dance for me, love?"

"Oooh, I do," Storm said as she closed her eyes and allowed Dollar to finger her pussy through her costume bottoms.

"Cool," Dollar said.

Dollar finished off his drink and followed Storm into the Champagne Room. He handed the one hundred dollar bill to the bouncer who was guarding the entryway and proceeded to get his sweet bud satisfied.

"Oooh oooh oooh ahh ahh ahh yeah yeah yeah what what what" were the words that crooned out of the ceiling speakers of the passionate room that was lit with one lamp that had a purple light bulb in it. The room was about the size of Dollar's old jail cell, but it was plush. It looked like something from out of the seventies. The lamp sat on a glass end table with a black metal frame next to a big, velvet-like couch with purple satin pillows to match the lighting. The walls were painted a shiny black and the floor was covered with black furry rugs. Across from the couch was a mirrored bar with a black pleather ice bucket sitting on it. Inside the ice bucket was a bottle of Asti.

Storm headed straight over to the bar and grabbed two of the champagne glasses that were lined up on the bar. She filled them to the top and then walked over to the couch where Dollar had sat down and made himself comfortable.

"Cheers," Storm said as she handed Dollar a glass of champagne. "Drink up, baby, but allow me to intoxicate you."

"Go on and talk that shit." Dollar winked as he spread his legs, sat an elbow on each one, with the hand free of champagne cupping his chin.

Storm began to roll her hips and allow her tongue to stroll across her top lip. All Dollar could imagine was her tongue strolling across the tip of his dick.

"'I'm just an R&B thug babe,'" Dollar lip-synched to the song. It must be a crime not to have R. Kelly's songs playing in a strip club. It surely wasn't the place for Luther. R's shit made a nigga wanna stop whatever he was doing and fuck. Damn that making love and making babies shit Luther specializes in. Gangsta niggaz wanna fuck. And for another Benji, that's exactly what Storm offered Dollar.

Dollar never thought in a million years he would trick, pay for some muthafuckin' pussy while there were hoes giving the shit away for free. But he had been locked up for eight years and the pussy was in his face. No nigga in their right mind, in his situation, could have turned it away. No nigga in their right mind.

Dollar went in his pocket and pulled out a wad of money. He peeled a one hundred dollar bill from the wad and placed it in Storm's hand. Then he pulled out his dick. It was hard from just thinking about getting ready to run up in some pussy. He had even pre-ejaculated in his drawers.

After properly placing a Magnum-style condom on his penis, Dollar watched as Storm's pussy sucked in all ten inches of his dick. Dollar felt like he was watching a magic show the way Storm made that shit disappear.

Storm put on a brief rodeo show for Dollar. She wrapped both legs around Dollars neck and bounced it out. Dollar watched as his dick went in and out of her, pussy juice flowing, dripping down his nut sack. Then Storm flipped it on him backward so that her ass smacked down on Dollar's six pack. That's when Dollar exploded. She rolled them hips like an ocean, and Dollar couldn't hold back the tidal wave.

Storm could feel Dollar's muscle flexing inside of her, so she proceeded to make the appropriate moans and groans to enhance his climax. Her pussy was working Dollar's dick like it was an old Atari 2600 joystick and she was playing *Centipede*. Once she knew Dollar had shot out all the juices he could, she then rested back on his chest and wrapped his arms around her body.

It didn't last as long as Dollar would have liked it to, but it had been awhile since he busted one up inside some pussy. There was no way to prolong it. It was quick, easy, and greasy, but it was pleasing.

"Did you like that, baby?" Storm asked as she sucked on Dollar's middle finger. "Did you, poppa? Did it feel good to you?"

"You know that shit was on point," Dollar moaned while kissing Storm's neck.

"Stop it. That tickles." Storm giggled, putting her head down and getting off of Dollar.

"Oh, now you wanna play the shy role."

Storm blushed. "So when you gonna come back and see me?" she asked as she began gathering her costume, which was Dollar's hint that it was time to keep it moving.

"I ain't really into trickin', ma. This was just a one-time thang, but I'll hook you up with a drink or two the next time I roll through. Is that all right? Is that all right with you?" Dollar said, zipping up his pants.

"Yeah, that's what they all say," Storm said. "But you'll be back. Trust me; you'll be back."

Storm vanished through a doorway leading into the changing room and Dollar let himself out of the Champagne Room. The first thing he saw was Tommy hugged up with some gold-tooth grill dude. Dude was all up in Tommy's face, playing in her hair.

Dollar took a seat back at the stage and made eye contact with Tommy. He widened his eyes and nodded his head as a sign to let her know that he was waiting to talk with her.

Five minutes went by and Dollar was becoming impatient. Eventually Tommy stood up and headed Dollar's way, but the dude who had been hawking her was right behind her. Tommy looked at Dollar and held up her index finger telling him to wait a minute. It didn't take Dollar long to figure out that she was headed to the Champagne Room.

Just then everything started going in slow motion. Dollar pictured ol' dude doing to Tommy what he had just done to Storm. That shit wasn't about to go down with him up in the spot. Dollar got up from his chair and approached Tommy as she was just about to head inside the Champagne Room.

"Yo, T," Dollar said. "I need to holla at you for a minute."

"It's Wine," Tommy corrected Dollar through gritted teeth.

"Yeah, whatever. I need to holla at you real quick," Dollar replied.

"Is this yo' man or somethin'?" the dude said to Tommy with a crooked face.

"Naw," Tommy replied. "We just friends."

"Then your friend needs to step. You workin'," the dude said, pushing Tommy on into the room.

"Mafucka, you don't know nothing about this here," Dollar said, pointing to Tommy and then to himself.

Smelling that some shit was about to go down any minute, Tommy put her hand on Bear the bouncer's chest to calm him as he began to flex.

"Look, let me talk to my homie for a minute. You go in there and wait for me," Tommy said to the dude. "When I get back, I'll play an extra song for you, baby. I promise you it will be worth the wait."

Dollar wanted to puke, but he laughed instead. This scene was unreal.

"It's cool, Bear," Tommy said.

The dude followed Tommy's instructions, and once he was out of sight, Tommy turned toward Dollar with devil eyes and said, "Follow me!"

Tommy escorted Dollar out to the parking lot of the club. She was steaming mad. She couldn't wait to get his ass outside so she could let him have it.

"Do I come up on your job and interrupt what the fuck you doing?" Tommy scolded as her breath created a fog from the cold.

"Look, my bad," Dollar said. "You right. I don't even know what got into me. I just couldn't sit out there and wait for you while you went in that room to do God knows what."

Tommy was silent. She looked at Dollar in disgust. "Is that what you think of me? You think I was about to fuck ol' dude just because I was going into the Champagne Room with him? Why, because you fucked Storm?"

The look on Dollar's face gave Tommy the answer she was looking for.

"You triflin' ass," Tommy said. She shook her head and looked down at the ground. "Well, I'm not like Storm. I get paid to dance and that's what I do. That's all I do and I'm offended you would think otherwise. Yeah, like I said, I sell a little bud on the side to some of these cats, but that's it."

"T, I'm sorry," Dollar said with his head down like a puppy dog.

"Sorry for what, fucking Storm or thinking I'm a slut?"

"Whoa," Dollar said. "I don't have to apologize to you for who I fuck, do I?"

"I didn't mean it like that so don't flatter yourself. Besides, Storm's a dyke anyway."

"You said that like a true hater. Is Tommy jealous?" Dollar said, cooing at Tommy like she was a little girl.

"Hell no, I ain't jealous. What do I have to be jealous of? Storm really is a dyke."

"She might be bi, but she sho ain't no dyke," Dollar said, grabbing himself as to insinuate that he had beat that pussy up.

"Remember when we checked Ral into Short Stay and I was talking to those two chicks? Well, Storm was one of them. The other one was her wife, girlfriend or whatever. Her name is Thunder. They been together for four years. Storm does dick on the side for money only. Thunder is straight pussy. And them bitches is raw."

"I knew I recognized her face from somewhere. They live at that hotel?" Dollar asked.

"No. They work up out of there. They got a nice-ass crib out there in Merrillville. Storm got two daughters who go to private school. The girls call both Storm and Thunder Mommy."

"But I thought you said ol' girl was a strict vegetarian, no meat," Dollar said.

"She is. Thunder don't get down with men. Them kids are Storms'. When the two of them put in work, they exin' a nigga," Tommy replied.

"What?"

"They gettin' a cat high off that liquid ecstasy and robbin' his dumb ass. Storm does what she needs to do and Thunder strips him for his goodies. Don't let them find out the muthafucka married." Tommy laughed. "They will blackmail his ass 'til Kingdom come."

"Hell no. Them bitches got hustle like that?" Dollar was impressed.

"As quiet as it's kept, they done put a couple of fools to sleep on that ex. They don't even look like the type, especially when you see them out with their daughters. They be lookin' like the perfect little mothers. Up in here, we call them Murder Mommies, also known as hit hoes." Tommy was referencing one of Biggie's songs with the nicknames.

Tommy could see the wheels in Dollar's head churning. "What you thinking?" she asked.

"Oh, nothing. I'm just storing this info for future reference. You never know when a couple of hit hoes might come in handy." Dollar winked. "Damn!" Dollar said, turning his attention to a girl getting out the passenger side of a yellow Hummer in a full-length mahogany mink coat. "Who's that lookin' like Lil' Kim?"

Tommy turned to look. "That's Becka. Her brother, Wayne, the guy dropping her off, he sells them coats. She's his walking advertisement," Tommy answered.

"Oh yeah, legit?" Dollar asked.

"Actually, he does sell them legit. Their dad has a store in Chicago. He gets them for next to nothing. You know how they do it in Chi-Town with the furs. I hear they're nice. Tiwana, the barmaid, her boyfriend is getting a load of them.

He's going to try to push them up North for double what he pays for them here."

"When's he supposed to be coppin' them?" Dollar asked.

"I don't know."

"You need to find that shit out so we can just happen to be around when the transaction takes place." *Game on!*

CHAPTER 14

Back In Business

It was midweek, about 7:45 p.m. Dollar wasn't comfortable with an early evening stickup his first go-round since '95, but hell, he was confident with his skills. He would have preferred a midnight or early a.m. stickup, but who runs around selling furs at midnight? Legit ones, anyway.

Dollar's big, buff self was crammed in Ral's little hooptie. He felt like a clown at the circus in one of them li'l buggy cars. He had just dropped Ral off around the corner. All the pieces to the game were in place with the exception of the queen, which was Tommy. Dollar was awaiting her call on his cell.

"Damn," Dollar said, fiddling with the radio dial. "This bitch ain't even got a tape deck in it. What was I thinking hooking my boy up with some shit like this?"

As Dollar tapped his fingernails on the dash-
board, he noticed how dull and rigid they were.
"My nails are fucked up," he said out loud as
he began to gnaw on them. "I'm trippin'." He
laughed. "Since when do I give a fuck about
my fingernails? I'm acting like a ho. Just relax,
Dollar. Just relax."

Dollar continued to tap his nails on the dash-
board. For some reason, even though he was
wearing a ridiculously overpriced Phat Farm
denim hookup and some clean AND1s, and was
sporting a nice, fresh cut, which left him with a
shiny, bald head, his nails were messing up his
total look.

"Niggaz get they nails done too," Dollar said,
trying to convince himself. "Fuck it! I'm gettin'
these shitz did."

Just then Dollar's cell phone rang and he
answered it.

"He just dropped Becka off, so it's on," Tommy
said.

"Good lookin' out. Peace," Dollar said, closing
the flap on his cell phone.

A few minutes went by before Dollar saw the
bright yellow Hummer H2 pull up across the street
from him and park. Dollar sat at attention.

"Dis mafucka rollin' an H2 in the heart of the
hood," Dollar said, laughing as he used his cell

phone to call Ral's pager and key in the code. "This cat deserves to get got."

On cue, Ral cleared the corner. He was wearing an olive green down coat with feathers poking out, some dirty jeans, and a funky baseball cap. He was looking like the recovering addict he was. He killed time by digging in garbage cans, collecting cans and whatnot. In the meantime, Wayne had gotten out of his Hummer and knocked on the door of Tiwana and her boyfriend's apartment. Once assured that Tiwana's boyfriend was home, Wayne returned to his truck. With three coats in arm multiplied by a total of four trips, he hauled the dozen minks into the apartment.

Back in the day, Dollar would have probably pretended to be a customer looking to buy some furs. Once Wayne showed up, Dollar would have robbed him for whatever he had on him. But according to Romeo, that was one of Dollar's mistakes. There wasn't a need to befriend a mark and play pretend. Just sneak up from behind and handle them. All that other miscellaneous crap took up too much time and left room for error. Romeo brought up the point that if Cartel and his boys hadn't been shot dead, they would have known exactly who to retaliate against. Now, with the situation at hand, if anything, Wayne would feel as though he had been set up by Tiwana's boyfriend and that's who he would look to seek revenge on.

After Wayne's fourth and final trip, Tiwana's boyfriend closed the door behind him. That was Dollar and Ral's sign that money was about to exchange hands. After ten minutes the apartment door opened and Wayne exited.

As soon as he opened the door to the Hummer, Ral caught him off guard. "You got some change?" Ral asked. "Driving a fine automobile such as this, I know you got some change."

"Man, kick mud," Wayne said. "I ain't got shit for you."

"Then maybe you got something for me," Dollar said, coming up behind Wayne and placing the gun he'd copped from Tommy into his back.

"Oh, shit," Wayne said, being caught off guard.

"Yeah, oh shit is right, nigga," Dollar said, cocking the gun.

"Here's my keys," Wayne said. "Take it. Fuck it. Just don't kill me."

"Look, we don't want to kill you and we don't want your truck," Dollar said. "Just empty your pockets."

"Empty my pockets?" Wayne repeated.

"Yeah, pull 'em out, nigga. Turn 'em inside out."

Wayne nervously put his hands down in his pockets and said, "Don't shoot. I'm just doin' what you said. I'm going in my pockets."

Wayne pulled his pant pockets inside out and gave Dollar the contents, which was only a few thousand dollars.

"Empty those pockets too," Dollar said, pointing to Wayne's jacket pockets.

"These pockets too?" Wayne repeated.

"What the fuck are you, an echo?" Ral added. "Yes, them pockets too."

Wayne emptied his inside jacket pockets that made the proceeds of the stickup around $30,000 in all hundred dollar bills. Meanwhile, Ral had raided the truck and retrieved a woman's long black mink coat.

Dollar forced Wayne to get into the back of his Hummer and ball up in a fetal position on the floor.

"Count to one hundred Mississippis before getting up," Ral ordered Wayne. "If you get up, our other partner who's watchin' all this go down is going to blow your muthafuckin' head off. You got that?"

"Yeah, yeah," Wayne said nervously and then started to count. "One Mississippi, two Mississippi, three Mississippi."

As Wayne continued counting, Dollar and Ral headed for Ral's car. Ral had trouble lugging the huge mink that was secured inside a clear clothing bag. Since Ral was frail, weighing in at about a buck twenty-five, the weight of the coat slowed Ral down. He even tripped and fell running with it and had a hard time getting the car door closed because he kept shutting the coat in the door. This bootleg scene from a *Three Stooges* episode was starting to piss Dollar off.

"Why the fuck you always gotta do some extra shit?" Dollar asked. "We got the money. You need to learn how to keep your eye on the prize. That's what fucked us up eight years ago. We doin' things different now, Ral."

Dollar steered the car with one hand while fondling the coat on Ral's lap with the other. "That's a bitch's coat anyway. What the fuck you gon' do with a woman's coat?"

"Do you know how much pussy this can get me, amigo?" Ral replied.

"Man, Ral, don't fuck with me." Dollar gave Ral the side eye, letting him know this wasn't the time for his clownin'.

"Seriously, how much loot we get away with from ol' dude?"

"I don't know. It looks like it's about thirty, thirty-five thousand," Dollar said handing the neatly stacked wads of crisp hundred dollar bills to Ral to count.

"So that means dude bought a dozen of these bitches for around three thousand each. Shit, I know I can get between four and five Gs for one."

"I swear to God, Ral, if I find out you swapped that coat for a hit . . ."

"Come on, man," Ral said. "Give me a little bit more credit than that. I ain't did no drugs, man. No hard shit anyway. Yeah, I might have blazed on a couple of those fat ones, but that's it. You can ask your li'l bro. He checks my piss every time I go to the clinic. He done already warned me about the bud leading me back to more glamorous pharmaceuticals. But I'm straight. Ask him, man."

"I'll take your word for it," Dollar said.

"What's the deal with you and your bro, anyway, man?"

"I ain't trying to talk about my brother," Dollar said, becoming a little uneasy. "I'm trying to talk about money."

Inside, Dollar wanted to talk about his brother. He wanted to ask Ral if he had asked about him. He hated the fact that he would probably never have the kind of relationship he longed for with Klein. But Dollar couldn't let that weigh on his mind. It was impossible for him to turn back the hands of time. So for now, he decided to keep his mind on money.

"So, what's our next move?" Ral said as he studied the food menu at Jimmy's Coney Island as he, Dollar, and Tommy prepared to talk shop.

"These cats from T town—" Tommy started.

"Toledo, Ohio," Ral confirmed.

"Yeah, they rolled through the bar last night. They were ballers on their way to cop some of them thangs," Tommy said, taking a sip of her ice water.

"What the hell some dudes from Toledo stopping off in Gary for?"

"Making a li'l pit stop," Tommy answered.

"So did all that pussy up in the spot get them cats to telling they business?" Ral asked.

"Well, I know that some dude named Ant over in T town is expecting about twenty Gs via FedEx," Tommy said in a bragging manner, being she was the one responsible for the lead.

"Okay, keep the info coming," Dollar said as he listened intensely. The talk of money made Dollar's dick hard. Contrary to popular opinion, fuck dogs; money is man's best friend.

"I know dude stays by a park on Hollywood and is expecting the loot next Friday," Tommy said. "Ol' dude was making it a point to let me know that throwing twenty at his boy wasn't nothin' but a thang."

"Showoff niggaz," Dollar said. "These young bloods don't know shit about the game."

"Oh well," Ral said. "That's where we benefit."

"Y'all know what y'all want yet?" the waitress approached their table and asked with pen and pad in hand.

The three proceeded to order their soul food entrees and discussed their next move as they waited on their meals to be prepared. Like a game of chess, Dollar was meticulous about the moves that were to be made. He didn't want to do too much too fast. Actually, he didn't want to do too much at all. He wanted to hit the jackpot; some big-type stickup that would put them on easy street for a long spell. He would then turn around and invest his money in something that would pay off well enough to take care of him for life. But no amount sounded remotely enough to take care of Dollar for life. Nah, he wanted too much. He wanted to live like one of the Good Fellas, although Romeo had warned him that that type of attitude leads to downfall. But, of course, Dollar's attitude was fuck it. He wasn't like these Similac-drinkin' wankstas. He would take heed of the words of the elders. He would be the exception to the game. He would win.

Just as the waitress brought the food out to their table, through the restaurant window Dollar noticed a familiar face walking by. He never forgot a face, especially one belonging to such a beautiful body. Obviously she recognized him too, because as she entered she told the girl who she was with to grab a table while she hollered at Dollar for a minute. Dollar acted like he didn't see her coming his way as he took a bite of his collard greens.

"Excuse me, sir, do you have the time?" the soft-spoken voice said over Dollar's shoulder.

Dollar looked up, replied, "It's time for you to get a new watch," and continued eating his food.

"I see you holdin' a grudge," she said, smiling.

"Naw, Miss Lady," Dollar said, cracking a smile: the "I'm that nigga" smile. "I'm just messing with you. Hennessey, right?"

"Umm, you're good. Yes, Hennessey Monroe," she said, turning her attention to Tommy and Ral who were sitting across from Dollar.

Tommy was eyeballing Hennessey from head to toe, checking out her Donna Karan casual pantsuit, Donna Karan purse, and Donna Karan casual-like flip-flops.

"Ahem," Tommy cleared her throat.

"Oh," Dollar said, "forgive me for being rude. Hennessey, this is Ral and Tommy."

Hennessey stuck her hand out to shake their hands. The diamonds from the five-karat tennis bracelet that appeared to be making love to her wrist nearly blinded them. Tommy really wasn't feeling Hennessey's presence, so she left her hand hangin' and gave her a "what up?" nod instead. Ral's hand was greasy from the fried chicken, but that didn't keep him from giving Hennessey a courteous handshake.

"Oh my," Hennessey said as she looked disgustingly down at her greasy hand. Tommy couldn't help but giggle.

Dollar was embarrassed and handed her a napkin to wipe her hands. "Uhh, yeah. These are my boys," Dollar said as Tommy kicked him underneath the table. "Well, this is Tommy, he's a girl. I mean, she's a girl. We're all just friends." Dollar was attempting to make it clear to Hennessey that Tommy was not his girlfriend.

"Oh, very nice," Hennessey said. "Well, I'm here with my cousin, Trini. She lives around these parts."

"And what part do you live around, Miss Lady?" Dollar inquired.

"I'm over in the windy city," Hennessey replied. "Well, I just wanted to say hey. I better go join Trini now."

"Well, it was nice meeting you, bye-bye," Tommy said, rushing Hennessey off with a wave.

"Uhh, let me walk you over to your table," Dollar said, excusing himself and, at the same time, giving Tommy an evil look.

"Oh, well, thank you," Hennessey said as she turned to Tommy and Ral. "It was nice meeting both you fellas." She put her hand over her mouth. "Ooops, I mean lady and gentleman. Take care." She gave Tommy the same wave she'd given her.

"Tah, tah," Tommy said sarcastically under her breath as Dollar and Hennessey walked away. After taking a bite of macaroni and cheese she said, "I don't like that bitch."

"You don't even know that bitch," Ral said, sucking the grease off of his fingers.

"I know her all right. I know her kind and I don't like her kind."

"What's her kind?" Ral asked.

"Bitch. She's a bitch who thinks she better than everybody else. But underneath it all she's got something to hide. I can tell she's fake. I just hope Dollar can tell too."

CHAPTER 15

This Is a Stickup

Stickin' up the FedEx carrier was the easiest $20,000 the trio ever made. Dollar, Ral, and Tommy drove over to Toledo on Thursday night in two separate cars and camped out on Hollywood. The park split the street, so each car manned one end of the block. There was no way they were going to miss the FedEx truck turning into the neighborhood.

The FedEx driver didn't put up a fight. Hell, as far as he knew, it was a set of stainless steel pots in the package and his life was worth more than that. He turned over the package with ease and even offered them all of the other packages he had in his truck waiting to be delivered.

Dollar felt bad holdin' up the driver. He looked like a little, young brotha tryin' to make a living, trying to earn money for college or something. He reminded Dollar of himself. Dollar tucked

five Benjis in the FedEx guy's uniform pocket
before they dipped and apologized for the incon-
venience.

It had been over six months since Dollar was
released from prison. He had been content bank-
ing his ends while living at the Y, but that got
old. Dollar used his entire cut from the FedEx hit
for the security deposit and first three months'
rent for some little apartment near the shore in
Chicago. Dollar couldn't believe how high rent
was in Chicago. He paid three times as much
for the monthly rent for his place than he had
put down on Ral's. And Ral's place was bigger.
You couldn't compare the atmosphere though.
Dollar's bachelor pad was like his little kingdom.
He fell in love with it the first time the manager
showed him around. He was nervous that his
application wouldn't get approved. Although he
didn't share his criminal history on the application, he didn't know just how extensive their
background check on him would be.

Dollar convinced Redd to nigga rig some
paperwork for him stating that he had been
doing work for his agency for the past three
years. Dollar agreed to work for Redd on a
fifty-fifty cut for an entire month in exchange for
the favor.

Dollar's credit was clear because he didn't have any. He concealed his felony bid from the apartment manager and spoke of how he had gone to school and graduated from The Ohio State University. It was a partial lie. He put in a few years at the state of Ohio, but it damn sure wasn't at the university.

Dollar bragged to the apartment manager about how he briefly played football for the university, but seriously injured himself during a practice. The injury would end his football career. The apartment manager praised Dollar for continuing his education in spite of his football letdown. As far as Dollar was concerned, doing time in the pen was like schooling. It was the school of hard knocks. He learned how to survive. No university could teach him that.

Dollar enjoyed creating a new life for himself. He felt like Omar Tyree, the Urban Griot, making up stories, telling people what they wanted to hear. Dollar had plenty of tales and very little of the truth. He started to believe the stuff he was making up himself. Dollar's demeanor and attitude began to change to accommodate his fables. He was on top of the world. He was about to have his game on lock. "Do it easy, easy does it," was what Dollar had to remember. He couldn't rush. He had to take his time and do the damn thang right, no guerilla-style type of endeavors. But while he waited on the pipe dream of living in style to manifest itself, he had to make sure he kept up his own style and appearance.

"Damn, my nails are shiny, ain't they?" Dollar asked Mya, the nail technician at the salon.

"Sir, they'll stay shiny for about two weeks," Mya replied as she continued to massage the smooth side of the buffer over Dollar's thumbnail. "Do you want a clear coat of polish on them? That will keep them shiny and strong for a long time."

"Naw, I'm straight on that, ma," Dollar replied.

"You ready for your pedicure, sir?" a small Asian lady said to Dollar.

"Yes," Dollar said, but at the same time Mya replied for him as well.

"No," Mya said. "I haven't given you your hand massage yet."

"Oh, that's okay. You did good." Dollar pulled out a ten dollar bill and placed it in the palm of Mya's hand. She clenched the tip and thanked Dollar with a stimulating smile.

"It would have been my pleasure. Enjoy the rest of your treatment." Mya then brushed a piece of her long, blond hair from her face and turned to the little Asian woman to say, "He's ready."

"You follow me now, sir," the Asian woman ordered Dollar.

She led Dollar over to a small refrigerator and offered him a drink and some fruit before taking him over to the massage spa chair. She then ran water into the attached foot tub and poured some lilac-smelling powder into the water, which formed a layer of suds. She showed Dollar how to operate the massage control buttons on the chair and then pampered him with a forty-five minute pedicure that included a foot massage.

After paying for his services, and tipping the Asian woman ten dollars as well, Dollar went on to get his head conditioned and massaged. This is how Dollar spent every other Saturday. Afterward, he would normally cop a DVD and some grub, then head back to his spot. But Dollar thought it was safe, and about time, to start finding him some hoes to keep company with.

This Saturday night would be different. Dollar was going to find a club that was jumpin', but not thugged out. He didn't want to mess with the ballers' scene. He just wanted to go somewhere where he could groove to a little bit of R&B, hip-hop with a touch of jazz, clock some hoes, and not have some ol' jealous niggaz mean muggin' him.

Joy

Dollar decided to go to one of Chi-Town's low key spots called the Art Bar and cool out. He heard it was a nice chill spot: not uppity, but not ghetto either. It was a mixed crowd.

When Dollar arrived at the club in his black long-sleeved CK dress shirt and black CK dark dress pants, he turned every woman's head up in the spot. And once he was out of their sight, the scent of his CK1 cologne left them with something to remember him by.

Dollar found an empty stool at the end of the bar and hugged it all night. Honeys deliberately brushed up against him while in an attempt to get the barmaid's attention to order a drink. This made Dollar smile, but none of the women coppin' free feels had "it." Some of the girls were tight, but Dollar would have rather paid for some ass than to have to listen to some gabby-ass chick talk about nothing, have to buy her a couple of drinks, and take her to the Waffle House before knowing if he even had the slightest chance of fucking her. So he decided to call it a night. He swallowed down his last taste of Hennessy and went for his wallet to leave the barmaid a tip. As he pulled his wallet out, a small body bumped into him.

"You got that out to buy me a drink?" the owner of the small body said. "I'll take Sex on the Beach."

"'Sex on the Beach', huh?" Dollar said.

"Yeah, and after that you can buy me a drink." Kera winked as she slightly stumbled. Dollar grabbed her arm, which was hanging out of her short-sleeved dark-colored Coogi dress, in order to help her balance.

"You're not even old enough to drink," Dollar said, trying to help her balance. It was obvious she had had a little too much to drink already, yet here she was in Dollar's face begging for a drink.

"I'm old enough to do lots of stuff." Kera giggled.

"How did you even get up in here? You're not even old enough to be in here," Dollar said to her.

"Shhhhhh," Kera said, spraying Dollar with spittle.

"Who you wit'?" Dollar said, standing up from the stool in authority.

Kera looked around and replied, "See that little number over there on the dance floor in that sky blue tube dress?" Kera pointed and Dollar's eyes found the girl she was talking about.

"Is that who you're with? Wait right here," Dollar said as he stomped toward the dance floor.

"No, wait," Kera said, trying to grab hold of Dollar before he took off. She wasn't quick enough though. Dollar had already walked over to the dance floor and began talking to the girl in the sky blue dress. The conversation was intense as Dollar pointed to Kera and then scolded the girl for allowing Kera to get to the drunken state she was in. The girl began to snap her neck and scold back at Dollar. This went on for a couple of minutes before Dollar returned to the bar where Kera was standing. Dollar was plum red and Kera was laughing hysterically.

"That wasn't cute," Dollar said.

"I tried to stop you," Kera replied. "Nobody told you to race over there and play daddy."

Just then a tall dark-skinned girl in a red one-piece pantsuit came over, tapped Kera on the shoulder, and said, "You ready to go?"

"Leece, this is Dollar," Kera introduced the two. "Dollar, this is Leece, the girl I'm really here with."

"Nice to meet you," Leece said before turning to whisper in Kera's ear. "Girl, you were right. He is a fine-ass LL Cool J–looking muthafucka."

"It's nice to meet you too, Leece," Dollar said. "You don't look old enough to be in here either."

"Thank you for the compliment," Leece said. "But I just turned twenty-one today."

"'It's my birthday,'" Kera sang.

Kera and Leece continued with their version of "In Da Club" that would have made 50 Cent proud. They had everyone within ear distance shouting, "Go 'head, go 'head."

"That's enough, ladies," Dollar said as Kera and Leece high-fived one another. "I hope there is a third party with you two because neither one of you look like you're in any condition to be leaving up out of here alone."

"We cool," Leece said. "My man and his boys are up in here. We ridin' out with them back over to Indy."

"How many of his boys?" Dollar asked, worried about Kera being taken advantage of in the condition she was in.

"Oh, we straight. I ain't gonna let nothing happen to my girl," Leece said.

"Oh, I can see how well you take care of your girl," Dollar said sarcastically. "I'll take care of little mama here." He looked to Kera. "I'll see to it that you get home. Do you need to get your coat from coat check or anything?"

"No, I'm straight. Are you sure you don't mind seeing to it that I get home?" Kera said, giving Leece a thumbs-up on the low-low. "I don't want to put you out or anything."

"I'm sure," Dollar said. "Leece, where's your man? I want to make sure you straight too."

Dollar saw to it that Leece caught up with her man; then he led Kera outside of the club and immediately hailed a taxi. The taxi driver pulled over, rolled down his window, and asked Dollar, "Where to?"

Dollar would have the driver drop him off first, then take Kera home. "Where do you stay?" Dollar asked Kera as he scooted into the taxi and held his hand out to help her in.

"A fucking taxi," Kera said. "You offered to see to it that I get home and you didn't even drive your own shit. I stay all the fuckin' way over in Gary. You gonna pay my fare?"

"Look, fast ass," Dollar said. "We in Chicago, not Alaska. Gary is thirty minutes away. Even if you lived right here in Chicago, like me, you'd still take a taxi. Half the muthafuckas here own a car and still take public transportation. Parking is always a bitch and damn near cost more than a monthly insurance premium. Now you can get your ass in this taxi or catch up with Leece and chance getting gang raped by her dude's boys."

Kera huffed and puffed but eventually hopped into the taxi.

"Now, where to?" Dollar asked her.

"I'm going where you going," Kera said, closing the door as the taxi driver pulled off.

"The hell you are," Dollar replied.

"Why, yo' bitch lying up waiting on you?"

"Ain't nobody waiting on me, but your ass is going home."

"I can't go home. My father would kill me if I came home drunk. Just let me sober up at your spot, pleazzzzze," Kera pleaded with her big, innocent eyes.

She looked good in that Coogi dress she had on, and she was giving Dollar mad sex appeal. He knew that if he took her home he'd want to do her. If only she were a little older. Young girls don't know the true definition of a one-night stand. She'd be sweating him and he knew it, so taking her back to his place was out of the question.

"Pleazzzze," Kera said, poking out her lips and rubbing on Dollar's knee.

"Stop whining," Dollar said, pushing her hand off of his knee.

"Look, seriously. I can't go home like this. Redd will trip. I'm eighteen and I want him to trust me; to see that I'm a responsible adult now."

"The meter's running and I'm just driving around. Are we sightseeing, folks, or are you going to tell me where you want to go?" the taxi driver said.

Dollar looked out the window and thought. He then looked into Kera's sexy, pleading eyes. His mind was made up as he directed the driver to his apartment off of South Shore Drive.

Damn, she got a tight-ass pussy, Dollar thought as he slid the tip of his penis inside Kera.

Dollar tried not to think about how his actions were violating everything he said messing around with Kera would lead to. It was getting easier not to think about it as he was succumbed by the warmth of Kera's pussy. Even through the condom, it felt so good and natural.

Once Dollar and Kera arrived at his apartment, tucking Kera in on the couch wasn't good enough for her. Dollar should have chained her ass down. It was a matter of minutes before she appeared buck naked in his bedroom doorway, and shortly thereafter, in his bed.

There wasn't any foreplay or nothing involved. Kera just jumped in the bed and started ramming her tongue down Dollar's throat while fondling his dick. What did Dollar have to lose at this point, he thought. This was easy pussy, the next best thing to easy money.

It had been a minute since Dollar had been with Storm. He was going hard. *Ease up, Dollar*

Bill. He decided to give himself a pep talk. *Just the tip. Just the tip. But damn, this shit is so wet.* Dollar was being hypnotized by the sound of Kera's wetness. Sounded like waves smacking up against the shore of an ocean.

Kera was moaning and squirming. Dollar figured that must have meant it was feeling good to her. On that thought he supposed he could give her another inch or two. Slipping in another couple of inches, Dollar gently kissed her on the forehead. He figured she'd like that, make her feel safe and secure. Next he kissed her eyelids, then her nose, and finally her lips. Once he got to her lips, Kera stuck her tongue in his mouth. Since she was sticking her tongue deep down his throat, he went on and stuck his penis deep inside of her.

Dollar positioned himself to be able to drive his dick inside of Kera while watching her facial expressions. She wanted the dick so bad; well, he was going to give it to her. Seeing the expression of pain on her face let Dollar know that little mama had bitten off more than she could chew.

"Ooouuuu," Kera screamed out as Dollar attempted to insert more of his penis into her. "Be gentle, it's my first time."

"What?" Dollar said in shock, stopping the motion of his hips.

"Despite what you may think of my fast ass, I'm a virgin," Kera said.

"Then what are we doing?" Dollar asked as he started to remove himself from on top of her, but Kera grabbed him closer. "Why didn't you tell me? Little mama, we can't do this. Your first time can't be some drunken night you won't even remember. Your first time should be special."

"Was yours?" Kera asked.

"Naw," Dollar sighed.

"You are special, Dollar," Kera said, rubbing his face. "That makes this special." Kera pulled Dollar's face to hers and began kissing him.

"We can't do this," Dollar said as he breathed heavily. "We gotta stop." He didn't want to, that was for sure.

"No," Kera said. "I want to do this. I really want to do this with you. It's too late anyway. You've already put half your dick inside of me. I can take it. I take it all. Please don't stop. Please don't stop," Kera repeated over and over as she began to roll her hips. She wasn't throwing that thang like no virgin. She buried her hands into Dollar's ass cheeks and pulled him into her gently. Dollar would dip in and out of her softly until she would pull him inside of her even more. Then, finally, half of his penis burst through her walls. Yep, she was a virgin.

The entire situation was blowing Dollar's mind. He imagined that Kera probably felt the same way he did when he got his first experience of the birds and the bees with Pam. He just wanted to get it over with so that he could peel the "V" (Virgin) off of his chest. That's probably what Kera wanted to do with her hot ass: rid herself of virgin status so that she could go on a fucking spree. All of a sudden Dollar felt used, but who cared. He was damn near all the way up in her now. As he pumped in and out of Kera, he didn't mind being used. Her pussy sucked in his dick like a leech until he exploded inside of her. Hell, he wished every eighteen-year-old female virgin would use him.

The feeling of Dollar busting through Kera's walls and her screaming and tearing down his back with her nails aided in his ultimate climax. After he and Kera had sex, Dollar led her into the shower where he washed her down with his hands and a bar of Irish Spring soap.

At that moment, Kera felt like a woman. She felt special, that she was probably one of the very few people Dollar had let into his world. Dollar played in Kera's hair, her beautiful hair that curled up even more from the moisture of the water.

"So what were you in jail for?" Kera asked as the water pounded against their skin.

Dollar paused at Kera's candidness. "It don't matter."

"I just want to know." Kera smiled. "I mean, I just gave you my virginity. You can't answer me a simple question?"

As they stood in the shower, Dollar told Kera, in very little detail, about his spending years in jail. He had already taken her virginity; why complicate the situation even more by laying all his business out on the table? But she already knew he had done time in jail, so he fed her some insignificant details to satisfy her craving.

Dollar's story to Kera was that he got pinned for a murder that he didn't commit and copped a plea on the advice of his lawyer. Being the young, naïve, "I just want a bad boy" type of girl Kera was, she ate the story up and digested every word of it.

Dollar felt a degree of guilt as he held the young, innocent thing in his arms. She had given him her virginity, and he had given her lies and false hope. *Poor thing*, Dollar thought. He felt bad in advance for breaking her heart.

Dollar's conscience didn't keep him from running up in Kera one mo'again before sending her home in a taxi with a fifty dollar bill for fare. The second go-round, Dollar had to get Kera wet before he could stick it back up in her. He wasn't about to go down on her, so he put his fingers in his mouth, then massaged the saliva onto Kera's private spot.

Kera wanted to prove to Dollar to some degree that she wasn't all little girl, so she went down on him. Dollar could tell she didn't really know what the hell she was doing, but she did well enough to make him cum all over her face. Kera did more lickin' and kissin' all over Dollar's dick than she did just straight out sucking it. When he felt a nut coming on, he held her head stiff on the tip, forcing her to keep her lips in one place and suck until he came.

Coming face to face with Kera again at work felt a little awkward, so for the next couple of weeks, Dollar avoided her as much as he could. The more distance he kept between the two of them, the more quickly Kera would realize that her one night with Dollar was just that: one night.

Dollar would show up at Redd's and wait outside with the other fellas instead of going inside the office first like he usually did. He wanted to keep from running into Kera. She hadn't done any unannounced drive-bys by his apartment like some other chicks might have, and she never came outside to see if Dollar was around. Perhaps Kera wouldn't be a problem after all.

CHAPTER 16

What's Good to You

Turning eighteen didn't make Kera feel like a woman as much as being with a man for the first time did. Kera couldn't get Dollar off of her mind, off of her tongue. She would go over to Leece's house just to talk about Dollar for hours.

"He's poison, girl, I'm telling you," Leece said as she and Kera sat on her bed eating a bowl of cherries.

"Nuh huh, girl. He's the antidote," Kera said as she sucked a cherry off the stem, spit out the pit, and placed it in a napkin. "And the way he calls me little mama, girl, it's so cute."

"I just can't believe you finally did it. You've been like the biggest tease in the world, clockin' dollars and shit from niggaz on the hope of them gettin' some pussy from your ass."

"Girls need to learn that they can play the ho, they don't necessarily have to be the ho."

"I guess you got tired of role-playing the ho." Leece laughed.

"You stupid," Kera said, play punching her on the shoulder. "This is different. Dollar ain't like all them wannabe wankstas I done fucked with in the past. They deserved to get played. Dollar's been there and done that. I can see that he ain't about the drama, the games and shit. And girl, he don't have no kids."

"Fine-ass catch like him and he ain't got no babies' mamas running around Gary? What's his story, Kera? Come on, girl, you can tell me. He got a wooden leg, don't he?"

"Will you stop being stupid?"

"A glass eye?"

"Dammit, Leece," Kera paused. "Okay, okay, girl. I guess I have left one thing out."

"I knewed it, I knewed it!" Leece said. "Go on, spit it out." Leece watched Kera fondle a cherry with her tongue before sucking it off the stem. As she slushed it around her mouth, trying to weed the pit out, Kera spoke.

"He been locked up the last few years," Kera said very quickly as she spit the pit out into the napkin.

"Oh, an ex-balla, huh?" Leece said. "Once a balla always a balla, you know that shit. You know he probably just using your pop's business to keep the feds off his ass. I thought you was through fuckin' with them street pharmacists."

Kera listened to Leece without making eye contact and continued sucking down cherries.

"Why do I have the feeling that you still leavin' some shit out?" Leece said without getting a reply from Kera. "What?"

"He wasn't in jail on no drug charges. He was kinda in jail for murder."

"Get the fuck out of here," Leece said. "That fool done killed somebody before?"

"More like killed three people," Kera said nonchalantly as she put another cherry to her lips.

"Bitch, are you crazy?" Leece said, snatching the cherry out of Kera's hands.

"He didn't really do it."

"Oh, twelve jurors and a judge just locked him up for being so damn fine?" Leece said sarcastically.

"That's why I didn't tell you. I knew you were going to overreact and try to rain on my parade. It's not even like that. He really didn't do it. He didn't want to risk the death penalty so he copped a plea. You know black men are guilty until proven innocent."

"I can hardly believe you," Leece said, taking offense. "So you caught that fish hook, line, and sinker, huh? His word is bond, huh? I'm your girl; I'm going to always have your back. But I'm not going to sit back and watch you fuck around with no killer. How long he been out? Is the fucker rehabilitated or what? I ain't feelin' this, K."

"Dollar's a good man. If you could just look into his eyes and see what I see. He's good."

"He might be good, but he ain't good for you. You need to spit his ass out the same way you spittin' those pits out. Walk away from this one, baby girl. Write it down in your diary for memory sake. You ain't ready for him."

"What the fuck is that supposed to mean?" Kera said, not giving Leece a chance to answer. "I'm a grown woman. I can handle anything. You know what? I don't even want to talk about it anymore. Jealousy is one thing I can't deal with."

"Jealousy!" Leece said. "Oh, now I'm jealous because you got drunk and gave up your virginity to someone who you hardly know?"

"Fuck you!" Kera said as she got up from off the bed and began to gather her things to leave. "I knew I should have hung around white girls. They don't hate like black girls do."

"And they won't beat your ass like a black girl, either," Leece said, rising up off the bed in flex mode. "Nigga, what?"

"Look, I'm out," Kera said as she walked over to the door with her sweater, purse, and car keys in hand.

"Oh, so now you gon' run away. Stick around and let's deal wit' this woman to woman. You a woman now, ain't you? Isn't that what you wanted, someone to make you feel like a woman? A man, a real man like Dollar!"

"I hate you so much right now," Kera said as her eyes began to swell up with tears.

"You can hate me all you want, but I'ma keep lovin' you. You my girl. I'm not about to sit back and watch you get hurt. Ever since you laid eyes on him your entire conversations has been Dollar this and Dollar that. How many times do you think your name comes up in his conversations?"

The tears that had welled up in Kera's eyes were now rolling down her face.

"How often does he call you?" Leece continued. "Has he ever called you?"

Kera stood there looking stupid.

"Does he even speak to you at work?"

A tear fell from Kera's eyes. No, Dollar didn't break his neck to check for her at work, and even though he was heavy on her mind, she didn't go checking for him either. For one, she didn't want people to start talking and it get back to her dad.

For two, she wanted to come off as a woman and not some young, stupid girl chasing after the dick.

"It's obvious he already got what he wanted," Leece continued. "He's done, Kera. You be done too."

Kera looked to her friend and through gritted teeth said, "I am done. I'm done with you." She then slammed the door behind her.

"Hey, it's me, Kera," Kera said through the phone receiver. Leece's words had been penetrating Kera's thoughts for the last couple of hours. Leece was wrong about Dollar just using her. Her relationship with Dollar was special. She'd prove it. She'd catch up with him after work hours where he would be free to express himself to her and vice versa.

"Hey, what's up, little mama?" Dollar replied rolling his eyes up in his head. The number she had called from was restricted. But even if it wasn't, he still wouldn't have known it was her, as he hadn't even bothered to ask her for her digits.

"Nothing, just wanted to see what was up, what you were getting into."

"Oh, uhh, I'm 'bout to head out to the movies," Dollar replied, not able to come up with anything else quick enough. He just didn't want her to think that he was chilling at home for the night and her offer to stop by.

"Oh," Kera replied, wanting so badly to ask Dollar who he was going with. But heck, it was ten o'clock at night; of course he was going with a female. "What are you going to see?" she asked instead.

"Uhh, uhh, what's it called?" Dollar thought, "Oh, yeah, *Deliver Us From Eva.*"

He was going to see a chick movie on top of that. Kera was almost positive he'd be going to see that with a female. "Oh, okay, well, I won't keep you. Call me sometime, okay?"

"Yeah, yeah, sure," Dollar replied.

"Okay, well then."

"A'ight, peace out," Dollar said, hanging up the phone.

Kera hung up the phone and sat staring at it in disbelief. She couldn't pick which emotion she wanted to keep company with. Instead of being angry or hurt, she convinced herself that she and Dollar didn't have any ties, so he could do what he wanted to. But still, everything in her wanted to go over and camp out at Dollar's apartment and stalk him to see for sure if he was with a broad.

While Kera fed herself excuses why she shouldn't be hurt, Dollar had rolled over and gone back to sleep, which was exactly what he had been doing when Kera phoned him. It was exactly what he planned on doing for the rest of the night.

CHAPTER 17

He's Got Game

Although Dollar wanted to scream out to the world his existence in the game, he didn't want a reputation. He didn't want niggaz knowing how hard he was; therefore, it would be easy to sneak up on them fools. Nobody living the street life really knew him; maybe a few cats from back in the day, but that's it. As far as he was concerned, Dareese Blake was a dead soul rotting away in jail. Dollar Bill was back: reincarnated. He would be a shining light to the game of life. Not the one that could be bought in the stores, but the one that was learned then earned on the streets of Gary.

Moving from Gary to Chicago gave Dollar peace of mind.

Gary was too damn small. It cluttered his mind and didn't allow him to think. Dollar liked living in Chicago and wished he had grown up there. It had way more opportunities than little Gary had. Dollar was actually born in Chicago, but his father had convinced his mother to move away with him to Gary. Dollar's father wanted to get his mother as far away from her controlling, overbearing parents as possible. Dollar's mother believed in that emotion called love and followed her heart, which meant following her man and his dreams instead of her own.

Shortly thereafter, Dollar's grandparents, Grandpa and Grandma Davis, his mother's parents, passed away. They died in their sleep of carbon monoxide poisoning. Auntie Charlene took over their house and tried relentlessly to get her only sibling to move back home to Chicago. She even said that she could bring her husband with her. Dollar's father convinced his mother that Auntie Charlene only wanted to pick up where her parents had left off; that she wanted to control their life and would eventually break the two of them up. So, Dollar's mother decided against moving back to Chicago. Instead, she lived in a one-bedroom, run-down apartment in Gary with her husband and baby.

Dollar could only imagine what life would have been like if his mother had moved in with Auntie Charlene. So much would have been different. But no, she had to be a down-ass chick and have her man's back. And in the end, he'd left her hangin'. Define irony.

It was Sunday morning and Dollar had been out the night before with Mya, the manicurist from the nail salon. He knew it was only a matter of time before he hit that. He could always tell that she wanted him by the way she gave him an extra ten minutes on the hand and wrist massage. Mya had the same unspoken persistence as Kera did, so like Kera, Dollar had to break Mya off a li'l somethin' somethin'.

The evening before, Dollar had only gone into the salon for a manicure, but he left with Mya. Dollar had been Mya's last client for the day and she insisted on taking him out to have a drink. After several drinks, he found himself in her apartment; then he found himself between her thighs.

As Dollar pulled the cover from over his head, through the cracks of the window blind, the sun screamed, "Wake up, nigga!" Dollar lay in bed wearing nothing but a morning hard-on. He stretched and flexed his muscles as one of them popped, causing an ache.

"Damn," Dollar said to himself. "I need to find a gym or something. Get this body back in shape.

It sounds like a box of Rice Krispies, all this damn snap, cracklin', and poppin'."

Dollar looked over at his digital clock that read 11:45 a.m. After a night of wild sex with Mya, Dollar was exhausted, and to add to it he had a hangover. He thought back on all the positions he had Mya's limbs pinned up in during their sexcapade.

Dollar rubbed his penis as he thought about how Mya allowed him to cum inside of her and then she sucked the juices off of him. The taste of her own pussy was like a delicacy to her. She managed to get all ten inches of Dollar down her throat without even gagging. Dollar felt like he had a starring role in one of his *Jake's Freaks, Hoes and Flows* porno tapes.

What really tripped Dollar out was that, as small and petite as that li'l white girl was, she took it in the ass like a champ. Dollar had never gone there before, and probably never would again, with a sista anyway. It didn't matter how long he had been locked up in prison, it was common knowledge that a guy had to be extra careful of what sexual acts he asked a sista to perform. Heck, they took offense to all kinds of sexual request. They didn't even like for a man to ask them to suck his dick. "Don't ask me to do it. Just let me do it on my own," they would say. And God forbid a man tried to push their head down to his spot. A sista would straight clown. So, asking a sista for some anal sex might get a brotha cut. They were always talking about they were saving that ass for their husband. But Mya was an exhibitionist. Dollar couldn't believe half the stuff they had done, and on top of that, he couldn't believe he had gone up in her raw.

What in the hell was I thinking? Dollar thought as he lay in bed and rested his body a little while longer. His mind roamed from one thing to the next.

Dollar's mind managed to drift into thoughts of his little brother. Ral bringing him up the other day must have struck a chord with Dollar because ever since then he caught himself thinking about his baby bro. He and his brother had been inseparable as kids. They were each other's keeper, and now here they were living a half hour from one another, yet a world apart.

Dollar desired to have a good relationship with Klein. He wished they could even ride together in his own mischievous endeavors. He'd never have to worry about trust if his own blood was part of his crew. But he knew that he and Klein were living in two separate universes.

Maybe once Dollar went legit he could see to it that things between them were on the up and up. But until then, it wouldn't hurt to at least try to carry on a decent conversation with him. So, Dollar decided that he'd invite Klein to play a game of ball with him. He was the older brother. He could set an example, be the bigger person, and make the first attempt to warm down the ice.

Dollar looked up his home phone number as he had done to get his address the night he went to his house with Ral. He grabbed his cell phone and dialed up Klein. Klein answered after a couple of rings.

"Hello," Klein said, almost out of breath. He had just walked in the door from visiting their mother's grave, which was what he did every Sunday after church.

"Hey, little brother," Dollar replied. There was silence on the phone. "You busy? You sound out of breath."

"I'm just walking in from church. I heard the phone ringing."

"Oh, cool. That's cool. I was wondering if you knew of a gym or someplace with a court," Dollar asked.

"Where you staying?" Klein asked.

"The shore. North," Dollar replied.

"Yeah, they got a California Fitness not too far from where you at. It's about a mile from the pier."

"How about you meet me over there for a game of ball?"

"Man, I haven't shot baskets in years." He laughed. "I'd need a doctor if I even attempted."

"Oh, you chumpin' out on me? You sceered?" Dollar joked.

"I didn't say I couldn't play. You know ballin' for me is like riding a bike. I ain't forgot how it's done."

"So, does that mean I'm gonna see you up at the gym?"

Klein paused while he contemplated, then replied, "Give me an hour."

"See you then," Dollar said, hanging up the phone. He took a deep breath and hit the shower to rid himself of Mya's scent.

When Dollar got out of the shower, he threw on his black-and-white And1 T-shirt with cutoff sleeves, the matching shorts, and his And1 black-and-white kicks. When Dollar went to leave, he noticed a pink envelope lying in front of his door. Someone had obviously placed it through his living room door mail slot. Dollar picked it up and was greeted by the sweet, flowery scent of the envelope. He recognized the scent as he pulled out and read the letter inside.

"The Gift"
Sleep don't come easy with you on my mind
I think I've found something it takes most people years to find
You tell me things so smooth and so clear
You make me feel like I have nothing to fear
Dreams of giving you my body, all of me,
the way I thought making love should be
My insides are burning as I explode in ecstasy
This feeling I'm feeling is greater than any feeling I've ever felt
Then I feel a sweet release and I start to melt
Stroking your hand through my hair,
holding me knowing I need you there
Kissing my neck, nibbling my ear,
your arms around me, keeping me near
I've given you all of me and all I want is for you to, at least, think about me every day
Cherish, adore and please don't throw my gift away
Love Always, Kera

Dollar closed his eyes and put his hand on his forehead.

What he had expected from sexin' up a young broad was coming to pass. Dollar balled up the note, pitched it into the trash, and then headed out to meet up with his brother.

"You don't want none of this. Buuuyaaa. Nothin' but net," Klein said as he dunked on Dollar, who was sticking him.

"Oh, you showing off now," Dollar said as he dribbled down the court, followed by the other players. Before Dollar could get halfway down the court, Klein stole the ball from him and took it to the hole.

"Game point," Klein said, showing his pearly whites.

Dollar bent over huffing and puffing. He managed to get out, "You da man," then gave Klein a five. The two shook hands with their teammates, then headed into the locker room to shower and get changed.

"You wanna go get some grub?" Dollar asked.

"Nah, I gotta study for my classes I'm taking over at Northwestern."

"How many years of school do you have to do?" Dollar asked.

"Well, you know I skipped my senior year. Hell, I earned college credits my junior year."

"Get out of here," Dollar said.

"Yeah, I got to graduate with the current seniors while I was a junior. Man, Ma was so proud."

"I'm proud of you too, man," Dollar said sincerely. "I just wish I could have been there. My brother, an MD."

"Yeah, I still have a lot of schooling left before I can put an MD behind my name, but I'm getting there. I'll be an MD in no time, and it will all be worth it." Klein smiled. "That's why I gotta hit the books."

"Oh, all right then. Well, maybe we can go some other time."

As the two continued to get dressed, Klein noticed the disappointing look on Dollar's face. He'd just enjoyed spending time with his big brother, but a game of basketball was different from having to sit across the table from him. He could handle constant activity between the two, but he didn't know if he could hold a conversation with Dollar without it turning sour. As Klein focused on Dollar's expression, he found himself staring at Dollar and noticing how much he looked like their mother.

"You've got her nose," Klein said to Dollar.

"Huh?" Dollar replied.

"Sadie. You've got her nose."

Dollar didn't reply to Klein's comment. He grabbed his gym bag and pulled out his keys. "I guess I'll talk to you whenever," Dollar said.

"Yeah, I guess so. Take care, man."

The brothers gave each other pound and Dollar headed toward the locker room exit.

"I guess it don't make sense to try to study on an empty stomach," Klein said on second thought.

A huge grin took over Dollar's face as he replied, "Fat's BBQ."

"And you know this, man," he said as he grabbed his belongings and followed Dollar out.

Dollar and Klein talked and laughed over their quarter chicken BBQ dinners. Holding a pleasant conversation didn't turn out to be such a hard feat after all.

"So, Doc," Dollar asked, tearing a piece of chicken off the bone with his teeth. "You got a woman in your life?"

"You mean a girlfriend?" Klein said.

"Yeah, man."

"Nah, don't have the time. Relationships take too much time and effort. I only have enough time and effort for success right now."

"But I thought every man needed a good woman in their life." Dollar smiled in a suggestive manner.

"I do have a woman in my life," he replied. "Mama. I visit her every Sunday, just to talk. Her spirit guides me, you know?"

"Yeah, I know what you mean," Dollar said, staring off in thoughts of his mother's loving spirit.

"Mama pushed me to this point and supported me to the end. I'm not going to let anything stand in my way."

"Mama was always there backing up every one of our big dreams," Dollar said. "Remember when we set up that lemonade stand? Mama helped us with the sign and everything."

"Man, do I remember. We used to do some crazy stuff trying to get money," Klein replied.

"What about that time we tried to sell decorated Easter eggs for a dollar each?" Dollar laughed.

"Yeah, and you forgot to boil them."

The two laughed hysterically. Dollar almost choked.

"The things a little nigga gotta do to make it out of the hood," Dollar said after clearing his throat.

"Tell me about it. I remember when Mom wouldn't buy you that Michael Jordan jersey. You were set on getting it yourself so you sold sips of Canadian Mist to the drunks in the hood from an old bottle Dad had left behind. You charged them one dollar a sip. You got your name honest, Dollar. You probably would have sold nickels for a dollar if you could have. Selling sips of liquor for a dollar . . . you was crazy. I thought Ma was going to kill you when Old Lady Parker ratted you out. Man, Ma was heated. I remember her saying how if Dad were still around she would have had him beat your tail black and blue. But then she thought about it and said, 'Boy, if your daddy was around, all he'd probably want to know was how much money you made so you could split it with him.'"

Klein began laughing. He found himself laughing alone.

"I don't have a dad, and neither do you," Dollar said as he stood up and walked over to the trashcan to throw away the remainder of his meal. He had suddenly lost his appetite.

Dollar returned to the table where silence was still present.

"What are you going to do with yourself, Dollar?" Klein asked with sincerity. "You just gonna walk around mad at the world, holdin' grudges?"

"Why not?" Dollar replied. "Ain't that what you doin'?"

Klein sighed and continued. "Why don't you go to school, man?"

"Me, go to school." Dollar laughed. "School ain't for me."

"You've got a brain, don't you? You're capable of thinking, aren't you? So, why isn't school for you?"

"I don't know nothing but the street, Doc. I mean, I read a lot, but even the majority of that is just some ol' gangsta shit," Dollar said.

"You know just as much as me."

"Yeah, right." Dollar laughed.

"I'm serious, man. Remember when I was younger, before you went to j . . . Well, anyway. You used to ask me all of those questions and pay me twenty-five dollars if I answered them correctly. A couple of times I gave you the wrong answers and you made me find out the true answer. I used to give you the wrong answers on purpose just to see if you even knew the answers to the questions yourself. And you did know."

"Yeah, I did, didn't I?" Dollar said, grinning proudly.

"Yeah, you did."

"Well, that was then and this is now," Dollar said, becoming more adamant. "School is not an option for me. That's your thang."

"And what's your thang?" Klein said, waiting for Dollar to respond. Dollar simply looked away. "Oh, let me guess, the thug life is your thang: big ballin' and shit. Fuck that street life, man. Fuck the streets."

"Fuck the streets," Dollar repeated angrily. "The streets is all I got. I love the streets and the streets love me back. Besides, I don't see you inviting me to come live out there in the 'burbs with you."

Klein couldn't say anything. Dollar had shut him down.

"Well, I guess I better get going," Klein said. "It's getting late and I, uhh . . ."

"You have to study," Dollar reminded him.

"Yeah, I have to study."

Dollar stood up and took his brother's trash to the garbage. He walked back over to the table where Klein was preparing to leave.

"You always been a friend to the streets, Dollar. I know this. I know you missed your freedom on the streets, but it ain't the answer," Klein said. "The streets don't love nobody. I'm stitchin' up bullet wounds, knife wounds and treating AIDS patients daily. Do you think the streets love them? Look at Stephan Crouse. He sleeps with the streets every night. Does it look like the streets love him?"

Dollar looked away from his brother in silence.

"Look, Dollar, man. I'm not trying to end this on a sour note," Klein told him as he turned to leave. "So let's just squash it. It was good kickin' it with you."

"Yeah, me too, man."

"You got a number or something?" Klein asked.

Dollar, surprised he's asked, responded, "Yeah, I have a cell phone."

"No home phone?"

"Naw, all I need is a cell phone. The feds can't tap that," Dollar joked.

"You staying over by the shore. That must mean your job is panning out pretty good for you. Those places over there are high as hell. You gettin' lots of gigs?"

"I can't complain. What about you? How's work at the clinic?"

"Oh, it's good. We just got a new grant from a private donor."

"Well, that's good. Hell, free money is always good," Dollar said.

"Not always," Klein replied. "Not always." There was dead silence. "Well, uhh, I guess I'll holler at you later."

"Yeah, man." He gave Dollar a hug, a passionate, brotherly hug. He looked up at Dollar then walked away.

"Yo, Doc," Dollar called to him. "What athlete was on the cover of *Sports Illustrated* more than any other athlete?"

Klein stood and thought for a minute. "I don't know. Who?"

"Muhammad Ali," Dollar replied.

"Oh yeah, that's right," Klein said, winking, knowing the answer all along. "Muhammad Ali."

Dollar smiled and watched his little brother until he was out of his sight, taking in the words his brother had just spoken to him. Perhaps Klein was right. Maybe the streets didn't love nobody. Dollar's ego wouldn't even allow him to entertain this concept for long. Of course the streets loved him. Didn't they?

CHAPTER 18

No Sex in the Champagne Room

"Did I look sexy up there for you?" Tommy said to her perspective Champagne Room client.

"Oh, hell yeah, ma," the man who called himself Kube replied. "You looked good as hell dancin' up there on stage." He had a toothpick hanging from between his lips.

"I bet you would like to take me in a dark room and let me give you a private dance, huh?"

"Yo, you'll do dat shit?" Kube said with his New York accent telling on his city of residence.

"You see that room back there?" Tommy said, pointing. "I can make it happen right there for you, baby."

"You gon' take some shit off?"

"You tippin' proper?"

"Fo' shizzel," Kube said, fondling the toothpick with his tongue and rolling it with his fingers.

"A'ight then," Tommy replied. "You and Benji follow me."

"Benji?" Kube questioned.

"Ben Franklin," Tommy said, screwing up her mug.

"Damn, it's gon' cost me a hundred?"

"Oh, you a baller on a budget?" Tommy asked.

"No, ma. It ain't even like that," Kube replied.

"Oh, you one of them cheap-ass wankstas frontin' like a gangsta." Tommy knew the more she insulted his pockets, the deeper he would go into them to prove her wrong. She'd met his kind a thousand times.

"You see this shit right here?" Kube said, pulling out a thick wad of cash. "Do this look like *Monopoly* money to you?" Kube proceeded to peel off twenties and throw them at Tommy, who kindly scooped them up. "Let's go." Kube took a sip from his drink and signaled to his two homeboys he rolled in with that he'd be right back.

Tommy showed Kube the way to the Champagne Room where Kube paid Bear one hundred dollars to enter. Tommy led him over to the couch and fetched the champagne.

Kube sat on the puffy black couch that many niggaz and hoes had fucked on over the years. He bobbed his head to the beat of the music as he stroked one of the purple, satin pillows that was on the couch.

"That's my shit," Kube said, referring to the song that was coming through the speakers. "Can you turn that up?"

"Sure, baby, whatever you want," Tommy said, turning the music up. With her back toward Kube, she began to pour the champagne.

"Can you turn it up a little more?"

"Just a little more. I want you to be able to hear me when I talk shit in your ear," Tommy joked.

As soon as Tommy turned the music up a notch, she felt Kube's hands groping all over her.

"Slow down, baby. Let me finish this here and I'll be over to do my thang. You just go back over to the couch and wait for me."

"I want my shit right here, right now," Kube said.

"You want me to dance for you right here?" Tommy asked. "Don't you think the couch would be more comfortable? You can sit down and—"

"Bitch, stop playing games," Kube said, cutting Tommy off. "I ain't pay no hundred dollars to get back here for no dance. Hell, you could have danced for me out here. A nigga trying to get some ass."

"Well, you got me bent," Tommy said. "Ain't no sex in the Champagne Room with me. You get a dance and that's it, nigga."

"I thought hoes play when ballers pay." Kube placed his hand down Tommy's crotch.

Tommy fixed her mouth to start cussing Kube out, but when she went to open her mouth, he rammed his tongue down her throat. Tommy knew if she got herself in the right position she could take Kube, but the trick had caught her off guard. The feeling of Kube's fingers plunging in and out of Tommy made her want to throw up.

Tommy was able to draw her hand up and slice her nails down the side of Kube's face. In retaliation, Kube grabbed Tommy by her hair and pulled her down to the ground, still kissing her and using his other hand to finger her. Tommy's resistance only excited him more.

As Kube was forcing Tommy down to the ground, she managed to grab onto the neck of the champagne bottle. Taking the bottle of bubbly down with her, she cracked Kube right over his head. This dazed him momentarily.

"You fucking cunt," Kube said, grabbing his head as blood streamed down his face. "You're dead, whore. You hear me? You fuckin' dead!"

Tommy had already made her way to the door and summoned Bear to handle that nigga. Bear took one look at Tommy's desperate face and disheveled hair and could tell something wasn't right. He picked Kube up like a rag doll and escorted him out of the Champagne Room. The two dudes Kube was with noticed the commotion and darted across the room to have their homeboy's back. The two dudes were no match for Big Bear, who put all three of them out the club. Their punk asses knew they didn't want none of Big Bear. But at least they had the heart to run up on him.

"You all right, girl?" Storm said, entering the Champagne Room where Tommy stood, still shaken up, but was more pissed off than anything.

"Girl, yeah, I'm all right," Tommy replied. "Son of a bitch. Niggaz kill me thinkin' just 'cause you dance for a living you fuck for a living, too, or that a big tip equals a quickie. Fuck this shit!"

"He didn't fuck you, did he?" Storm asked.

"No, but he was kissing me, and he stuck his fingers . . ." Tommy couldn't even finish she was so mad and disgusted.

"It's okay, Wine. It's okay. Girl, it's gon' be all right," Storm said, hugging Tommy.

"I'ma get that New York bastard," Tommy ranted.

"Girl, you know how these niggaz are. They think they can cut through our neck of the woods from the big city and treat us like trash. Fuck 'em, girl. Let it go. Trust me, they know better than to come up in here with that bull shit again."

Tommy shook her head. Negative. Try as she might, she was a grudgeable bitch. She couldn't let this shit go if she wanted to. "I want you to handle his ass, Storm," Tommy said.

"Girl, you just scared and angry right now," Storm replied.

"No, I want you and Thunder to handle that fucker. How much is it gon' cost me? I got money."

"Come on, Wine. You trippin'."

Bear knocked on the cracked open door and peeked through. "You all right, Wine?" Bear asked Tommy.

"Yeah, I'm cool," Tommy replied.

"I got that buster's license plate number and shit if you wanna press charges or anything."

"It was probably a rental," Tommy said pessimistically.

"Naw, that shit was customized," Bear responded. "It wasn't no rental."

Bear handed a piece of paper with the license plate number on it to Storm, who was closer to him, to give to Tommy. Storm took it from his hand. "I got this," Storm told Bear. Enough said, Bear closed the door behind him. Storm tried to hand the piece of paper to Tommy, but Tommy pushed her hand away.

"Naw, you keep it. You gon' be needing it to track that nigga down. How much?" Tommy was hell bent on utilizing Storm and Thunder's services.

Storm thought for a moment. There was no way she could refuse to help Tommy. One way or the other, Tommy was gonna get at old dude. Storm figured she might as well let professionals take care of him.

"You know what, boo? This one is on me," Storm said, lifting up her purple Crown Royal bag and sticking the piece of paper down inside it along with her tips. "As a matter of fact, by the time I finish cleaning out that nigga's pockets, it's gon' be on him." Storm turned to exit.

"I want the full package, you know, M&M."

Storm stopped and turned to face Tommy. "You sure about that?"

Without blinking Tommy said, "I'm sure."

Storm shrugged. "All right then; Murder Mommies it is. And don't you worry. We gon' melt in that mafucka's mouth for sure: just like M&Ms."

***

Dollar was standing outside of the work building talking to Jay when Kera walked up. *Please don't let her walk over here and speak to me. Please, God,* Dollar thought as he continued on with his conversation with Jay.

"Hey, Dareese," Kera said as she approached Dollar.

"Damn," Dollar mumbled under his breath as he tried to ignore her. He'd told himself not to mess with that young girl. Now getting rid of her was going to be like getting rid of ants at a picnic.

"Dollar," Kera said, putting a little bass in her voice.

"Oh, hey, Kera, hey. Uhh yeah, hey," Dollar stuttered. By this time, all eyes were on the boss's daughter. All eyes were green. Every one of them guys had used Kera as a motivating factor to jacking off. Their dreams were Dollar's reality.

"Yeah, uhh hey," Kera replied as they each stood in silence. "Well, I just wanted to say hey."

"Hey," Dollar said.

"Hey," Kera said, looking stupid as she walked away in humiliation. As she entered the building, she could hear the men begin to whistle and salute Dollar for his conquer.

"What's the matter, baby?" Redd said to his baby girl, seeing that she was a little disturbed.

"Nothing really," Kera hesitated. She had a pretty close relationship with her father. She could talk about almost anything with him. When she started her period in school it was her father she called to talk to and not her mother. He took away the dirty feeling she had about having a period and made her feel clean again, like she was normal and entering womanhood. Well, right about now she needed to feel good and normal again. She turned to Redd. "Daddy, can we talk?"

"Yo, T, come on. Answer the door. It's me, Dollar," Dollar said, knocking on Tommy's door like he was SWAT. After a few more pounds the door cracked open.

"Damn, girl, what took you so long? You ain't answering your phone or nothing," Dollar said, but before he could get another word out of his mouth, he saw that the person who answered the door wasn't Tommy. It was her older niece.

"Hi," the girl said. "You Dollar?"

"Yeah, I'm Dollar."

"My aunt always talks about you. I'd know you anywhere. She has pictures of you in newspaper articles. You were going up the courthouse steps in one picture. You were in the courtroom in another. You look bigger in person."

"Yeah, I'm a little bit bigger," Dollar said. "Where is your aunt?"

"She's not feeling well. She's 'sleep, but I'm sure she'd want me to wake her up for you."

"Is something wrong with the phone?" Dollar asked. "I tried calling."

"Oh, the ringers are off. The phone kept waking her up. Do you want me to get her?" the girl said.

"No, it's cool," Dollar said. "Just let her know I stopped by to talk about some work I got lined up."

"'Kay," the girl said as she watched Dollar walk away.

Dollar walked back to the car where Ral was waiting on him.

"She ain't home?" Ral asked once Dollar was inside the car.

"Yeah, she's home. She ain't feeling well or some shit. I need to holler at her when her head is right."

"So you still wanna head over to Jimmy's to grab a bite and talk business?"

"Yeah, we can do that," Dollar replied.

Dollar and Ral went on to Jimmy's, without Tommy, so that they could discuss their next move. The stickup Dollar had lined up was one that Ral and Tommy could handle on their own.

Dollar wanted them to rob Mr. Owens. Dollar knew for a fact that Mr. Owens always carried a good amount of cash money on his person, and another good amount in the glove box of his Navigator. He wasn't a check writing or credit card using man. He liked dealing with straight-up cash. Mr. Owens always said that when you use cash money you get more for less because money talks. Dollar knew that they'd get no more than $9,000, but he still upheld the theory that free money was always good money.

CHAPTER 19

From Hood Life to the Good Life

After a couple days of cooling off from her awful experience with Kube, Tommy put her high-heeled boots back on and hit the grind. She also handled her business with stickin' up Mr. Owens. She and Ral pulled off the robbery with ease. There was a good chance he would have recognized Dollar had he participated.

They caught Mr. Owens first thing in the morning, 6:00 a.m., as he was getting ready to pull out of his driveway for work. Dollar had been to Mr. Owens's house before and had given Tommy and Ral directions on how to get there. It just so happened that Mr. Owens was making a bank deposit that day and had an extra few grand on him, which made the total stickup worth $13,000.

Dollar took his share, purchased some odds and ends for his place, and tightened up his

wardrobe. He invested in a fourteen-karat gold
Figaro necklace and bracelet set. He wasn't
trying to mess with that platinum jewelry that
just drew attention to him.

It hadn't taken Dollar long at all since his
release from jail to get a nice place to rest his head,
a nice li'l ride, and a nice li'l wardrobe. He had a
couple of options on pussy and he looked good as
hell. On top of all that, he had a legit job so Uncle
Sam couldn't fuck with him.

Dollar kept a nice little bank account, but he
kept his real loot in a safe at his apartment. He
made it a habit to always deposit one half of the
money he made working at Redd's into his bank
account. He didn't deposit the money from his
mother's life insurance policy. This way he could
always say that any purchases he made were
made with that money.

At this point, Dollar felt all he needed was
one big hit. Redd had been talking to him about
some investments he'd made that damn near
quadrupled his money, and Dollar was looking
to do the same. With the money he earned from
his investments, he wouldn't mind opening up
a spot similar to Redd's. Maybe he could open
up a barbershop/massage parlor or something.
Dollar didn't know what he was going to set
up for himself, but he knew that he had to do

something. All good things came to an end and he wanted to be the one to put an end to them; not the police and not some jealous thug. He would live the good life, but on his own terms.

The line at the bank was long and Dollar was becoming agitated. There were two security guards on duty. One in particular, who was standing at the bank entrance right underneath the surveillance camera, kept eyeballin' Dollar. The security guard didn't try to hide his suspicions, as he never once turned his eyes away from Dollar, even when Dollar decided to stare back at him. Dollar wanted to go over there and whoop his ass. After all, security was standing underneath the camera, so the assault wouldn't get caught on tape.

Dollar should have known better anyway than to go to the bank at lunchtime on a Friday afternoon. There were only five more people ahead of him out of the eleven that were initially standing in front of him. Although Dollar had already been waiting a half hour in that line, he didn't think he could stand to wait much longer. Just as he decided to pull out of line someone tapped him on the shoulder.

"I didn't mean for you to have to stand in line. You can come back to my desk now," a voice said to Dollar.

He turned around and to his surprise standing there was Hennessey.

"Huh? What?" This was the third time she just happened to pop up. In Dollar's mind, this was clearly no coincidence, this was fate. This was a sign that he was indeed supposed to hook up with this chick and the gods were on his side. He'd let her slip through his fingers the first two times, with not so much as getting her phone number. He was getting yet another chance, which would probably be his last. Hopefully the third time really was a charm.

"I said, you don't have to wait in line again. Come on back." She winked and began walking toward the back office area. "Right this way," Hennessey said, signaling with her hand for Dollar to follow.

Dollar smiled and followed Hennessey back to a cozy little office where she offered him a seat.

"I didn't know you worked here," Dollar said. "I've never seen you here before."

"That's because you've never looked into investing in your retirement," Hennessey said. "That's what I do here; make sure people are taken care of when they're old and gray."

"I'm anything but that," Dollar said with conceit, which lightweight turned Hennessey off, evident by the corners of her mouth slightly turning downward.

"What can I help you with today, Mr. Blake?" Hennessey asked Dollar.

"A deposit . . ." His words trailed off as curiosity took over his thoughts. "How did you know my last name?" Dollar asked. He was almost certain he'd only given her his first name, and not even that, but his nickname.

Hennessey's eyes went left, right, then downward. "Well, it's not that hard to read upside down, you know," Hennessey said, referring to the personalized, preprinted pink deposit slip Dollar had in his hand. "I can make that deposit for you."

"How do I know you're not going to run off with all of my money?" Dollar joked.

"You don't know, do you? I guess you'll just have to trust me," Hennessey said, holding her hand out to take Dollar's deposit.

Dollar stuck his hand out to give Hennessey his deposit, but instead he grabbed her by the arm. "Fuck the deposit," Dollar said, looking into Hennessey's eyes. "Let me take this money and spend it all on you."

Hennessey couldn't help but laugh as she took the deposit out of Dollar's hand with her loose hand. "That's quite all right, Mr. Blake," she said as she proceeded to log the deposit into her computer.

Dollar watched her pounding away at the keyboard, thinking all the while what he wouldn't do to get with her fine self. She was playing hard to get, but he could tell that she wanted him. But what could she possibly want him for?"

Dollar second-guessed himself. What did he have to offer her? He wasn't exactly company Christmas party material. *Hello, I'm Dollar. I do construction for a living and, oh yeah, on the side I rob people.* Dollar laughed to himself.

"Something funny?" Hennessey asked.

"It's funny why you won't go out with me," Dollar answered. "Come on, just dinner."

"Nah," Hennessey said. "You look like the type who might feel as though I'd owe you something afterward. Being in debt is not my thing."

"Naw, Miss Lady. It ain't even like that. It will be kinda like me returning the favor of you rescuing me from that long-ass line out there."

Hennessey proceeded to log in Dollar's deposit and hand-write him a receipt. "Here you go, Mr. Blake," she said, slightly smiling and blinking almost in slow motion.

"Thank you," Dollar said. "But anyway, that was good looking out, not making me stand in that line."

"It wasn't a problem," Hennessey said. "I'm glad I could be of some assistance. But waiting on customers in line really isn't my job."

"That's right; you're an investor."

"Yeah, but my official title around here is personal banker."

"Personal banker, huh? So what all does the word *personal* include? Perhaps I'm in need of a personal banker."

"Perhaps you are, so it would be my pleasure to assign your account to one of my colleagues."

Dollar's face twisted up. Had old girl just put him off on someone else? "What's wrong with you being my personal banker?"

"Ummm, I think it's better that we don't get too *personal*. You know what I mean?" Hennessy winked and started typing away at her computer.

Dollar stood before her not knowing what his next move should be. He wasn't used to waiting around for a woman to say something to him. What was it with her? Dollar was going to make it his mission to find out.

"There we go." Hennessey punched a final key on her computer then looked up at Dollar. "Someone will be in touch." She smiled.

Dollar smiled.

Awkward silence.

"Can you find your way back out?" Hennessey asked Dollar.

And now she had the nerve to dismiss him just like that. This was a first for Dollar for real.

"Oh yeah, yeah," Dollar said. "I see you're busy, and this isn't really your job," he mimicked, "so yeah, I'll just go ahead and find my way back out."

"All right then," Hennessey said as she went back to typing something on her computer. "Oh, and, Mr. Blake?"

"Yeah," Dollar said, stopping in his tracks. *I knew she couldn't resist me.* He had a huge grin on his face.

"Can you close the door behind you?"

"Uhh, sure. And thanks again."

"Anytime," Hennessey said as Dollar walked out of her office and closed the door behind him, his tail dragging between his legs.

He shook his head. "Damn, I can't believe I froze up," Dollar said as he looked down at his deposit receipt. Just then his eyes lit up. Underneath his deposit verification was a note that read:

You can return the favor at 8:00 p.m.
tonight. 1777 Lake Wave Loop,
   Hennessey
   855-2755

A huge grin of victory spread across Dollar's face. He guessed Hennessey wanted to get personal after all.

It wasn't as chilly as it had been the past few nights as the cold season was coming to an end, so Dollar sported his Fonzie, from the old *Happy Days* sitcom, leather jacket over his V-neck, long-sleeved ribbed sweater and Hard Knock Life Wear jeans. He couldn't wait to meet up with Hennessey at her place.

Dollar wasn't sure exactly how to get to Hennessey's address, so he left his house a few minutes earlier than he had originally planned. He only had to stop and ask for directions one time when he saw that there was a chance that he might be late. Hennessey didn't seem like the kind of chick who would wait around on a late-ass nigga. She was the type that kept a brother in check, on his toes. Perhaps she was exactly what Dollar needed in his life.

Hennessey was smooth like the cognac she was named after, but Dollar knew her chaser was bitch mode. Her words were fly, as if they were rehearsed. This is one of the things that attracted Dollar to her.

When Dollar finally turned onto Lake Wave Loop, he saw that the scenery wasn't residential at all. There were hotels, cafés, and drug stores. Dollar followed the numbers carefully until he found 1777. It appeared to be a lovely, high-class hotel.

"That's what I'm talking about," Dollar said out loud as he searched for a parking space. As he drove by the hotel he realized that it had valet parking. He turned his car around, drove up to the hotel door, and utilized the valet services.

Dollar walked into the hotel and headed straight toward the registration desk to find out what room number Hennessey was in, prayerfully waiting for him buck naked.

"May I help you, sir?" the clerk asked Dollar.

"Yes, can you phone Miss Hennessey Monroe's room and let her know that Mr. Blake has arrived?" Dollar replied.

The clerk punched a few keys on her computer before saying, "I'm sorry, sir, but we don't have a Hennessey Monroe checked into this hotel."

"Well, there must be a mistake. I'm sure she's here."

"There's no mistake," a voice crept up on Dollar from behind.

Dollar turned around to see Hennessey standing in a black floor-length halter gown with a split in the front that almost played peek-a-boo with her kitty cat.

"You look good," Dollar said to Hennessey, turning away from the desk and walking toward his beautiful date.

"Thank you," Hennessey replied. "You're lookin' fine." Hennessey circled Dollar like he was her prey, nodding her fondness of the fineness before her. Hennessey licked her lips and winked. "I hope I don't have to come out the heels tonight and beat down nobody over you."

"Would you do that for me, baby?"

"Umm hmm." Hennessey smiled.

Hennessey had a smile that humbled even a hardheaded dude like Dollar instantly. The contour of her lips allowed for just enough of her beautiful white teeth to show. She had a memorable smile, like Laci Peterson, the woman whose smile was plastered on every news channel and newspaper when her husband was accused of murdering her and her unborn child.

Dollar stood before Hennessey, mesmerized by her smile. The two stood there looking each other up and down. Hennessey especially admired Dollar's chest muscles peeking up out of the V on his sweater. She could have stood there and counted every chest hair if time had permitted.

"We should head to the hotel restaurant," Hennessey said. "We have reservations, so we don't want to be late."

Dollar followed Hennessey over to the restaurant where the hostess led them to a quaint table for two.

Dollar slightly nudged the hostess, who was about to pull Hennessey's chair out for her, and pulled it out himself. He then removed the little black evening bag she was carrying from her shoulder and placed it on the back of her chair by its gold chain strap.

"Thank you," Hennessey said, surprised at Dollar's manners.

"It's my pleasure, Miss Lady," Dollar replied.

The hostess presented them with menus and said, "Take as much time as you need to look over the menus. Your waiter will be right with you."

As the hostess began to walk away, Dollar stopped her. "May we see the wine menu?" Dollar asked.

"Certainly," the hostess said. "I'll bring one right over."

Upon the hostess returning with wine menu in hand, Dollar allowed Hennessey to scan it and order the wine of her choice.

"By the way," Hennessey said to Dollar, "Rutherford Alleghany is your new personal banker. He said he has some great investment ideas in order for you to make money, so he's going to put something together for you."

"I appreciate it," Dollar replied. "But why didn't you just be my personal banker in the first place since it looks like we are getting personal after all?"

"Didn't want to mix business," was Hennessey's short reply.

Dollar and Hennessey shot the breeze over a bottle of Zinfandel and a nice, elegant dinner that consisted of steak and lobster, preceded by an appetizer of crab-stuffed mushrooms, and followed by a delicious dessert of cheesecake covered in caramel syrup.

When the waiter had originally brought out Dollar and Hennessey's main course, Hennessey sent her steak back to be prepared a little longer. Instead of diving right into his delicious-looking food, Dollar waited the ten extra minutes for Hennessey's plate to be served and then ate with her. That had to have gotten him bonus points with this class act of a woman.

After feeding Hennessey the last bite of the cheesecake the two had shared, Dollar signaled the waiter over to the table. He was ready to get out of there in hopes that Hennessey would invite him back to her place . . . just to talk.

"Is there anything else I can get you two tonight?" the waiter asked before handing them the bill.

"No, we're fine," Dollar said, sticking his hand out. "Unless the lady would like something to go, for, perhaps, a midnight snack or something."

Hennessey put her hand up and shook her head. "Oh, no, thank you. I'm fine."

"The lady says she's fine," Dollar told the waiter, then looked to Hennessey. "And I'd definitely have to agree."

Hennessy put her head down to hide her blushing.

"Then here you are." The waiter laid the bill down on the table. "I'll be back to pick it up whenever you're ready." He smiled and walked away.

Dollar reached for the bill. Hennessey stuck her hand over top of Dollar's to stop him from picking up the bill. She then reached into her little black evening bag for money.

"Hey, I thought I was supposed to be returning the favor," Dollar said.

"You did by having dinner with me. Your company is opulent. I feel like a priceless, angelic antique."

"Well, damn, does that mean we fuckin'?" Dollar quickly raised his hands in both surrender and defense before she could catch and attitude. "I'm playing," Dollar said as Hennessey shook her index finger at him.

"You are so bad," Hennessey said, smiling. She then whispered, "But, between you and me, that's how I like 'em."

"Really, Miss Banker with a personal office throwing words around like 'opulent' and 'angelic' and shit? I find that hard to believe."

Hennessey couldn't help but laugh as Dollar imitated her. "Shut up, Eddie Murphy, and kiss me."

"Huh," Dollar said, being caught off guard by Hennessey's forwardness.

"Lay one on me. Pucker up. Stick your tongue down my throat. Am I speaking your language now?"

Dollar looked around the restaurant to see if anyone was watching them.

"You embarrassed?" Hennessey asked.

"Who, me?"

"You know what? Forget about the kiss. I'm sorry for putting you on the spot like that. Excuse me, waiter," Hennessey said, raising her hand and signaling the waiter over.

Dollar couldn't figure out if this woman had an attitude with him for not kissing her. Had he bruised the lady's ego?

"You mad, baby?" Dollar asked. "Well, I'm sorry. I don't know who you mistook me for, but I'm not one of those guys who kisses on the first date. You think just 'cause you buy me an expensive meal I'm supposed to let you stick your tongue down my throat?" Dollar said, enjoying his and Hennessey's role-playing.

"I understand. I ain't trying to rush things. I don't want you to do anything you don't want to do. It's cool," Hennessey said, winking at Dollar.

When the waiter came over to the table, Hennessey handed him the leather check presenter with the bill and two one-hundred dollar bills inside of it. Dollar tried to leave the tip, but Hennessey wouldn't allow him to do so. Hennessey laid a thirty dollar tip on the table and then excused herself to go to the ladies' room.

Dollar stood up when Hennessey stood up. Upon her return, she and Dollar exited the restaurant and hotel.

"So, where did you park?" Dollar asked Hennessey once they were outside. "I'll walk you to your car. Or did you valet?"

"It was much too lovely of an evening to drive. Besides, I just live a few blocks around the corner," Hennessey said.

"Then let me walk you home," Dollar insisted.

"No, that's okay. But if you're up to it, I wouldn't mind going for a walk. There's a little park behind the building with a penny fountain. I'm in the mood to make a wish."

Dollar obliged Hennessey by walking her to the fountain. He dug all of the change from out of his pockets and he and Hennessey threw coins into the fountain and chatted.

"So, Dollar," Hennessey said. "How did you get the name Dollar?"

Dollar laughed and replied, "When I was a kid I had big dreams, dreams of becoming a thousand-naire. I did and sold everything I could think of to try to make a dollar. I would try to sell eggs to a chicken if I could. And no matter what it was I was selling, everything had the same price."

"A dollar," Hennessey jumped in.

"You got it," Dollar said, mocking his days as a child. "Dollar Bill. It's just one dollar, dollar bill, y'all. Pretty soon folks in the neighborhood started calling me Dollar."

"Oh, I bet you were so cute," Hennessey said pinching Dollar's cheek.

"Well, Miss Hennessey," Dollar said, turning the tables. "How is it you were named after an alcoholic beverage?"

"Actually, I'm not named after an alcoholic beverage. My name is spelled 'e-y' at the end instead of just 'y.'"

"Okay, aaannnd? It's still pronounced the same."

"Let me finish, why don't you?" Hennessey continued. "My mom was going to be a lawyer if it was the last thing she did in life, only she could never seem to afford law school. So, until the day she could afford it she studied law by watching every court show that existed. The last name of one of her favorite characters on one of the court shows was Hennessey, therefore, naming me Hennessey. My mom was a homebody. She had no idea that Hennessy was a cognac."

"Nice story," Dollar said.

"It's the truth," Hennessey said, play nudging Dollar on his shoulder. "Besides, she was a geography buff as well. Hennessey is the name of a city in Oklahoma, but see y'all black folk only know about where da liquor store at," Hennessey joked.

"I get where your moms was coming from," Dollar said. "It's like that Justice shit in that movie with Pac and Janet Jackson. What was it called?"

"*Poetic Justice.*" Hennessey laughed. "You know I never thought of it like that."

"Well, did your moms ever make it to law school?" Dollar asked.

"I'm putting her through it now," Hennessey said proudly, almost as if she wanted to cry at just the thought of it.

Dollar turned Hennessey's face toward him with his hand and kissed her softly on the cheek. The tear that had made its way from her eye slid onto his lips. The warmth from the tear melted Dollar. He could feel where Hennessey was coming from. His own mother had been his motivation in life. Dollar wanted so badly to share his thoughts with Hennessey, but for the first time in a long time, he was afraid. He felt that there was something special about Hennessey. Dollar couldn't risk losing something before he even had it. He wasn't going to make the same mistake his father made.

Dollar sat holding Hennessey for a few more minutes.

Hennessey ended up walking Dollar back around to the hotel where he waited on the valet driver to bring his car around. When the driver drove up in Dollar's car, he exchanged the twenty dollar bill in his hand for the keys to his car.

"Well, Ms. Monroe, we must do this again sometime."

"We must," Hennessey said, placing a kiss on the side of Dollar's neck. Dollar tried to push up on her, but Hennessey pulled away. Her eyes said, "Not yet," as she watched him drive away.

As Dollar drove off he was in complete bliss. He looked in his rearview mirror at Hennessey who was standing in model stance, leg stretched out, one hand on her hip, and blowing him a kiss good-bye with the other. He wanted so badly to catch it in the air and place it on his lips, but he knew that would be some corny-ass shit. So instead, he drove on.

Honey had Dollar cheesin' all the way home. Just the thought of Hennessey put a smile on his face. She was beautiful, smart like his mother, and no-nonsense like his auntie Charlene. She was two of the most influential women in Dollar's life rolled up into one. And on top of that, Dollar saw that same look in her eyes, that determination to do anything she could for her mom by any means necessary. That same look he used to possess.

Dollar made it up in his mind that Hennessey was going to be his main girl. He liked her style. She wasn't necessarily going to be the only one, not just yet. But she damn sure would be number one. Maybe, in time, the little spark that existed between the two would grow into a flame. Who knew what the future held for the two?

CHAPTER 20

Hit Hoes

"So, how was you and your wife's little trip to the NYC?" Becka asked Storm as they got dressed in their dance costumes.

"It was very productive," Storm replied as she looked over at Tommy who was lining her lips with a chocolate Mary Kay lip liner. "I ran into a dude there who said he had been up in here the last time he came through the city."

"Oh yeah?" Becka replied, none the wiser that Storm and Tommy were having a conversation over her head. "Small world. Well, I'll holler at y'all hoochies later. It's show time." Becka put on her cover-up and walked out of the dressing room.

"By the way," Storm said to Tommy. "This is yours." Storm handed Tommy a wad of cash. Tommy flipped through it, puzzled.

"What's this?" Tommy asked.

"That dude I ran into," Storm said as she headed for the door, "well, he said the last time he was here he forgot to tip you. He wanted you to have that."

Tommy's eyes almost watered as she flipped through the $3,000 Storm had just handed her. Storm winked at Tommy and then closed the door behind her.

"Now that's a down-ass chick," Tommy said to herself. She tucked the money in her Crown Royal bag that was down inside her gym bag. It was almost show time for her as well.

That night at the club Tommy was supposed to handle a situation with some young buck named Rob from LA. It was something Ral had hooked up through some cat he used to cop crack from named Kill Dog. Ral had started to make runs here and there for him for a little change. Dollar thought it might have been smart of him to let the streets know he had a source of income. It wasn't worth taking the risk of someone figuring out he was behind some of the stickups going down.

Through Kill Dog, Ral learned that some kid named Rob and a couple of his boys were going to be hitting Chi-Town to check this nigga named Steelo's shit in. Supposedly, Steelo had set up a deal that went raw with some boys from

LA. The LA boys were paying them Chi-Town niggaz a personal visit. Ral was getting paid to be their host while in town. Of course, after the hit he would lead them straight to the Chocolate Factory, where they, themselves, would get hit in the parking lot.

Tommy waited all night for Ral to show up with them so that she could make the call to Dollar. As it turned out, Ral and Rob and his boys were a no-show. So finally Tommy made a call to Dollar, but it wasn't the one he'd been expecting.

"Ral been spending mad loot lately," Dollar said to Tommy.

"Have you noticed? He got all kinds of shit up in his place, and did you see the sounds he got installed in his li'l ride?"

"Umm, not really. Well, I guess," Tommy replied, focusing on the television show she and Dollar were watching in her living room.

It had been a week since their failed hit on them LA cats. "I mean, I heard he been trickin' like mad lately, but what's new? As long as he ain't fuckin' with that shit, he straight. He could have bartered for half the shit he got. You know how he is. He'll sell a rope to a man threatening to hang himself."

"Word," Dollar replied, nodding his head, but not 100 percent convinced.

"This is the funniest show in the universe," Tommy said as she continued watching television.

"Yeah, that's a funny-ass muthafucka," Dollar said, referring to Dave Chappelle of *Chappelle's Show*. His thoughts went back to his friend. "Ral probably just been holding on to his loot from the hits, huh, and that little bit of change he gets making runs for Kill Dog? You know how sometimes people get the urge to just start spending? Yeah, he's probably just going through one of them phases."

"Yeah," Tommy replied, half listening to Dollar. "Ah ha ah ha. I love this show. Dis nigga crazy!"

"You probably even dip into your stash every now and then to treat you and the girls to a little something nice, huh?"

Tommy took a deep breath and looked at Dollar. She picked up the remote and turned the television off. "Dollar, what's on your mind? Just spit it out. What are you trying to say?"

"Things just ain't been feeling right lately. I mean, there's been too many interferences and circumstances. Like when we was gon' stick up kid from LA, but he turned out to be a no-show;

like somebody gave him a heads-up, dropped the dime or something."

"Ral said them niggaz wanted to handle their business and dip back out of town. What's so strange about that? Shit happens," Tommy said in Ral's defense.

"I know, but now all of a sudden Ral got all this spending money. I guess I just been adding two and two together."

"So, what you trying to say?" Tommy asked. "You think Ral getting paid behind our backs; that he don't want to split the pot no more so he handling shit on his own? That's ridiculous. You just noided. That means it's time for you to give this shit up, especially if you gon' start worrying about how much money your boy is spending."

"It ain't like I'm clockin' his dollars. I'm just saying."

"You just saying what? Next thing I know you'll be thinking Ral getting paid to talk, like he's some informant involved in a conspiracy to put you back in the joint." Tommy laughed.

Dollar remained serious as he glared off into space.

"I was just joking. You can't honestly be thinking that," Tommy said.

"Lately I just can't erase the thought that Ral was a hard fiend. The shit a fiend would do for a hit, you'd never know."

"Yeah, but not turn on their partners. Not Ral. He'd die first. Besides, it wasn't a concern back when you wanted him on the team, so why should it be a concern now? He's the same Ral. Besides, he hasn't been high any of the times he's been around me."

"Yeah, you right. I'm trippin'," Dollar said. "Turn that show back on."

Tommy turned the show back on and in moments was back to laughing hysterically. Dollar tried to enjoy the show and Tommy's company, but something was itchin' at him. That something was Ral. Dollar couldn't help but think that his loyalty to Ral, to clean him up and help him get his shit together, might have gotten in the way of his better judgment.

"So what's been up with Storm and her girl?" Dollar asked Tommy out of the blue.

"They cool," Tommy said. "Why do you ask?"

"No reason," Dollar replied with a snide look in his eye. "No reason at all."

CHAPTER 21

Can We Talk?

"Yo, Dollar Bill," Redd called to Dollar who was getting ready to climb inside of Mr. Owens's Navigator. "I didn't know you were out here. You didn't come in today. Matter of fact, you haven't been coming in at all lately. Can I talk to you for a minute, just real quick?"

"Oh shit," Dollar said under his breath. He hoped Kera hadn't been running her mouth and he wouldn't have to beat down her pops for stepping to him.

"Yo, Mr. Owens. Can you hold up a sec?" Dollar asked him, who he tried not to act awkward around knowing that he had set him up for a robbery.

"Sure," Mr. Owens agreed. Dollar then followed Redd into his office.

Redd sat down at his desk, took a long, deep breath then stared at Dollar. He paused momentarily before speaking. "I won't beat around the bush with this," Redd said. "So, I'll just get right to the point. Kera has been acting really strange lately."

"Look, Redd," Dollar interrupted.

"No, let me finish," Redd continued. "I could tell she was hiding something from me."

"Redd," Dollar tried to intercept.

"Just listen," he said sternly. "Kera told me about the night at the club and I'm not going to lie, I was completely shocked."

"I can explain," Dollar said.

"No need to explain. I mean, hell yeah, I'm pissed that you didn't tell me. But teenagers need someone they can trust and I'm just glad she chose you."

At this point Dollar was mystified. Since when did a father approve of who takes his daughter's virginity?

"I still can't believe my baby snuck into a twenty-one and over club and drank alcohol," Redd said. "If you hadn't been there to see to it that her and Leece got home safe, then I don't know what could have happened to my baby girl. Some pervert probably would have taken advantage of her and I'd have to go back to prison on a 187."

Redd began to laugh as Dollar contributed his fake laughter.

"Well, Mr. Owens is waiting on you so you better get going. I just wanted to say thanks for looking out for my baby girl. I'm glad I can trust you. Loyalty is priceless."

"No need to thank me, sir; anytime," Dollar said as he headed back outside.

"By the way, did you hear what happened to Mr. Owens? He got robbed. Two thugs did it, I think. It's a fucking shame," Redd said.

"Yeah," Dollar added. "A fucking shame."

Dollar and Tommy became a little nervous as they sat in Jimmy's waiting on Ral to show up. He was already twenty minutes late. It wasn't Ral's absence that had them nervous. It was the fact that two cops came in and were dining at the table right behind Dollar and Tommy.

"You two ready to order or do you still want to wait on the other person?" the waitress asked.

"Uhh, actually, he just called me on my cell phone," Dollar said. "He's stranded so we have to go pick him up."

"Yeah," Tommy said as she stood up from her chair. "We got to go pick him up. Thanks anyway though. If it doesn't take too long, we might be back."

Joy

Dollar and Tommy exited the diner suspiciously. Tommy was walking a hundred miles per hour.

"Slow down," Dollar said to Tommy. "Relax."

Tommy slowed her pace and began to take quick breaths. "Now what?" Tommy asked as Dollar walked her to her car.

"Let's just drive to your house. We'll talk there."

"Not my house," Tommy said. "What if those cops follow us?"

"Girl, you talking silly," Dollar said.

"Meet me at the DQ on Broadway instead."

"Okay," Dollar agreed. "Drive slow. Stay calm and relax, dammit."

Dollar followed Tommy to the DQ where they each ordered a small vanilla ice cream cone and sat in Tommy's car to eat and talk.

"Now you see what the fuck I'm talking about when I say interference and circumstance?" Dollar said to Tommy.

"What's going on, D?" Tommy said, confused. "I mean, Ral should have at least called you on your cell or something."

"I paged him on the way here and he ain't hit me back yet," Dollar said. "I should have listened to you in the beginning. You said we shouldn't fuck with Ral."

"What we gon' do, D?" Worry covered Tommy's face. "I can't do this. My nieces. This is too much. I'm sick of this shit. I can't do this."

"Come on, T. Be cool. Everything is going to be okay."

"I don't want the cops sniffing around my tail, and for what, a few punk-ass stickups? I got enough saved to maybe start doing my own thing. Fuck this shit!"

"Dammit, Tommy, stop talking like that," Dollar said. "We can't let one monkey stop our show."

"We not fucking teenagers anymore, Dollar. Can't you see that? I might as well have done that fucking bid nine years ago because I'm locked up anyway. I'm locked up between these fucking city walls. They trapping me, man," Tommy said out of frustration. "I don't think the game was designed for us to win, D."

"Stop pumpin' out that negative energy," Dollar snapped.

"We can do this shit. Just you and me. We can make shit happen."

"Yeah, but Ral knows everything. He knows what we're about. If he's playing us while he's part of the plan, imagine what he'd do if we cut him off."

Dollar sat listening to Tommy who was on the verge of frantic. His soft serve vanilla ice cream cone began to melt down his hand. He rolled down the window and threw it out.

"Well," Tommy interrupted Dollar's thought. "What are we going to do about Ral?"

"We don't have a choice," Dollar said. "He's poison. We got to spit his ass out."

"I told you that you'd be back," Storm said as she straddled Dollar who was sitting on the couch in the Champagne Room. Storm slowly crooned to the music.

"I guess you were right," Dollar replied as he stuck a twenty dollar bill between Storm's breasts after already having paid Bear the one hundred dollars just to get back in the room.

"I'm always right." Storm put her hands behind her back and began to untie her bikini top. Dollar grabbed her hands and stopped her.

"What's wrong, poppa, don't you want me?" Storm said as she pulled Dollar's head to her breasts.

"Yeah, I want you," Dollar said as he began to lick them. "I want you to do something for me."

"Anything. Tell me what you want and tell me how do you want it," Storm said as she began caressing Dollar's penis.

"I want M&M. Exes, overdose," Dollar said while pulling Storm hard against his penis.

Storm immediately pushed away from Dollar and got off of his lap. She went and poured her a glass of champagne and started drinking it.

"Did you hear me? M&M."

"I don't know what you're talking about," Storm said as she took another sip of her champagne.

"Oh, you don't hear me now? It ain't like I'm muthafuckin' 5-0. Don't even try to front. I already know underneath all that sex appeal you ain't nothin' but a hit ho."

Storm continued to ignore Dollar.

"Well, maybe you'll hear this," Dollar said as he pulled out fifty one-hundred dollar bills and waved them in Storm's face.

The corners of her mouth turned up. "Well, as they say, money talks," Storm said, removing the money from Dollar's hand nice and slowly.

Never once did Dollar think twice or even reconsider his decision. Ordering a hit on Ral was preventative maintenance. As far as Dollar was concerned, it was only a matter of time before Ral killed himself anyway. Ral had been missing meetings with the drug counselor and word on the streets was that he'd been lacing his blunts with cocaine. Dollar felt that Ral's

destructive ways would somehow be the downfall of his mission. Boys or no boys, friend or no
friend, Dollar couldn't just sit back and let that
shit happen. This was his second chance at the
game and he'd be damned if he let a dope fiend
be the cause of his downfall.

Dollar paid Storm a portion of the money for
the hit up front and promised her the rest once
he received the call from her stating that the
deed had been done. And on that note, Storm let
Dollar hit it from the back on the strength.

CHAPTER 22

Pro-choice

Dollar had finally given in to Kera's persistence. She wasn't going to stop hounding him until she got with him again. Dollar had already hit it once, so why not hit that twice? Kera wasn't anything he couldn't handle, so he invited her into his home. No dinner, no movie, no nothing. Dollar refused to butter up to Kera. If she wanted to be like Stevie Wonder and pretend she couldn't see the real, then that was her own mistake. Like all sleeping beauties, Kera would someday find that Prince Charming to wake her up with a genuine kiss. Until then, Dollar might as well keep doing what he do.

Dollar couldn't really enjoy being inside of Kera. His thoughts were on Hennessey. He had been kickin' it with her for a minute now, yet he hadn't gotten into her head. He hadn't gotten into her drawers.

Dollar would have definitely wanted to spend most of his time with Hennessey, but she always made it seem like she was so busy. The most time she would allot Dollar was lengthy conversations on the phone. It seemed like that was the closest he was going to get to her. Talking dirty after dark just wasn't doing the trick for Dollar anymore. One could say that Hennessey had Dollar questioning his manhood.

Hennessey was a real woman, not like Kera and Mya who were barely a class up from being chickenheads. As Dollar lay on top of Kera, the more he thought about Hennessey and how she continued to reject him, the deeper he shoved himself inside of Kera.

"Oh shit, Dollar," Kera cried out.

"Umm, you like that, bitch?" Dollar said, pumping harder and harder. "You like that shit?"

"Dollar, stop it!" Kera cried out. Her cries were silent to Dollar's ears as he aggressively assaulted Kera's insides.

Kera had shown up at Dollar's house that evening on the inevitable drive-by; no call before coming, just an "I was in the neighborhood." All that meant was that she wanted to be screwed. This was the third time she had pulled this stunt.

"Oh shit. I'm cummin'," Dollar roared. "I'm cummin'." He wrapped his hands around Kera's throat as he ejaculated.

Tears of pain and anger strolled down Kera's face as she lay beneath Dollar who was breathing heavily. Eventually he got up and showered. Normally he probably would have led Kera into the bathroom with him so that they could shower together. Just like the last time, she would have probably let him get one more off up in her, but this time Dollar showered alone, leaving an emotional Kera alone in his bed.

As the water ran down Dollar's butter pecan toned six pack, for the first time he saw his life for what it was. He had put in work hustling. He had the riches, jewels, and a nice crib out of the hood, yet his mind was still in the ghetto. Did he ever really want to leave the streets alone, no matter how much money he had? It must be true what they say about being able to take the boy out of the ghetto, but not being able to take the ghetto out of the boy.

Dollar realized why a lot of cats didn't leave the hood. It was like an addiction, a fear. They were scared to leave what they had learned to love and what loved them back. Dollar loved the streets. He was married to them, forsaking all others.

After Dollar got out of the shower he dried himself off and wrapped the towel around his waist. He went back in the bedroom to find a fully dressed, teary-eyed Kera grabbing her purse and sweater.

"Aren't you going to take a shower?" Dollar asked Kera.

"Fuck you, Dollar," Kera said.

"Little mama, what's wrong?" Dollar said, none the wiser to the situation at hand.

"What's wrong? I don't know what that shit was," Kera said as tears flowed down her face.

"What what shit was?" Dollar asked, completely ignorant of what was going on in Kera's mind. "You didn't cum?"

"That sex, fucking, screwing or whatever you want to call it. It sure wasn't making love."

"Making love." Dollar laughed. "We ain't never made love. People who care about each other make love. You and me ain't like that."

"You are one big piece of shit, do you know that? I can't believe I fell for you. Fuck you, Dollar. You don't ever need to say two words to me again, ever."

"Am I supposed to be mad? Are my feelings supposed to be hurt? Ma, this was just a fuck thang. I thought you knew," Dollar said, spelling it out in black and white to Kera.

Dollar's words were destroying Kera. He felt it was time to get rid of her anyway so he might as well go for the jugular. "You let me hit that the first night you were ever with me. That was a ho move. Did you think I was going to make a ho my girlfriend?"

Anger took over Kera's emotions. She looked around the room to see what she could pick up to throw at Dollar. Her eyes settled on a crystal base lamp that was on the nightstand.

Dollar, noticing Kera's intentions, quickly walked up on her. "Bitch, don't even think about it," Dollar said.

"Now I'm a bitch, too," Kera cried. "I can't believe this is happening. What's happening to you?"

"You talking like you know me. You done popped over here a few times to get laid and now you know me? You don't know me, girl. I'm Dollar Bill. I'm that muthafucka. You lucky to be one of my chosen ones."

"Well, I don't feel so lucky. I feel like I've just been raped."

"Oh, so now you 'bout to pull a Mike Tyson situation and scream rape. I guess I better walk you down to the car so that I can avoid catching a case," Dollar said.

"Funny you should make the comparison. You're an animal just like him, and it didn't take twelve jurors to convince the world of that."

"Here, call 911," Dollar said, throwing the phone at Kera. She tried to block it from hitting her. It skimmed across her fingers, breaking one of her nails. "If you think I raped you, go ahead and call the police on me. Put me back in jail. But don't play games with me, girl. You really don't know who you fuckin' with. I'm a grown-ass man. You do what you need to do. Either call the police or step. You make the choice."

"Nah, I don't need to call the police," Kera said. "Your punishment will come from a much greater wrath. Mark my words. You think I'm a bitch? Wait until you meet karma."

"Get the fuck out," Dollar said, throwing himself on the bed as if nothing mattered to him in the world.

Kera began crying harder. She watched Dollar lie on the bed as if he could do no wrong, as if he had done no wrong all of his life. How could he be so cold? Kera asked herself this question over and over as she walked outside, not caring that tears were flowing down her face.

The people she walked past looked at her with such pity. A couple even stopped to ask her if she was okay.

Kera knew in her heart, and her head, that this would be the last time she would ever make the walk from Dollar's apartment, and that she would never hear him call her little mama again. But fuck that shit! She wasn't going to be the young and dumb little number Dollar had taken her for. She wasn't going to keep falling. Her actions weren't going to mimic the words to an Alicia Keys hit song.

Kera jumped into her white Saturn that was parked a couple of blocks down. She could hardly get the key in the ignition she was so upset. Once she finally started the car, she sat there and recalled the words her mother had told her during "the talk."

"The man that breaks your cherry will break your heart, and even ten years down the road when you bump into him on the streets, he'll still make your heart beat fast and your palms sweat," her mother had told her.

Instead of going home, Kera went where she could be comforted. She needed someone to talk to who would understand what she was going through.

Kera pulled up to Leece's house and parked on the curb in front. Her legs wobbled the entire journey to Leece's doorstep. Her body honestly felt as if it had been abused. She hesitantly knocked on the door.

Leece, wearing her girlie pink J Lo terry cotton short set, peeked through the peephole. She hadn't talked to Kera since they'd gotten into that argument a couple months ago. She had no hard feelings though. No matter what, Kera was her girl. They'd been friends too long to ever let a dude come between them. She didn't hesitate to open the door.

When she opened the door, Kera was standing there with her head down. She tried to stop crying long enough to say "hello" and to say "I'm sorry" to Leece, but she couldn't.

Leece's eyes watered and her bottom lip trembled at the sight of her heartbroken friend standing before her. She put her arms around Kera. Leece stood there holding Kera for what seemed like forever, holding back the words, "I told you so."

"You haven't been in the salon in a while," Mya said to Dollar as he sat down at her table to get his fingernails worked on.

"I been busy," Dollar said short.

"Too busy to call?" Mya pried.

"Something like that."

"I tried calling you all last week," Mya said as she placed Dollar's hand in a bowl of water that she knew was too hot.

"Damn!" Dollar said, jerking his hand out.

"Oh, is that too hot for you?" Mya asked sarcastically without getting a rise out of Dollar. She poured some of the water out and added cold water to the bowl. She then placed Dollar's hand back into the bowl. "Is that better?"

"That's cool."

"But, like I was saying," Mya continued. "I tried calling you all last week." She began to file the nails on Dollar's hand that wasn't in water.

"Oh, for real?" Dollar said, knowing darn well he had seen her number on his cell phone caller ID and ignored the calls. "Ouch."

Mya had accidentally jabbed Dollar with the nail file. He pulled his hand away from her and checked out his finger to see if any blood had been drawn.

"Is there something on your mind?" Dollar asked Mya. "If it is just cut the crap and spit it out, ma."

"I need to talk to you," Mya said.

"I'm listening," Dollar replied.

"Not here. Can we get together tonight?"

"Here you go," Dollar said, throwing his hands up.

"And what is that supposed to mean? Oh, let me guess, you just get women left and right wanting to talk to your fine ass, huh? Well, what I have to say is far more important. Trust me," Mya said.

"Let me just go on and put it out there to save us both the time. Your shit was good, ma. I won't deny that. But I ain't really trying to get down like that on no permanent kind of—"

"Don't fucking flatter yourself," Mya said, raising her tone. Customers and workers turned their attention to her. "I'm sorry," Mya apologized to the onlookers before gearing her words back to Dollar. "Look, what I have to say won't take up much of your precious time."

Dollar could tell Mya was becoming emotional. *That's what I get for fucking with a white girl,* Dollar thought. In the future he knew to stay away from young girls and white girls. He was pretty sure he'd gotten rid of Kera; now for Mya.

"I'll meet you at your spot at about nine tonight. Is that cool?" Dollar said.

"Yeah," Mya replied. "I'm sorry for raising my voice and cussing at you."

"No problem," Dollar replied. He knew Mya's dramatics were just an excuse for her to get Dollar back over to her place and in bed again. He didn't blame her for being addicted. Hell, she had gone black so she couldn't go back. That was a well-known fact.

Mya finished up Dollar's nails. He skipped the pedicure today. He had a little bit of business to take care of before meeting up with Mya. As the time neared to meet with Mya, he really just wanted to stand her up and find a new nail tech, but he couldn't put off the inevitable. So he kept his word and went to her place.

When Dollar showed up at Mya's, she had a candlelit dinner prepared for the two. Dollar gobbled down the roasted duck, red potatoes, and green beans. He wasn't impressed with the fancy meal as much as he was hungry.

During dinner, Mya went on and on about her sister and her husband and their two children, about how happy they were. Dollar couldn't have cared less. He had no intention of ever meeting them.

After dinner, the two engaged in intercourse that wasn't even worth describing. It was off the hook the last time. Maybe all that liquor had something to do with it. Dollar humped on Mya for about two minutes before he felt himself ready to cum. He snapped the condom off and jerked on Mya's belly. Dollar then got up, went into her bathroom, and cleaned himself off. When he returned he had a towel in his hand that he had already used to wipe himself off.

"Here you go, ma," Dollar said, throwing the towel at Mya. "Here's a towel to clean yourself up. I'm fixin' to go."

Dollar was hoping that Mya caught on to the significance of him throwing in the towel. He was finished with her. As a matter of fact, he was finished with hoes, period. He wasn't about to let them fuck up his game by fucking with his head with all of their emotions and drama.

"Dollar, remember, I invited you over here to talk," Mya said, getting up from out of the bed to slip on her robe.

"Well then talk. I have a lot I have to do tomorrow."

"I'm pregnant," Mya blurted out, before she could lose her courage.

Dollar stood speechless momentarily before bursting out laughing. "You're kidding, right?" Dollar continued laughing. "And I guess I'm the daddy."

"Of course you are," Mya said. "I haven't—"

"Been with anybody else," Dollar mimicked. "Here we go. Okay, humor me. How much is the abortion going to run me?" Dollar said, pulling money out of his back pocket.

"I'm having this baby. I can't have an abortion," Mya said to Dollar as she sat back down on the bed. "It's against my religion."

"Oh, and having sex unmarried isn't?" Dollar said. "Mya, you don't even know me. I'm just some dude you slept with."

"And that's my fault. I'm the one who will have to explain that to the world. But why should I punish this unborn child?" Mya said, rubbing her belly. "I can't do it. I won't. Abortion is murder."

"I don't even know why you're laying this on me," Dollar said. "We were only together one time."

"News flash; all it takes is one time."

"And I'm supposed to believe the baby is mine?" Dollar asked.

"Don't go there," Mya said. "Please don't go there."

"Look, Mya, honey, sweetheart," Dollar said in a condescending manner. "I've never wanted kids. I don't want any kids now, tomorrow, or yesterday. This baby, if it is mine, ain't gonna happen."

"Dollar, I understand where you're coming from, but you don't have a choice at this point. I'm having this baby."

"It's a no-win situation with bitches," Dollar snapped. "When y'all get pregnant, the man doesn't have any choice over whether he wants to be a father."

"The man has a choice before he lies down and sticks his dick in a woman," Mya retaliated. "You made a choice not to wear a condom. That's where your choice started and ended."

"I am so not hearing this. I am so not fucking hearing this," Dollar said swinging his fist in the air. No way in hell was a kid in the plan.

"I'm sorry this happened. I didn't plan for it to happen," Mya cried.

"Yeah, right," Dollar said, disbelieving every word Mya uttered.

"Forget it. You don't have to be a part of this child's life. This child never has to know you exist. I'll tell him you were a casualty of war or something." Mya paused. "I knew telling you was a mistake."

"You're not paying attention, Mya," Dollar said. "This baby is not going to happen. No seed of mine is going to be born. You feel me?"

"I'm sorry, but you can't tell me what to do with my body. The baby didn't get to choose whether it wanted to be conceived. It's not fair to take the baby's choice of life away."

"That's all good, but I believe in pro-choice," Dollar said. "Abortion isn't always bad depending on the circumstance. And in this circumstance, where the father doesn't want the baby or the mother, abortion is the answer."

"I'm not asking you to want me, Dollar. I believe in pro-choice too, and my choice is to have this baby. Abortion might be the answer for other women, but not me. I won't have that on my conscience."

By this time, Dollar was heated. His conversation with Mya wasn't going anywhere. This dumbass white girl was determined to have this baby. He didn't want it to get to this point, but it was time for him to pull out his wild card.

"Well, since you believe in pro-choice," Dollar said as he flipped through his wallet, "here's five hundred dollars. Bitch, it's your life or the baby's. You make the choice." Dollar threw the money at Mya who had the fear of death in her eyes. She stood trembling as she didn't mistake Dollar's words as an idle threat.

Dollar walked up on Mya slowly as he stared her down. "Here's another two hundred," Dollar said, throwing the money at Mya. "This is for the couple of days of work you might have to miss while you recuperate after the procedure." Dollar kissed Mya on the forehead then left her apartment.

A baby, Dollar thought as he stood outside of Mya's closed door. Maybe a li'l Dollar Bill wouldn't be so bad. But what did he have to offer a kid? What could he teach a kid? How to hustle? That's about the only thing his old man had taught him. Maybe things would be different between him and his kid though.

Dollar contemplated walking back into Mya's apartment and talking things out, maybe hear her out. He was so torn at that point. The fate of another human being's life was in his hands. Dollar turned around and put his hand on the doorknob to turn it. Mya, who was standing on the opposite side of the door contemplating going after Dollar, watched the knob turn. Maybe she wouldn't have to go after Dollar after all. Maybe he had changed his mind on his own.

Just before pushing the door open, Dollar said to himself, "I can't curse my baby. I can't bring no child into this ghetto-ass shit. Naw, it's better off dead."

Mya could hear Dollar's footsteps walk away. She leaned up against the door and slid down to the floor. Her wailing filled the apartment. She knew what she had to do.

Later on that night Dollar was tossing and turning as sweat dripped from his body. He opened his eyes, which weren't asleep, just closed, and looked at the clock. It was two o'clock in the morning.

On top of all the female drama Dollar had been dealing with, concerns about Ral had been eating at him as well. The situation with Ral just didn't feel right at all anymore. Dollar remembered Romeo once telling him that if shit don't feel right, then it ain't right.

But this was Ral, not some new jack on the street. This was the same comrade Dollar traded in eight years of his life for. This was the same comrade he had invested so much time in saving. This was his best friend, Ralphie Boy from the playground.

Dollar felt like someone had put a dinner plate covered with delicious foods in front of him right after he had eaten a large pizza. The dilemma between throwing the food out or just eating it so that it didn't go to waste was tormenting Dollar's soul.

I should have listened to Tommy in the first place, Dollar lay in bed thinking. Ral was a junkie. A junkie wasn't any good to anybody. He'd tried to fix him. He'd done his part, hadn't he? Dollar had given Ral a chance. It was only a matter of time before Ral messed up and took Tommy and Dollar with him.

CHAPTER 23

The Perfect Gift

Dollar, Ral, and Tommy sat in the living room of Ral's crib. Since Dollar and Tommy's scare with the po-po at Jimmy's Coney Island, they hadn't met back up there since. Dollar suggested they meet at Ral's until they decided on a new location to discuss dealings. Ral was clueless to the fact that Dollar and Tommy had no intentions on ever meeting with him again.

"Damn," Ral said. "I didn't even think you remembered my birthday."

"How could we forget? We're family," Tommy said. She nodded to the envelope she'd just handed Ral. "That's from Dollar and me."

Ral opened the envelope and pulled out another piece of paper. It was a gift certificate for a suite at the W in downtown Chicago. "Man, for real?" Ral said with excitement. "This is what I'm talking about."

"I'm glad you like it," Dollar said.

"A suite at one of the dopest overnighters in the city, shiiitt. There's only one other thing that could top that," Ral said, raising his eyebrows.

"You think I ain't on top of that?" Dollar winked at Ral. "I knew you'd get lonely up in a big ol' place like that so I arranged for you to have a little company."

"See, that's why you my mafucka," Ral said, beating on his chest with one hand while pretending to wipe away invisible tears from his eyes with the other.

"That's all men think about," Tommy said.

"And good thing we do or else you wouldn't have a job," Ral said. "Y'all excuse me. I have to go to the bathroom." Ral got up from the couch and went into the bathroom.

Tommy waited until she heard the bathroom door close before she spoke. "I knew one of the two would be Ral's downfall," Tommy said to Dollar. "Pussy or drugs."

"Yeah, but who ever thought it would be both?"

Tommy had already bumped her head twice on the pole. She even stumbled and almost fell off the stage. "Wine." The DJ chuckled. "I think you done had a little too much of your name." He shouted out to the bartender. "Tiwana, just give that ho Shirley Temples the rest of the night." The patrons in the Chocolate Factory laughed along with the DJ as Tommy exited the stage and went and sat next to Dollar in a corner booth.

"You okay?" Dollar asked a nervous Tommy.

"Hell no. Are you?" Tommy replied. "He's our boy, D. Maybe we should have just talked to him."

"Talk is cheap, Tommy. Unless you up in a piece like this, talk is free and gets you nowhere."

"Look, I can't think straight. I can't be up in here, not tonight. I'm gon' go tell Shay I need to go home." Tommy excused herself and headed toward Shay's office.

Dollar sat at the table looking at his watch, knowing that in a few minutes, like two-day-old milk, Ral would be expired.

"Hey, Dollar, right?" some cat said as he strolled up to Dollar.

Dollar put his hand on his chin and eyeballed this cat up and down. He didn't recognize this fool whose pants were about five sizes too big. "Who wants to know?" Dollar said.

"Oh, it ain't like that, partna. I'm Kill Dog, ya dude Ral's boy. I've seen you with him a couple of times." Kill Dog put out his hand to shake Dollar's. Dollar reluctantly did so.

"Ral talks about you twenty-four/seven. It's good to meet you up close and personal. I'd expect to see some gleaming halo over your head, a beaming light behind you like you Jesus or some shit." Kill Dog laughed.

"Oh, yeah?" Dollar lightweight laughed.

"Word. Ral's my boy, with his crazy ass. That wigga would take candy from a baby and sell it to its mother if he had to. He's good peoples though. Always got a mafucka's back."

Kill Dogs words were starting to eat away at Dollar's conscience. They only reminded Dollar of how loyal Ral was and had always been. But people changed. The game changed people.

"Me and my girl had got into it and Ral was there to have my back," Kill Dog continued. "Ma had just caught me getting down with a Chiquita from 'round the way."

As Kill Dog went on and on, Dollar saw first-hand how niggaz get to running their mouth off in the spot. This cat was telling all of his business.

"Ral's ass shows up out of nowhere with a mink. I shut my ho up with that coat. I ain't even have the money on the spot to give Ral but he looked out. As a matter of fact I just paid his ass a couple three weeks ago. I hit him up with an extra two grand. Hell, ma is the mother of my four kids. She special like that. Ral saved my ass."

"Hold up," Dollar stopped Kill Dog before he could continue gabbing. "Ral sold you a coat?"

"Yeah, a mink," Kill Dog said. "He was gon' bring my dude Rob from LA up in here not too long ago to try to cop one. He said dude's who sells them sister works up in here and shit, but them boys had drove up to Chi-Town and put in work and wasn't trying to hang out. But they said the next time they roll through they gon' check out this spot. I told them niggaz they didn't know what they were missing. Don't nobody roll through the interstate without jumpin' off at the Chocolate Factory."

Dollar had left Kill Dog standing there talking to himself. One of the biggest mistakes Dollar could ever make was about to go down and he had to stop it.

"Nigga, what the fuck you doing in here?" a dancer shouted as Dollar busted into the dressing room.

"T, it's a mistake. We gotta stop that shit!" Dollar shouted to Tommy.

"Whoa, hold up," Tommy said, confused. "What's going on?"

"Are you crazy busting up in here like that?" Bear asked Dollar as he snatched him up.

"Man, get your motherfuckin' hands off of me," Dollar said, going for his piece.

"Wait!" Tommy yelled. "Come on, Dollar. What's wrong?" Tommy said as she peeled Bear's hands off of Dollar.

Dollar rambled on and on to Tommy about Ral having money because he'd sold the mink coat to Kill Dog. He told her about why them LA niggaz hadn't shown up at the club that night they were supposed to rob him in the parking lot. Tommy wasn't fully comprehending everything. All she knew is that a big mistake had been made. It was like a ghetto version of the sitcom *Three's Company*. All the wrong conclusions had been jumped to.

"Call Storm's pager," Tommy shouted as she began to tremble.

Dollar searched his person for his cell phone and it was nowhere on him. "Fuck, I must have left my phone in the car."

Dollar and Tommy ran out to Dollar's truck to retrieve his phone. Dollar dug through his pockets and glove box for Storm's number.

"Dammit, D, hurry the fuck up," Tommy said. By this time, she was shaking and tears were running down her face.

"I can't find it," Dollar said.

"Your cell phone; is it stored in your cell phone? Numbers called, received calls or something?" Tommy screamed.

"Yeah, yeah," Dollar said. He felt around under the seat until he located his cell phone. "Found it." He sat down in the driver seat and fumbled through the address book, but couldn't recall what name he had stored the number in as. "Fuck," Dollar said. "It's not under Storm."

"Try M& M," Tommy suggested, which Dollar did.

"It's not under that either."

"Hit hoes. You called them hit hoes. Try that."

Just as Tommy suggested, the phone number was stored under Hit Hoes. Dollar hit the quick dial button. The phone rang one time; no answer. The phone rang two times; no answer. The phone rang three times; no answer. The phone rang four times.

"Hello," a seductive voice answered.

"Storm," Dollar shouted.

"No, this is Thunder. Just a moment and I'll get her," Thunder said.

"No, wait a minute," Dollar shouted, but Thunder had already put down the phone. Dollar could hear his heartbeat as he waited on the phone.

"This is Storm," she said into the receiver upon picking up the phone.

"Baby girl, this is Dollar," he said.

"Hey, poppa, what's—"

"Have you done that shit yet?" Dollar said, cutting Storm off.

"My feelings are hurt that you doubted my skills," Storm said. "Don't worry. That black suit won't go to waste. It's done."

Dollar removed the phone from his ear. He dropped his head and closed his eyes.

"No, oh no," Tommy whimpered.

Dollar looked over at Tommy and D'ed up. He stuck out his chest, took a deep breath, and swallowed. He then put the phone back to his ear.

"You still there?" Storm asked.

"Yeah, I'm here," Dollar replied.

"Yeah, he's gone off that ex. Thunder and me 'bout to finish this shit off. I told you that I would hit you up when the deed was done, so let me do my thang and I'll call you back when—"

"Whoa," Dollar interrupted. "You mean he's not gone *gone?*"

"Didn't I say not to worry? My girl and me gonna handle this. We ain't amateurs," Storm said.

"No, no," Dollar said. "There's been a change in plans."

Storm paused. "Meaning what?" Storm huffed.

"Meaning I don't need M&M anymore," Dollar said.

There was silence on the phone. Dollar could hear some shuffling and could tell Storm must have been changing to a location where she could speak more freely.

"Look, muthafucka," Storm said. "I done already sucked Opey's little-ass dick, so if you thinking you getting this money back then you got another think coming."

"Calm down, Pocahontas," Dollar said. "You keep that shit and good looking out. We cool?"

"Hell yeah, we cool. We always gon' be cool as long as you don't try to fuck up my money. My daughter's tuition was due, so your shit was already spent."

"I hear you and it's cool, ma. Like I already said, you keep that shit. But since you are keeping it, why don't you go ahead and see to it that my man has a happy birthday after all. You feel me?" Dollar said.

"That's not a problem," Storm said.

"All right then, later."

"Hey, Dollar," Storm said before ending the call.

"Yeah!"

"It was a pleasure doing business with you."

Delighted that Dollar was able to stop Storm from finishing Ral off, he replied, "The pleasure was all mine."

Dollar hung up his cell phone, took a deep breath, and planted his head against his steering wheel.

"So, it's all good?" Tommy asked as Dollar sat hunched over the steering wheel.

"If you hadn't figured out what Storm's fucking number was stored under, then I don't know," Dollar said, becoming emotional. "I don't know what would have happened."

"Jesus." Tommy sighed. "I knew Ral wasn't no rat. I knew it."

Dollar looked over at Tommy who was in a cold sweat. Dollar put his hand on her knee and said, "You did it again."

"What?" Tommy said.

"You saved Ral. Once again, Tommy Gun to the rescue."

CHAPTER 24

Strictly Business

"Nice place you got here," Hennessey said to Dollar as she walked in his apartment dressed in a navy blue business suit with her butterscotch Coach briefcase in hand.

"Thank you, Miss Lady," Dollar replied. "This nice little place costs as much as a mansion it seems. It sucks up my entire paycheck, not to mention the extra fee for parking that's tacked onto my rent."

"What exactly do you do, your job?" Hennessey asked.

"Construction, pretty much," Dollar replied.

Hennessey couldn't help but giggle. "Construction, huh?" Hennessey said, twitching up her lips.

"No, I'm serious. I really do construction. I got the work boots to prove it."

"Construction," Hennessey said, walking over to Dollar and grabbing hold of his hand. "With nails like these?"

"I wear gloves." He slid his hand away from hers. "You wanna see those, too?"

"I'll take your word for it."

"Hey, I'm a hardworking brotha. Otherwise, I'd be spending more time with you. Not just talking on the phone like we usually do."

"I like talking to you on the phone," Hennessey said. "Besides, you know my job is always sending me out of town to seminars and stuff."

"And I like talking to you too, but I like seeing you in person more."

"Talking to you on the phone up until the wee hours of the night makes me feel like I'm in high school again," Hennessey said, reminiscing back to those days.

Being hypnotized by the scent of a woman, Dollar lifted Hennessey's hand to his lips and planted a kiss on it. He then proceeded to kiss up her arm until he made his way to her lips. Dollar planted three soft kisses on her lips. Hennessey responded with a deep French kiss. The two kissed for what seemed like an eternity. Dollar ran his hands down Hennessey's back until he reached her bottom. He then squeezed as if she were a package of Charmin.

Hennessey could feel Dollar's nature rising against her as he held her close. She had to remember that she was there on business, strictly business. She pulled Dollar's hands from off of her butt and pushed away from him.

"Let me grab the portfolios that Mr. Alleghany worked up for you," Hennessey said as she pulled some folders out of her briefcase. "He apologizes for having to cancel his appointment with you that was scheduled for this morning, but his little girl took ill."

"Oh, no problem," Dollar said. "I'd much rather go over it with you anyway." That was the truth, well, the half-truth anyway. Dollar would rather not go over the portfolio at all, but if he had to, he'd much rather do it with Hennessey.

Dollar couldn't have cared less about some financial portfolio. When his personal banker had called him up yesterday to even make the appointment to go over the portfolio, Dollar didn't want to waste his time—Mr. Alleghany's or his own. But then he realized that going into the bank for a meeting meant he'd probably get to see Hennessey too, so he made the appointment. When Mr. Alleghany called early this morning to reschedule, Dollar told him he had a pretty tight schedule for the week and only had today open, which he followed up by asking since Hennessey

was the one who referred Dollar to him in the
first place, if he could just meet with her instead.
Ask and you shall receive.

"We have all night to look at those," Dollar
said regarding the portfolio, walking up behind
Hennessey, pressing himself against her and
kissing her on her neck.

It was going to be hard for Hennessey not to
fall into lust with Dollar. She had to admit it, he
was the finest man she had ever worked with.
But business was business and even though it
was after work hours, this was supposed to be
a business call. After allowing herself to get a
little creamy in her panties from the kisses to the
tender spot on her neck, Hennessey pulled away
from Dollar.

"Well, I really don't have all night and Mr.
Alleghany said you seemed very serious on the
phone about wanting to make some long term
investments to provide for a secure future."

"I am serious, but damn, you got a nigga all
hot and bothered."

"Come on, Dollar. I'm serious. I'm sure there
are some interesting business opportunities. You
have no idea how much I'm going out of my way
here. I really want to help you. I really do. Let me
help you."

Hennessey's sudden sincerity showed Dollar that she was all business. She spoke with such passion. Dollar excused himself and went into the bathroom and handled his business. There wasn't any need in letting a woody go to waste.

As Dollar cleaned himself up in the bathroom, he asked himself over and over why he thought for one minute Hennessey was going to give him any. "I told myself I wasn't going to let these broads fuck up my head," Dollar said to himself as he straightened himself out in the mirror, and then headed out of the bathroom to rejoin his guest.

For the next hour or so, Hennessey followed Mr. Alleghany's notes and schooled Dollar on some high-risk investments that could either earn him ten times his money or put him in the poorhouse. That would be the risk he would have to take. Big risks always came along with big money. CDs and bonds didn't interest Dollar. The payoff wasn't worth the wait.

When Dollar realized that he only had $29,000 in his safe, he panicked. He told himself that he was going to live modest, but those "must-have" materialistic possessions had gotten the best of him. Lack of money to Dollar was what lack of crack was to a fiend. It made him nervous and jittery. It also made him anxious. He needed to flip his money. He was willing to take the high-risk investments Hennessey was suggesting to him. He was willing to risk every dime he had. But doing so meant he had to make a big move to back his shit up. If he was going to put all of his eggs in one basket and turn them over to Hennessey's bank in hopes of becoming a rich man, he needed to keep a golden egg for himself.

As Dollar listened to Hennessey go on and on about the type of investments her bank had made for people and how their investments had paid off, he realized that a bank mans a lot of money for a lot of people. When a person wants candy, where do they go? They go to a candy store. So when a person wants money, where do they go?

By now Dollar wasn't paying much attention to Hennessey's words. Dollar was fixated on candy: green candy with dead presidents on them. She finally wrapped things up and got Dollar's signature to move forward with the suggested investments.

Dollar offered her a nightcap, which she accepted.

Of course Dollar tried making moves on Hennessey, but she refused his advances by stating that she just wanted to cuddle. The two sat sipping on Alizé and watching television.

"So what do you want with me?" Dollar couldn't help but ask Hennessey.

"Excuse me?" Hennessey replied.

"I mean, look, I'm just a regular guy. I don't have much to offer," Dollar said.

"I don't want much," Hennessey replied. "Besides, I just like being with you. You're a good guy, Dollar."

"Ahmmm," Dollar laughed in an "if only you knew" sort of tone.

"You don't think you're a good guy?" Hennessey asked, taking a sip from her glass of Alizé. "Then tell me, what are you?"

"I'm just a man, you know," Dollar said, looking down at his glass of Alizé. "I mean, an everyday brotha out here trying to make it."

"Trying to make it how?" Hennessey began digging.

The door was opening for Dollar to be able to tell Hennessey about the man he really was. How he had spent time in jail. But that would only make her skeptical of him, maybe even drive her away. Dollar didn't want that. But what kind of future could they possibly have together? It would only be a matter of time before Hennessey found him out. Dollar couldn't see her wanting to have anything to do with a man who robbed people for a living. It wasn't as if robbing folks was something he was going to do for the rest of his life. He just needed to hit the jackpot and then everything would be good.

Dollar looked over at Hennessey's French manicured nails and sparkling tennis bracelet and knew that she would never give the real Dollar Bill the time of day. So on that note, Dollar figured if it ain't broke, don't fix it. Telling Hennessey his business was futile at that point. There was still plenty of time for their relationship to move forward. By then, robbery would be a thing of the past for Dollar.

As Dollar looked at Hennessey, he was convinced, now more than ever, that perhaps it was time for a change. Dollar wanted to get closer to Hennessey. It was hard to be real and open with her knowing that there was a side to him that he couldn't share with her, and telling her the truth about him wasn't the way to do it. He would just have to keep her at bay until he got his life straight.

"It's getting late," Dollar said, looking down at his watch. "Don't you have to work tomorrow?"

"Yes, I do," Hennessey said, setting her glass down on the living room table and standing up. "Besides, I know when I'm being told to go home."

"You don't have to go home, but you have to get the hell up out of here." Dollar laughed as he stood up with Hennessey.

Dollar walked Hennessey down to her car and made sure she was safe and sound inside. "Thanks for walking me down," Hennessey said, rolling down the window to her money green convertible Saab.

"Anytime," Dollar replied as he turned away and headed back up to his apartment.

"Dollar," Hennessey yelled, stopping Dollar in his tracks. "Can I tell you something?"

"Anything."

"I'm kinda diggin' you." Hennessey blushed.

"Oh yeah?" Dollar smiled. "Well, I'm kinda diggin' you too."

Hennessey smiled, blew Dollar a kiss, and then drove off. This time Dollar did catch it, and placed it on his lips. "Now her right there," Dollar said to himself. "She could have my baby. That's baby mama material if I ever saw it."

As Dollar walked back up to his apartment, all he could envision was Hennessey's smile. It warmed him. It comforted him the same way his mother's smile used to comfort him.

Dollar returned to his apartment. By that time it was after eleven and the evening news was on. Dollar walked over to the television to turn it off so that he could get ready for bed. Just then he heard the words from the anchorwoman.

"And now let's go to Barb McNeil for news around the country," the anchorwoman said.

"Hello, I'm Barb McNeil and I'm outside of Orient Prison in Orient, Ohio, where convicted felon Ramelle Blake has spent the last seventeen years of his life. Well as you know, after years of investigations, the State of Ohio found evidence that confirmed that Blake is, in fact, the Midwest Serial Killer. In less than forty-five minutes, Blake will be transferred to Mansfield Correctional Facility where death row awaits him.

"As you can see behind me, there are many protesters who oppose the death penalty out here on Blake's behalf. No appeal has been filed nor is one expected to be filed; therefore, no last-minute stay is expected to be granted. Both family members of the victims and supporters have signed a petition requesting that Blake be put to death as early as next month. If they have it their way, Blake will be transported from MCF to Lucasville Correctional Institution where he will be put to death via lethal injection. The mother of one of the victims said that the families have been living in hell for years not knowing who was responsible for the deaths of their daughters.

Now that the murderer's identity is known, it would be punishing the families even more if the state forces them, via use of their tax dollars, to keep this monster alive any longer. The same mother also stated that she's going to go out and buy a new dress to wear when she's escorted into the prison to witness Blake's death."

Dollar turned the television off and headed toward his bedroom as he mumbled, "See you in hell, old man."

As Dollar prepared for bed, a few thoughts ran through his mind. Dollar knew that going back to work for Redd was out of the question. He didn't want to be on pins and needles waiting for the drama to erupt, not with Redd, but with Kera herself. This was all the more reason why Dollar needed to make something happen. Did he think his big break was going to show up on his doorstep one day? Hell no. He had to go out and just do the damn thang. He couldn't go back to work for Redd, and he wouldn't even consider working for some fast food joint. That was out of the question. It was time to make that move. Forget these punk-ass stickups. Dollar needed to make a big move.

After hours of contemplation and running game plans through his head, Dollar phoned

Tommy and Ral to meet up with him. It was time
to share his master plan with them.

"You want to rob a fuckin' bank?" Tommy
asked Dollar as she squeezed the lemon slice into
her ice water.

"Shhhh," Dollar said. "You tryin' to tell the
whole fucking world?"

"You've lost your damn mind," Tommy said.
"We can't rob no bank."

"Why not?" Ral asked. "A stickup is a stickup."

"You two muthafuckas ain't got nothing to
lose," Tommy said. "I got two; two very important things."

"I'm so goddamn tired of you using them two
girls as your excuse to be soft," Dollar said as he
pounded his fist on the picnic table at the DQ.
"I'm sorry, T, but it's time you start using them
two girls as an excuse to raise up out of this town.
What about that bookstore you be talking about?
Niggaz in Gary don't read. What you gon' do,
open it up next door to Jimmy's Coney Island?"

Dollar always had a way of breaking Tommy
down, talking her into doing something. There
was one time when they were kids and Dollar
convinced Tommy that she could fly if she swung
high enough on the park swings and jumped off.
Her arm was in a cast for almost two months.

Tommy couldn't believe Dollar talked her into doing that dumb mess. But this time was different. They weren't twelve-year-old kids. Tommy was grown, and robbing a bank just wasn't her MO.

"I can't do it, D," Tommy said, putting her head down sadly. This was the first time she would ever not do something to please Dollar. From the moment she'd met him, all she ever wanted to do was please Dollar, but this time she just couldn't.

"Yeah, you pussy, all right," Dollar said. Dollar felt some degree of guilt for the way he was talking to Tommy. He hated having to appear to be so callous, but he knew that nice wasn't going to get him anywhere.

"Yo, Dollar, man," Ral said, feeling bad for Tommy. He knew how hard it was for Tommy to say no to Dollar.

"Speaking of pussy," Tommy said. "Why don't you let the bitch you fuckin', that Hennessey trick, help you rob the muthafucka? She can be Bonnie and you can be Clyde."

"That ain't even her style. She's on some entirely different shit. She's got far too much class for that," Dollar said. By the expression on Tommy's face, Dollar realized he had just hurt Tommy's feelings.

"She's got too much class, huh?" Tommy said.

"Besides, even if she was into this shit, I couldn't convince her of robbing her own shit. That's one of the rules of the game: you don't fuck with your own backyard. Outside of the fence is cool, but not your own backyard."

"So, you wanna rob your girl's bank?" Ral asked. "Damn. Won't she recognize you and rat you out, dude?"

"I'ma wear a mask, and in addition to that, that's where Tommy comes in," Dollar said, turning to Tommy. "You dress up in some of that dress-up shit you got, you know, wigs, makeup and shit. You pretend to be a customer. Tell her you wanna look into her designing a financial portfolio for you. You keep her occupied back in her office while the shit goes down. If need be, use your piece to keep her back there, but don't hurt her. Just keep her back there out of our way. She'll never suspect a thing. Besides, I just put twenty thousand dollars into that bank for investments. Why would I do that knowing I'm about to go rob them and have to risk my money being all tied up and shit?"

Ral thought for a minute. "Don't they got some kind of insurance for that?"

Dollar gave Ral the "shut the fuck up" look. He was getting inside Tommy's head and he could.

Tommy kept shaking her head as if she couldn't believe what she was hearing. Ral was most attentive as he rubbed his index finger under his nose.

"Look, all I'm asking you to do for now is to just at least think about it," Dollar said to Tommy. "This is our big move, T. Remember when I said we wasn't gonna do that robbin' niggaz shit forever? Well this is it, T. This is that big move that's going to put us in retirement." Dollar looked over to Ral to see where his head was at. "You in, Ral?"

"Hell yeah," Ral said, sniffling.

"It's all on you now, T," Dollar said. "The world is on your shoulders."

On Dollar's way home from meeting with Tommy and Ral he decided to stop by the clinic to see what his baby brother was up to. The clinic had standing room only. The fact that it was a Monday might have had something to do with it. Folks had been putting off seeing a doctor the entire week before. Come Friday at 5:00 p.m., once the doctor's office was closed, they realized just how bad off they were. They had to suffer through the entire weekend before seeking relief.

Dollar walked up to the sign-in counter and asked if Klein was in. "I'm sorry," the receptionist at the clinic said to Dollar. "He's in with a patient. We're extremely busy today."

"Just let him know that his brother is here to see him," Dollar replied.

The receptionist paused before lashing out at Dollar. "For your information," she said, "his brother is dead, which makes your statement very cruel. Now please just sign in and wait your turn like everyone else." She then mumbled under her breath, "Folks will do anything to keep from waiting."

Dollar was a little stunned by the fact Klein had actually told people he was dead. Sure he'd told both him and his mother to consider him dead, but he'd been back from the grave for a while now. Obviously Klein had no intention of ever making Dollar a part of his life. Dollar figured he'd cut his losses short now. "Look, never mind," he told the receptionist and then walked away. He wasn't about to set himself up for something that would never exist between him and his baby brother. Klein was now dead to him too.

Dollar walked back through the clinic lobby to the exit door. He pushed the door open to leave the clinic knowing that he had no intention of ever stepping foot back in there again. A hand from the person entering the clinic wrapped around the edge of the door as Dollar proceeded to leave. This hand displayed a very unique tattoo. It was a tattoo of a cross with barbed wire wrapped around it. A hand was grasping the cross as if it barely had an ounce of strength left. Underneath the design were the words HOLD ON.

Dollar remembered seeing this before. He knew exactly who it belonged to.

"Well if it ain't Dollar Bill," the man entering the clinic said. "Fancy running into you here. Oh, yeah. I forgot. This is your turf, huh; your hometown? What a coincidence bumpin' into you here."

Dollar stood still and frozen as the man continued.

"I don't know why anyone would want to live in this shithole of a town. How that ho talked me into moving here I'll never guess. I ain't got no plans on making this my permanent home, though. I just got some business I need to handle; then I'm moving West, Cali or some shit."

Dollar had no idea why this fool was standing here chumming it up with him like they were the best of friends. Still, he listened, having a feeling it must be leading up to something.

"What you doing up in the clinic? You catch something while you was in the joint? You got the clap or something? I know you probably been running up in everything with a pussy. You know how it is when you get out of the joint. Hell, a muthafucka would fuck a sheep on a farm." He burst out laughing.

"My brother works here," Dollar replied.

"Oh yeah. Is that so?" the man said, sticking his head around Dollar and peeking inside the waiting area. "If your brother is anything like your father, maybe he can hook me up, you know, tit for tat. I'd hate to have to wait for all these sick muthafuckas to be seen before I can see the doctor."

"What did you just say?" Dollar asked.

"I said I'd hate to have to wait for all—"

"No, I mean about my father."

"Oh, shit, you know what I mean. I do a little something for him and he does a little something for me. Like back when we was all in the joint."

Dollar stared into Wojo's eyes as if he had the capability of dissecting his brain. "My father," Dollar said, wanting to confirm that he and Wojo were on the same page.

"Yeah, Romeo, the ladies' lover, or should I say killer." Wojo laughed. "Can you believe they fell for that shit, Romeo, the Midwest Terror, serial killer or whatever?" His eerie laugh was like nails down a chalkboard to Dollar's ears.

Wojo stood in the doorway laughing hysterically. It was an evil, wicked laugh. At this point, he was the only one who knew the punch line.

"That old bastard held that shit over my head for years before finding a way to put it to use. You know how it is when you first get to the joint; you act like some ol' bitch and running your mouth."

"Naw, I don't know anything about that," Dollar answered the rhetorical question.

"Well, anyway, I was in for possession with intent to sell. Those funky-ass cops were so worried about trying to stick a drug charge on a brotha that they let all the real evidence slip right between their fingers: the rope, the gloves, the blade, all dat shit. Let's just say a nigga got away with murder, literally." He winked at Dollar. "Guilt and shame must have been eating your pops alive," Wojo said. "His boy was fixin' to spend the rest of his life behind bars, the son he had abandoned as a small child. How could he make it up to you? So, with nothing to lose, he decides to be someone he's not. Who admits to a crime they didn't commit to save the next bastard?" He shook his head. "Blood or no blood; fuck that. He could have easily been a free man, but he made you one instead. And me too for that matter." He let out another irritating laugh. "Memorized every detail I told him."

Dollar just stood there and glared at him. He couldn't believe he was hearing what he was hearing. Wojo was saying it, without saying it, that he was the one really responsible for all those murders. He held the truth. But what did Dollar give a shit about the truth now? Authorities finding out the truth would only mean him finishing off his time.

Dollar's stomach was turning ninety miles per hour. Dollar stood in the doorway watching Wojo's dingy off-white teeth open and close as he continued speaking.

"Your father was going to make good with you if it was the last thing he did. Nigga acted like he was God up in the joint or some shit. I guess that makes you Jesus. Whose soul will you sacrifice yourself to save?"

A woman walked up and brushed through Dollar and Wojo.

"Damn, that's one more muthafucka who's going to be ahead of me," Wojo said as the woman proceeded to the registration desk. "Let me get my ass in here and take care of my business. I'm sure I'll run into you again. Maybe we can do lunch sometime. And hey." He placed his hand on Dollar's shoulder. "I hope you don't hold shit against me from back in the joint. You know how a nigga gotta act hard up in there. It was all show; strictly business." Wojo chuckled and headed into the clinic.

Dollar put his hand over his mouth and bent over. He quickly ran off to the side and vomited up everything he had eaten and eventually the lining of his stomach. He stood still, unable to lift his feet, as the world spun around him. He couldn't see straight. He couldn't think straight. All he could envision was a man, his father, being injected with lethal fluids. His life had been taken for a crime he had not committed. In all actuality, Romeo had literally given up his life so that his son could have one.

Dollar reevaluated everything Wojo had just shared with him and put things in perspective. At the end of the day, in his heart, any man who abandoned his wife and kids deserved the death penalty. Romeo had only gotten what was coming to him.

CHAPTER 25

Dear Mama

It was late Sunday morning and Dollar lay in his bed flipping channels with the remote control. He had spent a couple of days earlier in the week casing the bank, the position of the tellers, cameras, and the daily routine of the security guards. He had ordered in food and ordered pay-per-view movies for the past two days. The only thing he got out of the bed to do was use the bathroom. He hadn't even showered. There were just so many heavy things on his mind. Life outside of the cage seemed to be taking more of a toll on him than inside. And he had to admit that his mind hadn't been right since running into Wojo and learning what his dad had done for him. The issue with Kera and the whole Mya pregnancy thing had been gnawing at him as well. He'd been a complete asshole to both women. Yeah, he wanted to be hard so whenever life knocked him down the fall wouldn't hurt. But somehow his heart had managed to harden in it all. If he didn't know any better, it was as if he'd inherited the God syndrome from Ramelle. Like father, like son.

There were thoughts of his brother. He didn't know if he'd ever be able to patch things up 100 percent with him.

A small, digital envelope was visible on his cell phone signaling to him that he had voicemail messages. He allowed all calls to go directly to his voicemail. He didn't want to be bothered by anyone. No distractions. He had to get his mind back right.

For some reason Dollar was feeling empty inside. Here he was, a free man, who was supposed to be spending the rest of his life behind bars but had been spared. A part of him felt he owed his father at least a thank-you, while another part of him felt his father deserved nothing more than a fuck you. Did Kera and Mya deserve apologies? Had he played them or had they played themselves? Then there was Tommy. She'd been trying to open up her heart, soul, body, and mind to him. His mind was too busy on the money to even acknowledge her feelings.

One thing after another constipated his head and overtook his thoughts where he could hardly function. Did any of it even matter though? Those chapters in his life had been written and read. There was nothing he could do to change it. He had to get over the madness. Now was not the time to get soft.

At the same time, though, Dollar knew that there was so much to be grateful for. He had a roof over his head and food to eat. He had big plans. Soon he would be living more comfortable than ever. Still, there was a major void. Something was missing. A detail had to have been over looked and it was nagging in the pit of Dollar's stomach.

Out of nowhere, Dollar rose up in his bed. He may have done many women wrong, but there was one who deserved an apology more than anybody. A sudden wave of energy took over his being. He went to his closet and picked out some garb to sport for the day. He jumped in the shower and hit the road.

As Dollar drove, he took in the city air. With no final destination, Dollar just drove while he listened to his *Best of Al Green* CD. Once he had listened to every song on that, he popped in his Tupac *Me Against the World* CD. As Dollar listened to the beat of song number nine, he knew why he was on the road. He knew what had lifted him up out of that bed and where he needed to be at that very moment.

***

"Dear Mama," Dollar said as he sat on the ground gazing at his mother's headstone. Choked up, Dollar swallowed hard and maintained his composure. "I haven't been able to bring myself to come back up here and I know I haven't talked to you in a while. I don't know what to say, Mama. I'm your oldest boy." Dollar put his head between his knees and fought back his tears.

"I made some mistakes, and despite my decisions, you taught me well, Mama. Me being in jail wasn't no reflection on you. That was all my doing. I was young and just wanted to find a quick route to taking care of you and my little brother. Can you believe he's about to be a doctor? My little brother, a doctor. I still can't believe it. I guess you know me and him ain't tight like we was when we was younger. I know that ain't making you happy. I know I ain't making you happy, Mama. I know you looking down on me and . . ."

Once again Dollar had to stay strong and fight back tears. "I'm sorry, Mama," Dollar said, breaking down. "Can you hear me, Mama?" Dollar cried. "Do you hear me, Mama? I'm sorry. I'm so sorry. I never meant for any of this to happen. I miss you, Mama. I love you so much. I wish I could do everything all over again. I would do what you did, Mama. I would work at every fast food chain in the city. I would catch the bus, ride a bike, walk even. I would be just like you, Mama. But things are different now, Mama. Klein and I, we didn't need no daddy. No man was as strong as you, Mama. No man."

By this time Dollar was crying and snottin' uncontrollably. His body trembled as he sat on the ground before his mother's grave, pouring his heart out to her, holding a conversation with her that he should have had with her years ago.

"I did wrong, Mama," Dollar continued. "But I ain't no killer. I ain't never took another man's life. You didn't raise a perfect son, but you didn't raise no killer, either. I just want you to know that. I just want you to have that peace of mind."

Dollar paused and collected himself. "I guess all you got now is peace. Please forgive me for not being strong like you. I'm about to do something that I know you wouldn't be proud of, but I promise you, Mama, after that, I'm gonna make you proud. I know I've got some nerve asking you to forgive me for a wrong I ain't even made yet, but it's something I just got to do, Mama. I've lost everything: you, my brother, and Auntie Charlene," Dollar said looking over at his aunt's headstone.

"All this loss can't be in vain. It just can't be," Dollar sobbed. This time Dollar couldn't control the flow of his tears.

"I miss you, Mama. God, I miss you. I miss your smile. Speaking of your smile; I met a woman, Hennessey. You'd like her. She has your smile. She's a good woman, Mama. I can see me with somebody like her. I think . . . No, I know I need somebody like her. She'll keep me on my toes just like you did, Mama. I wish you were here. Oh, Mama."

Dollar kneeled over his mother's grave for almost an hour crying. His once silent shouts were now heard throughout the cemetery grounds. Dollar couldn't hold back his cries, his yells, his wailing. He didn't care who saw a grown man crying. He had held in so many tears for so long. It was time. It was long overdue.

Just as Dollar wiped away his last tear he felt a hand on his shoulder. He knew the touch. He needed the touch. So, Dollar grabbed the hand tight and began to cry even harder.

"I . . . I," Dollar stuttered. "I'm sorry. I'm sorry for everything. I . . . I love you."

"Bro?"

Upon hearing the voice, Dollar looked up and saw his baby brother. Dollar had been oblivious that Klein had arrived for his usual Sunday afternoon visit and had been standing over him during his pleas to their mother.

"Doc, I'm . . . I'm . . ."

Klein walked over, kneeled down and put his hand on Dollar's back. "It's all right, big bro. We gon' be all right. Everything is good. We got each other . . . again," Klein said as he sat down next to his brother and held him tight.

CHAPTER 26

The Confession

Dollar banged outside of Tommy's door for at least ten minutes before it cracked open. Tommy stood in the doorway with a white towel wrapped around her hair and another one tubed above her breast.

"Why you knocking like you the police?" Tommy said.

"Why you fronting like you didn't hear me out here?" Dollar replied.

"I was in the shower, duh." She let Dollar inside. "The girls are at school, so it's not like they could answer the door for you."

"I been calling you for the last few days," Dollar said. "You ain't got none of my messages? I stopped by the club and you weren't there. Didn't Storm tell you?"

Tommy closed her eyes, turned her back to Dollar, and took a couple steps away from him.

She was prepared to lie to Dollar. Instead of a lie, the truth came out.

"Yeah," Tommy turned around and said. "I got your messages. Look, Dollar. This one just doesn't feel right and I'm not down with you trying to pressure me."

"I'm not trying to hear this, Tommy."

"I know. I've been trying to figure out how to tell you," Tommy said.

"Tell me what?" Dollar shouted. "Oh, you bailing?"

"It's not even like that. But I've thought about it like you asked me to and my answer is still the same."

"I guess that explains the FOR SALE sign in your front yard," Dollar said, nodding toward the sign of abandonment. "Fuck you, Tommy!"

"Dollar, please," Tommy said as Dollar began to walk away. "It's not what it looks like. I'm doing this for the girls."

"Naw, fuck you. I did eight years for you. I gave you eight years of freedom on these muthafuckin' streets and this is how you gon' repay me?"

"And I cried for you every day for eight years."

"Nigga, you cried," Dollar said.

"You made that choice," Tommy said. "I showed up at the courthouse prepared to admit my guilt."

"Here we go," Dollar said, downplaying Tommy's dramatics.

"You are so fuckin' clueless, Dollar. You're too worried about your own muthafuckin' self to notice anything or anybody around you. You haven't even taken the time to notice me," Tommy said softly as she approached Dollar.

"As luck would have it, I'm back out here on the streets, but I was willing to trade in my life for you, T."

"Why?" Tommy asked.

"What do you mean 'why'?" Dollar said. "You was my partner, my dawg, my boy. You know what I'm saying."

"Well, I didn't want to be all that. I never wanted to be those things to you; being your partner, dawg, boy. I wanted to be your girl," Tommy admitted. For so long she had wanted Dollar to notice the feelings she had for him. She wanted him to stop mistaking her love for him as though she loved him like a brother. She wanted him to just wake up and realize that she loved him like a lover.

"You are my girl," Dollar said, reaching out to put his hand on Tommy's shoulder.

"I mean your *girl* girl," Tommy said, trying to overcome the embarrassment of showing her true feelings, which was something she had never been good at.

Dollar was speechless. He just stood there dumbfounded.

Tommy, misconstruing Dollar's silence, moved in closer to him. She couldn't have been any closer to Dollar. The towel was still wrapped around her. She could feel his heartbeat as he could feel hers. With her eyes open, she leaned in and allowed her lips to touch his. She was hoping for some kind of response. There was nothing but awkwardness. She pulled back and just shook her head. Tommy stormed away to her bedroom. A few seconds later she returned with a shoebox that she slammed down on the table. "There!" Holding her towel up, she began pacing back and forth.

"What's this?" Dollar asked.

"It's for you," she said.

Dollar walked over and took the lid off the shoebox. The shoebox was filled with stacks of envelopes that were held together with rubber bands.

"Those are letters that I wrote you while you were locked up," Tommy said. She walked over, picked up the box and shoved it into Dollar's arms. "After the first dozen or so were returned, I still kept writing. I just never mailed them. Those letters are a diary. A diary of a woman in love with your black ass."

"Tommy, I don't want to do this," Dollar said, trying to give the box back to Tommy.

"Well, you are," Tommy insisted by pushing the box back toward Dollar. "One minute I think you're spending the rest of your life in jail and then one day you just show up on my doorstep ready to hustle. You never even asked how I'd been. I mean, we never just spent time together."

"What do you mean? I spend more time with you and Ral than anybody."

"Yeah, me, Ral, and a slew of hoes, but what about me? What about just me, Dareese?" Tommy said as her eyes watered. "Tell me why you did it. Tell me why you really did time in prison for me, Dollar. I mean, I really want to know!"

"Tommy, what do you want from me, for me to tell you a bunch of shit that you want to hear like I do these other hoes on the street?" Dollar shouted.

"Say it," Tommy said, snatching Dollar's face up by the chin. "Why'd you do it? Just say it. Just say it! Had the tables been turned, I would have done the same thing for you. Do you know why I would have done it for you? Because I loved you. I love you, you fucking asshole."

Tommy stood before Dollar crying. The only thing she wanted him to do was to put his arms around her and hold her. He didn't even have to say the words back to her. She just needed him to show his love by comforting her. She had concealed her feelings for Dollar for years. She had acted like just one of the boys almost all of her life just to be close to him. The charade was over.

Tommy looked up at Dollar. The expression on his face told the story that he hated to see Tommy hurting like this. He had never had a single inkling that Tommy felt this way about him. He stared into Tommy's eyes, trying to absorb her hurt. Tommy took Dollar's comforting gesture the wrong way and, once again, pressed her lips against his and just began to kiss him. He tried to fight her tongue but inhaled it instead. Dollar closed his eyes and kissed Tommy like a preacher had just granted him permission to kiss the bride. Suddenly, Dollar opened his eyes, snapped out of the fairytale and back to reality. He immediately pushed Tommy away.

"Dollar, I don't want to confuse things. I just wanna—" Tommy said as Dollar cut her words short.

"I know what you just wanna. You just wanna trick your way out of your debt to me like you do with those fake-ass ballers in the club. This is one debt you can't repay on your back, Tommy.

I need you in order for this shit to go down, so you can cut this big act you're putting on," Dollar said, throwing down the shoebox filled with the letters.

Dollar saw stars. He didn't know what had hit him. It took a few seconds before he realized that it was Tommy's uppercut that had him stunned. When he threw down those letters he might as well have punched Tommy in the stomach. He threw the letters down like trash. She'd given him her heart in those letters. It was like he was throwing her away too.

"Get out," Tommy said, swallowing a few tears along with her pride. She was crying so hard that she thought she would become intoxicated from the salt from the tears that had made their way from her eyes to her tongue.

"Thomasena," Dollar said.

"Get the fuck out, Dollar!" She pulled her fist back again.

"I'll go," Dollar said, licking the blood from his lip. "But I need you, T. Eleven o'clock. I need you there, T. You owe me. Put all this bullshit aside, dammit, you owe me, T. You know you do!"

"You're unbelievable," Tommy said. "Do you think I'm one of these women you manage to wrap around your finger and control? Well, I'm not, Dollar. I don't owe you. I don't owe you shit. You made a decision years ago, you live with it."

Dollar could see the pain in Tommy's eyes as she stood before him opening up her soul. This was so hard for her. It hurt her and he knew it. She'd survived by being a closed book. At that very moment she was wide open and he could see that Tommy loved him with pain.

"I'm not trying to hear this, Tommy," Dollar said, going back into hardcore mode. "You've got a choice to make: your debt to me, or these bullshit feelings you think you have for me."

"I love you. Loving you is my choice."

"Will you shut the fuck up with that shit, Tommy? Don't do this. Don't go catching feelings and fuck up things."

"I'm in love with you. I've always been in love with you. You can't tell me you've never felt it," Tommy persisted, unable to control that life-altering thing called love.

"Save that bullshit for a nigga who gives a fuck. Save it for one of them tricks down at the club. Save it for someone who loves you back, 'cause I don't." Dollar paused. His words cut Tommy like a knife. "I'm doing this shit with or without you, Tommy. You riding?"

Tommy stood frozen. Blood oozed from her ego. She had been shot down at high noon. She was dead and therefore couldn't speak.

"Fine," Dollar said as he stormed out of Tommy's house, slamming the door behind him. Dollar stood on the other side of the closed door. He couldn't believe Tommy had tried to drop the love bomb on him. He knew Tommy loved him, but never like that.

Mixing love with money was a definite no-no. Besides, Tommy was like one of the boys and Dollar just couldn't get past that. Crossing the line of a friendship was surely the end of one. Yeah, Dollar loved Tommy, but not like that. He loved her like a little sister. He loved her like she was blood. Once the friendship line was crossed, things would never be the same. Tommy meant too much to Dollar for that.

Dollar's rejecting Tommy was killing her softly. She probably hated his guts. But their love ran deep and he knew that, although she was mad at him now, she would get over it. If he were to cross the line just to appease her emotions, he would eventually break her heart. He had to choose the lesser of the two evils.

Instead of turning around, going back into Tommy's house and satisfying her feelings, which the dawg in Dollar was barking for him to do, he walked away. He walked away with a genuine friendship that he could take to his grave no matter what.

***

Dollar had just treated Hennessey to dinner at the same hotel restaurant where they had their first date. Dollar was cleaned up well; suited up with a hat to match. Although he ordinarily didn't get hardcore *GQ,* it was as if he subconsciously wanted to show Hennessey that he had another side to him that could perhaps be molded.

Hennessey, sporting a satin-like Oscar de la Renta pant and top set, rambled on and on the entire time during dinner about how well Dollar's investments she had made for him were doing. Dollar hadn't heard a word she'd said. He couldn't stop thinking about his fight with Tommy.

After dinner, Hennessey talked Dollar into a trip to the park behind the hotel building where she continued chitchatting about his portfolio. "I'm glad to hear those investments you made are looking real good," Hennessey said to Dollar as she pitched a penny into the fountain.

"Me too." Dollar had spoken with his personal banker and relayed to Hennessey that all was looking good.

Hennessey pitched another coin into the fountain.

"What was that one for?" Dollar asked.

"Huh?" Hennessey said.

"The coin you just threw into the fountain; what did you wish for with it?"

"If I tell you, then it might not come true."

Dollar dropped his head and stared off into space.

"Here," Hennessey said, placing a penny into Dollar's hand.

"Oh, you want me to make a wish too?" Dollar asked.

"No, that's a penny for your thoughts. You probably only said ten words max at dinner and now you're sitting here like you just lost your best friend. Like P. Diddy was lookin' after his and J Lo's split," Hennessey joked. "What's going on?"

Dollar wanted so badly to spill everything that was on his mind to Hennessey. He wanted to tell her about his bid, and about how he came about being a free man again. He wanted to share with her about Mya's pregnancy and the abortion he was forcing her to have. He wanted her advice on his situation with Tommy. He wanted to tell her about his brother and his mother. He wanted to tell her how he was really starting to have feelings for her.

Hennessey could sense Dollar's hesitation. She knew he wanted to talk. If only she could just get him to. "I know you think I'm just some stuck-up broad who works in a bank who probably ain't never did a day without. But that's not true. Shit ain't always been easy for me. So you can talk to me, Dollar. You'd be surprised that I just might be able to understand and help you out."

Dollar looked at Hennessey sitting there in her $200 Italian shoes and top designer outfit. He thought about how hard his mother had worked during her life and was never able to afford items like that. Dollar began to laugh.

"What?" Hennessey said. "Did I say something funny?"

"Oh, you've had it rough all right. The world can just look at you sitting there and see right away just how hard you've had it. Let me guess," Dollar said as he began to read Hennessey like a book. "You were born into a middle-class, two-parent home. Your mother's pregnancy with you was planned. Her and your father were married at the time and they probably still are to this day. As a little girl you took tap and ballet. Your mother put you in all sorts of beauty pageants of which, by the way, you always placed top three. You won spelling bees and shit throughout grade school and was captain of the cheerleading squad in high school. You were voted most likely to succeed and even gave the commencement speech at graduation. You turned down your acceptance to Yale and Harvard so that you could go to school close to home. You graduated college, on a full scholarship of course, at the top of your class and never once had to go job hunting because offers came pouring into you. Yeah, what a hard-knock life."

"You know what? Fuck you," Hennessey said as she pointed her finger into Dollar's chest. "I've tried to be nothing but kind to you and all you want to do is stand here casting these aspersions about me."

"Oh my," Dollar said, covering his mouth as if he were the monkey who could speak no evil. "I'm casting aspersions. Is that the same thing as casting stones? The next time I want to have a conversation with you I guess I'll have to bring my dictionary, seeing I didn't go to college and all."

Dollar was cracking himself up. This showed by the way he hunched over in laughter while holding his stomach. Of course only he knew that his mind was so heavy that he was laughing to keep from crying.

"I know what you're doing," Hennessey said. "I see right through you, Dareese. You tryin' to run me off because you're scared."

"Pssttt, scared of what?"

"You're scared that you're gonna fall in love with me." Hennessey paused. "And that I'm gonna fall in love with you back. You don't know how to act about that and it scares you to death. You're scared to let me in there." Hennessey pointed to Dollar's head, mugging him with her index finger. "And there."

Pointing to his heart Hennessey continued. "You're afraid of what I might find. So instead of facing your fears, you wanna try to run me off with words. How many other girls have you run off with your words, Dollar? Well, I'm grown and words don't bother me. I ain't going nowhere."

Hennessey walked over to Dollar and tried to run her hand down his bald head. Dollar pushed her hands away.

"Don't flatter yourself," Dollar said, angry at the truth Hennessey had just spoken. "You think you the only skirt in town? You think you the first chick to ever fall in love with Dollar Bill? Plenty of bitches love me. Love don't scare me. So why don't you take your one-woman act and perform it for a brother who gives a damn."

Hennessey put her hands up in surrender. "You win. I'm not going to fight you, Dollar. My job is done here," Hennessey said, walking away.

"What the fuck do you mean your job is done?" Dollar said, running up behind her and grabbing her by the arm. "Was I just some charity case, some thug you bumped into on the streets and decided to be nice to? Is that why you ain't never said, 'Hey, Dollar, come over to my place so we can just kick it'? You afraid I'm gonna steal your silverware or something? You afraid I'm gon' dirty up your couch if I sit on it?"

Hennessey could see the hurt in Dollar's eyes. There was still a chance that she could get to him, get inside him. She decided to be the bigger person. "I'm sorry," Hennessey said as she was swallowed up by the look in Dollar's eyes. "I didn't mean it like that. I just want to help you. That's all I've been trying to do. I wish you could see that."

Dollar released Hennessey's arm and just stared off into space.

"Look, I don't know where we took a wrong turn, but can we just start over, please?" Hennessey asked.

Dollar looked at Hennessey and sucked his teeth. After giving her the once-over he just walked away. Once again Dollar was running from emotions, not only his own, but the woman's he cared about.

If only these bitches would just let a nigga get money first, then everything would be cool, Dollar thought. He didn't need all this drama.

Not right now, not when he was trying to stay focused.

"Excuse me, sir, but do you have the time?" Hennessey said tapping Dollar on his shoulder.

"What are you doing, Hennessey?" Dollar asked.

"I'm starting over," she replied.

"You're oil and I'm water."

"Opposites attract."

"You're not going to give up are you?"

"Nuh huh," Hennessey said, giving Dollar a sexy smile. "Dollar, you want to be saved. I don't know all of the demons you're running from, but let me be your savior." Hennessey kissed Dollar on his lips and said, "Let me save you."

Dollar leaned closer into Hennessey and planted a kiss right on her lips. He allowed his hands to glide down to her butt and he pulled himself against her. Lost in the moment Hennessey began to kiss Dollar hard.

"Let's go to your place," Dollar said, as he pulled a hand around to Hennessey's breast.

"Huh, what?" Hennessey said in a dazed like manner. "Wait a minute. We just met. We can't do this on our first time meeting."

"Fuck this role-playing," Dollar said. "I want you."

"Umm umm. I can't," Hennessey said, drifting back into reality.

"Come on, Miss Lady. Stop playing," Dollar said as he pulled Hennessey tighter into him and started kissing on her neck.

Those heated kisses Dollar was branding on Hennessey's neck were setting her pussy on fire. The loud, short, deep breaths she was taking let Dollar know that she was feeling him. As Dollar grabbed Hennessey's crotch through her pants he could feel the warm moisture.

"Dollar, stop. Don't," Hennessey whispered.

"You know you don't want me to stop," Dollar continued.

"Yes, I do," Hennessey said, snapping fully back into reality.

Dollar stopped and looked at a less passionate and more serious Hennessey. "Fuck it!" Dollar said under his breath. "I'm not playing this games." He turned and walked away.

"Dollar, wait," Hennessey said, doing a light jog after him.

"I don't have time for your good girl/bad boy games. I'm not a fuckin' toy, Hennessey. Why don't you go find some suit you work with and pull this act on him?"

"Dollar, wait!" Hennessey called. "You don't understand. Please don't take this personal. It's not that I don't want to, I just can't right now."

"No, you don't understand," Dollar shouted as he proceeded to the hotel and signaled the valet driver to retrieve his car.

Once the driver brought Dollar's car around, Dollar gave him a twenty dollar bill and got inside and drove off, leaving Hennessey standing behind, alone.

CHAPTER 27

Get Money

Dollar stood outside of the salon watching Mya do some woman's nails for a half hour before going in. He hadn't talked to her since he had the fight about the baby with her. He knew he needed to holler at her to see where her head was at, but more importantly, he wanted to make sure her tummy hadn't grown any.

When Dollar walked inside the salon there was immediate dead silence and all eyes were on him. It did not take a rocket scientist to realize Mya had been telling their business. *Bitches always runnin' they mouth, black or white,* Dollar thought as eyes rolled at him and necks snapped.

"Mya, hey," Dollar said.

Mya pretended as though he wasn't even there and continued putting the finishing touches, a coat of clear nail polish, on the woman's hands she was working on.

"Can I talk to you outside for a minute?" Dollar asked.

"She no talk to you," the little Asian woman hurried over to intercede. "You hurt feelings. You go away."

"It's okay, Leila," Mya said to the Asian woman. She looked to Dollar. "Give me a second. I'll meet you outside."

Dollar headed back outside the shop and waited for Mya. She met him a couple minutes later. She was wearing a tight-fitting dress. No baby bump.

"So you doing okay?" Dollar asked her.

"I am now. It would have been nice of you to ask me that a few weeks ago. You didn't even call to make sure I was okay." Mya started to become emotional. "Anyway, I'm good. I need to get back inside. I have another customer waiting. Besides, I told Leila if I wasn't back in there in five minutes to call 911." Then she added before Dollar could respond, "Just joking."

Dollar smiled at her.

"I do have to go though."

"It's cool," Dollar said as he watched Mya head back inside. Relief overtook Dollar. He'd gone to visit Mya to perhaps right a wrong. Seeing she'd gone ahead with the abortion, there was no wrong to right. He had made it up in his mind, though, that had she still been with child, he would have had no choice but to step up to the plate and be Daddy. He didn't have to be her man, but he had to be a man for his child, if there was to be one. He'd dodged a bullet, or, who knew, maybe Mya was the one who had dodged the bullet.

After leaving the salon, Dollar stopped off and grabbed him a submarine sandwich from a deli before going home. He pulled into his space in the apartment parking garage, turned the car off and then pulled out his cell phone to make a call. This was the hundredth time Dollar had tried getting in touch with Tommy. Her phone either rang and rang and rang until voicemail picked up, or whoever answered the phone at the club said she was busy. This time wasn't any different.

"Fuck!" Dollar spat upon hanging up his cell phone, then getting out of his car. Not being able to get in touch with Tommy was just one more thing weighing heavy on him. He turned on his car alarm, then headed into his apartment building. As he walked down the hall he noticed a figure standing against his door waiting on him.

Once Dollar realized it was Hennessey he proceeded to take out his keys and unlock his apartment door. Dollar had never seen Hennessey in a casual getup, but tonight she was in a nice pair of indigo Guess jeans with a matching jacket. The jeans flared at the bottom where the heel of her three-inch black ankle boots could be seen. She was tight to death, which made it extra hard for Dollar to ignore her presence.

"So you don't see me standing here?" Hennessey said. "So it's like that? That's the game we're going to play with each other?"

"As far as I can tell, you like playing games," Dollar said, opening his door.

"Come out with me," Hennessey said. "Kind of like a makeup date. I've missed you."

"Not in the mood; got a lot of shit on my mind," Dollar said, with his back still to Hennessey.

Hennessey looked at Dollar and for some reason the sight of him just broke her heart. He was a big man, but there just seemed to be this little, hurt boy inside of him. That little, hurt boy was calling for her to rescue him.

"Look, baby," Hennessey said walking up behind Dollar, placing her head on his back. He smelled of the scent Domain. It made her want to stay there forever, or at least long enough for the scent to rub off on her so that she could go home smelling like him. "Let me take you out for a drink. No place loud, just this mellow joint

I know. Please," Hennessey said, pouting her bottom lip.

How could any man turn down such a plea? Dollar stood there for a moment taking in Hennessey's heart beating against his back. Her heartbeat was calm and tranquil, just the opposite of his, which was rowdy and turbulent. Before obliging to Hennessey's request, Dollar turned around and looked into her eyes, eyes that perhaps belonged to the one person who could tame his heart.

"I be trying to keep my shit straight. I be trying to keep my shit straight, but the world be going 'round. I said the world be going 'round, y'all," the poet spoke as the audience was mesmerized by his every word.

Dollar sat at the half-empty poetry spot drinking one shot of Henney after the next.

"Slow down," Hennessey, who had pulled her chair up next to Dollar, said to him. "You putting them drinks away tonight. You sure you're all right? Do you wanna talk to me about anything?"

It was almost as if Hennessey was trying too hard to get into Dollar's head. Dollar wished he had never agreed to go out on the makeup date with her.

"I'm good," Dollar replied, focusing on the poet's words, but not listening to them. His mind was off in a thousand places; those same places it had been for a while now, with a few other pit stops along the way. Removing Kera, Mya, and even Tommy from the equation, Hennessey, the woman he thought he could settle down with, even seemed to be playing games. Perhaps it was karma. The same way he'd asked himself not too long ago whether he'd played Kera and Mya or if they'd played themselves, in the back of his mind he couldn't help but wonder if Hennessey was playing him, or if he'd played himself.

"Sometimes I fall and I be going 'round. I said I be going 'round, y'all, 'round with the world, y'all. And I get dizzy. I said I be gettin' dizzy and I get off track. And I be callin' y'all, but y'all don't answer. Where y'all at? Where my niggaz is at? I'm callin' y'all. Answer me back like y'all be answering the wax. Where my niggaz is at?" the poet continued.

"I'm ready to dip," Dollar said to Hennessey, who was enjoying the poetry.

"You sure?" Hennessey asked.

"Did I stu . . . stu . . . stutter?" Dollar replied.

Hennessey looked at Dollar as if he was crazy. She could tell his mind was a million miles away, so instead of lashing back at him, she decided to try to comfort him. "Baby, let's go somewhere and talk. Wanna go to the fountain?" Hennessey asked.

"I don't want to talk," Dollar replied. "I got some shit I have to do."

Dollar needed to get home, sober up, and start going over his plan again as his big moment, the moment that would define him as a man of the streets, was only a couple days away. This was his meal ticket to easy street for life. With this transaction pending, he couldn't possibly give Hennessey the attention she deserved. He was liable to say some shit that would fuck up any chance of starting something real with her. He needed to take a break from her and then start fresh once his mind was back on track.

Robbing a bank was a major step up from sticking up people. He was taking on a franchise. A franchise that was always prepared for people such as himself. There wasn't no catching a bank slippin'. You just had to go in and set it off.

"What is it you have to do?" Hennessey inquired.

"What the fuck is it with all the questions?" Dollar said loudly, which made the poet forget his words. "I said I'm ready to go, so let's go!" Dollar quickly exited the club with Hennessey right behind him.

"You go ahead. I'm gonna catch a cab home," Dollar said to Hennessey.

"I drove you here so I'll drive you back home. You're in no condition to be trying to get home by yourself."

"I want to be alone," Dollar said.

"But I don't," Hennessey said, grabbing Dollar by the arm.

He stopped and looked into her passionate eyes. Before Dollar could reject her, she began to French kiss him. Dollar was beginning to get into it before he managed to push Hennessey away.

"Naw, I know what this is about. You just trying to cuddle and shit. You want to kiss all on me and get me all worked up and leave me hangin'. I'm straight on that bullshit."

"No, you're wrong. Not tonight. I'm ready," Hennessey said, as she grabbed Dollar by the back of his head and pulled him into her. She kissed him hard, tongue all down his throat. She pressed her breasts up against him and began to moan. She could feel Dollar's manhood getting hard. After a couple of minutes of kissing, Hennessey stepped back with her hands inside Dollar's and stared into his eyes.

"So what do you say?" Hennessey asked. "You wanna go to my place?"

"Yeah, but just to talk," Dollar said with a mischievous grin.

***

Back at Hennessey's condo she lit incense and candles. She fixed her and Dollar a glass of wine and excused herself into her bedroom to go get out of her street clothes.

When Hennessey returned, she was wearing a powder blue lace two-piece boy leg lingerie set. She walked into the kitchen and did a shot of vodka. She then strutted over to the Oriental rug in front of her fireplace and stretched across it. She signaled for Dollar, who was sitting on the couch, to come lie next to her by patting the floor with her hand.

Dollar, still buzzing from the Henney he had drunk earlier in the night and the glass of wine, made his way next to her. "You sure you wanna—" Dollar said as Hennessey cut him off.

"Shhhhhh," Hennessey said, putting her index finger over Dollar's lips. She showed him the condom in her hand. "I'm sure I wanna." She then put her lips against his and began to kiss him. She sucked the taste of the liquor off of Dollar's tongue. She slowly pushed Dollar down and climbed on top of him and began to aid him in the removal of his clothing.

Softly Hennessey kissed Dollar, first on the forehead and then on each eyelid. Once Dollar was fully undressed they each worked on getting Hennessey out of her lingerie.

Buck naked the two lay there on the floor caressing one another. They would hold one another for a while before Dollar would find himself below Hennessey's belly button. Dollar did not think about it twice, nor did he hesitate before lashing his tongue out at Hennessey's private spot.

Hennessey laid there moaning a silent shout before finding herself in a quiver. If she wasn't mistaken, Dollar had spelled out her full name with his tongue on her lips. His first time going down low was undetectable by Hennessey who produced gushes of sweet juices down Dollar's throat.

Looking up at the high beam ceiling as Dollar caressed her, Hennessey knew it was time to give herself completely to Dollar. She had fought it off for some time, but tonight, she would throw in the towel. There was no turning back. Now, she was in too deep. She closed her eyes and allowed him to enter her world.

Dollar had never been so nervous with a woman in his life when it came to laying the pipe, not even with Pam during his first time ever having sex. He'd been nervous with Hennessey though, up until he entered her special place. All his fears vanished. It was just something about Hennessey that made him feel faultless, that he couldn't touch her the wrong way, caress her the wrong way. He felt like he had already made love to her a thousand times before. She was a perfect fit.

"There's something about you, baby," Dollar whispered in Hennessey's ear as he slowly dipped in and out of her, mesmerized by the sound of her wetness.

"Talk to me," Hennessey whispered. "Tell me what that something is. I like to talk and fuck at the same time."

"Oh shit," Dollar said, turned on by Hennessey's words.

"What is it about me?"

Dollar continued to stroke in and out of Hennessey while looking into her eyes and talking to her. She wanted to fuck and talk, then he'd give her just what she wanted. "That something about you is everything that you are." Dollar plunged deep inside of her. Dollar passionately stroked his body against Hennessey's as the muscles in his arms flexed. It was as if he was doing push-ups over her body.

Tears began to flow down Hennessey's face. She had fought engaging into the act of giving her body to Dollar for so long, and now it was too late to turn things around. She hated the fact that he felt so good inside of her. She hated it because it made her want him. Hennessey let herself go.

She wasn't afraid to hump with Dollar as she rocked her hips back and forth, forth and back. The faster Dollar went, the more determined she was to keep up with him.

"Look at me," Hennessey said to Dollar, who had his eyes closed. He was taking in every moment of being inside of Hennessey. "Open your eyes and look at me."

Dollar followed Hennessey's orders and began looking into Hennessey's eyes. He wasn't even embarrassed as she witnessed the expressions on his face caused by the pleasurable feeling of being trapped by her walls. Formerly trapped between the walls of a jail cell, Dollar now felt trapped between the walls of paradise. He wanted to bottle up the way he felt.

"Go faster," Hennessey ordered.

Dollar began to increase his pace. In and out of her he plunged, not breaking eye contact once.

"Faster," Hennessey ordered.

Dollar pulled his dick out just enough to make sure the condom was in place before he pushed himself deep inside of her. Faster and harder he dove into Hennessey. He was on fire. He never wanted this feeling to end.

The faster Dollar pumped, the wider Hennessey seemed to open up for him. Still staring into one another's eyes, they ground and pounded like it was the end of the world, like it was the last time they would ever make love. Dollar could feel the blood rushing through his vessel.

"I don't want to cum yet," Dollar said, attempting to ease up.

"Fuck that," Hennessey said as she grabbed hold of Dollars ass and pulled him hard against her. Hennessey whirled her hips, flexin' her pussy muscle tight around Dollar's penis, which made Dollar lose it.

"Fuck," Dollar said as he began to jerk inside of Hennessey.

Sweat dripped off of his forehead onto Hennessey's face. She felt as though she was drowning.

"Oh, God," Hennessey screamed.

"Oh, shit, baby," Dollar said.

"Cum with me," Hennessey said as she began to kiss Dollar.

"Cum with me. I'm cummin'. Cum with me."

As the two climaxed together, they felt as though the room was spinning. They had both gotten caught up in the feeling. They were tipsy off of one another.

Dollar and Hennessey lay in position breathing heavily for a few minutes.

"Baby, you felt so good," Dollar said, finally rolling off of Hennessey.

"You too," Hennessey responded. Hennessey stared into space as if her mind was a million miles away.

"What's wrong?" Dollar asked. "Did I hurt you or something?"

Hennessey couldn't help but softly chuckle. "No, you were great," she replied.

"Then what is it?" For the first time in a long time, Dollar actually gave a damn about somebody other than himself. "Tell me what's wrong?"

"It's nothing," Hennessey hesitated. "It's nothing at all."

Dollar kissed Hennessey softly on her lips and lay down next to her, wearing what appeared to be a permanent smile.

Hennessey turned away from Dollar and closed her eyes. For the next couple of hours Dollar watched Hennessey sleep. He watched over her like a mother bear does its cub. Something about looking at Hennessey lying there made Dollar want to protect her. He wanted to pick her up and run far away with her to a place where it was just the two of them, to a place where he could forget about the rest of the world. At the same time he felt safe and protected. It was a feeling he had long needed. At that very moment Dollar knew that his life was about to change.

CHAPTER 28

The Final Chapter

Dollar spent the next day going over the plan with Ral. He sent Ral, with plan in hand, to relay to Tommy. Tommy might not have been trying to hear from Dollar, but he knew she would always have his back. When it came to Dollar Bill, her heart was more forceful than her head. Dollar wasn't ignorant of this fact.

With the big moment in their hustling careers being less than fourteen hours away, Dollar was in a zone. He hadn't turned on any lights or the television. At the moment the only sound that could be heard was the sound of Tupac and Scarface coming from his CD player. "Born with less. . . ." The words echoed through Dollar's head.

The sudden ringing of Dollar's cell phone made him jump to answer it. "Hello," Dollar said.

"I've got great news," Hennessey said with excitement. "I'm on my way over to share it with you."

"Not tonight, Miss Lady," Dollar said, as he lay in the bed in anticipation of the following day's event. In all actuality, he wanted nothing more than to be able to make love to Hennessey again. But he couldn't focus on that right now.

"What do you mean not tonight? This is absolutely, positively the best news ever. I'm going to grab a bottle of Dom and I'm on my way."

"Hennessey, not tonight," Dollar said with authority as silence occupied the phone line. "Look, I'm sorry. I didn't mean to yell. It's just that tonight is really bad. I got something really big going on in the morning, and I just need to get my mind right. I'll call you tomorrow."

"Oh, I get it," Hennessey said. "Now that you got what you wanted, you don't have time for me."

That wasn't the truth, and Dollar hated the fact that he had to allow her to think it was. He hadn't gotten what he wanted from Hennessey, not by far.

"You know it ain't even like that," Dollar said. "Look, Hennessey, I promise I'll call you tomorrow. If all goes well tomorrow, things are going to be different between us, you'll see. I promise."

Dollar hung up. He could hear Hennessey trying to get in one last word, but he closed the flap on his cell phone and closed his eyes. He felt bad, but he would make it up to her. But for now he needed to keep his mind focused and prepare for tomorrow. Although he adored Hennessey and wanted her to be a permanent fixture in his life, Dollar was in gangsta mode. No way was a bitch and her feelings coming before him and his money. Hennessey would be there after tomorrow. Opportunity might not.

With the hit of his life hours away and the possibility of Hennessey being in his future, Dollar had shrugged off his self-loathing and got refocused. Dollar picked up his phone and dialed Tommy's number. The voicemail picked up and Dollar left a message. "Eleven o'clock tomorrow morning. Eleven o'clock I need you, T."

It was 10:50 a.m. and Dollar was sitting across the street from the bank on a bus stop bench gnawing at his manicured nails. If he wasn't gnawing on his nails he was tugging at the knit hat he had rolled up on top of his head. He was nervous, not at the fact that he was about to rob a bank for major paper, but that he wasn't 100 percent certain that his backup would show.

Tommy said she wasn't with it, but Dollar knew in his heart Tommy wouldn't let him down. She couldn't. Ral was game, but if he got caught up in some pussy or the pipe, Dollar was screwed. But Ral had never, ever failed him before.

But his attitude, as always, was fuck it. Many men had robbed a bank solo. He could pull it off. He had been in the bank a hundred times. He had cased the joint. He knew they only had two security guards and that one took a ten-minute break at 11:15 a.m. At 11:00 a.m. Tommy was to specifically occupy Hennessey's attention while he and Ral handled their business as soon as the security guard left his post. He didn't want Hennessey's attention on him any longer than necessary, as she might surely recognize him.

I gotta shit, Dollar thought as his stomach rumbled in knots. This was it, though. Dollar wasn't about to turn back. Everything was going to go off without a hitch. He had to keep telling himself that.

"In and out, nobody gets hurt," Dollar recited. "I'm going in this bitch, get the loot, and live like a Don. Fuck it. If push comes to shove, I can do this shit. I don't need them."

Tommy and Ral had been Dollar's courage, his sidekicks who had always made him feel superior. But then he remembered Romeo's words: "Whenever a cat gets iffy on you, like they wanna bitch out, cut 'em the fuck off. They useless."

This may very well have been the best advice his father could have given him.

It was eleven o'clock and there was no sign of Tommy or Ral. All of Dollar's money was tied up in that bank. The quick easy change from Redd's place was no more. He had to do this. He'd never bitched out of anything in his life. He could do it. He could do it alone; after all, he was Dollar Bill. Twenty-two minutes later, Dollar picked up the gym bag he had with him and headed inside the bank.

"Excuse me, sir," Dollar said to the single security guard standing at the bank entrance, underneath the surveillance camera. "Can you tell me where the deposit slips are?"

"Oh sure," the security guard answered.

As the security guard turned to point, Dollar pulled his knit hat down over his face, grabbed the security guard's hand and bent his arm behind his back. He removed the security guard's gun from his holster and put it to his head. Lucky for Dollar, the fact that "all black people looked alike" would work in his favor.

"Nobody fuckin' move," Dollar said at an even tone, not too loud, but loud enough for everybody to know he meant business. "Put your noses on the ground."

No one hesitated to follow their given instructions. With the security guard in hand, Dollar made his way over to one of the tellers. He then handed her the gym bag and ordered her to fill it with money. The teller nervously hit up every drawer in the joint before handing Dollar the overstuffed bag full of money.

"Everybody count to one hundred Mississippis," Dollar shouted. "If anybody tries to make a move before then, they're dead."

Just then, Hennessey came running out of her office with gun in hand like she was one of Charlie's Angels.

"Detective Roe," the guard shouted to Hennessey. "Get down. He's got a gun."

"Detective Roe?" Dollar said, looking at Hennessey puzzled.

Hennessey trembled as she stood before Dollar, staring him dead in his eyes with a gun of her own in hand.

"Dareese," Hennessey said. "I know that's you. You don't want to do this. Let me help you, please. You don't want to go back to prison."

"Detective! You undercover? You a token?" Dollar shouted as he stood with his gun still aimed at the security guard's head, but looking at Hennessey. "So this is why you always wanted to help me. I was just a job. I was strictly business to you. Didn't want to get personal, huh?"

"That's not true. I wanted to help you, Dollar. You're a good guy. I know you are. You just need a chance; someone to believe you. I believe in you."

Dollar let out a wicked laugh. "Yeah right."

"I do. Otherwise you think I couldn't have busted your ass on those petty robberies a long time ago if I wanted to?" Hennessey replied.

Dollar tried to hide the shocked expression on his face. Hennessey had been trailing him; waiting for him to mess up big time so that when they locked him up, there was no way he would ever get out again. Stealing fur coats and those other hits wasn't the nail in the coffin like this, robbing a bank. Hennessey had told her superiors that she knew it was only a matter of time before Dollar went for something big. She'd been right; even though she had no idea his big hit would be that particular bank—as her luck and Dollar's bad luck would have it.

Everything in Dollar wanted to point the gun at Hennessey and blow her brains out. Dollar couldn't believe this was happening to him. Dollar couldn't believe he had been caught slippin'.

"Come on, Dareese," Hennessey said. "Let me talk to you for a minute. Just come back into my office so we can talk."

"I'm not going back to no fuckin' office. You talk to me right here and right now damn it!" Dollar spat. "Why, Hennessey? Why'd you do this to me?" Dollar asked, trying to hide the visible hurt from her betrayal in his eyes. "I thought you and me could . . . Fuckin' why?"

"Ohio put me on you, to get in good with you. When you slipped, I was supposed to be there when you fell. You didn't think they were really going to let a murderer walk free did you? I'm sorry, Dareese. God, I'm so sorry. You don't know how bad I wanted things to be different, how many nights I thought about how cool it would be to know you in another life," Hennessey confessed. "To help you. And I thought eventually I might be able to help you do right. That day I saw you here at the bank, I pulled you out of the line because I thought you were going to do something stupid then. But you really were here just to do business. It was then that a part of me hoped I was wrong about you. So I set you up with Mr. Alleghany; he was real.

My superiors had no idea I had him helping you with investments. That's something I did on my own. I thought maybe I could change you."

But you did change me, Dollar thought. "How in the fuck were you going to change me, Hennessey? Did you really think that 'love conquers all' shit was really going to work?"

Hennessey gave no reply. She just held her gun on Dollar.

"So when we made lo . . ." Dollar had to pause. He was so hurt and angry that he couldn't get his words out. "When you slept with me, was that work?" Dollar asked.

Hennessey remained silent.

"So what if, hypothetically speaking, I did fall in love with you, you know, just say that I was really diggin' you and decided to live in your world. Could we have, you know, been a couple?"

"Dareese, please don't."

"I just want to know, Hennessey."

Hennessey shook her head.

"Speak the fuck up!" Dollar shouted. "I can't hear you."

"No, no!" Hennessey answered. "I would have found some way to break it off with you, a job transfer or something. Then I would have gone back to Ohio with my husband and son."

"Husband . . . Son," Dollar said, fighting so hard to hold in the tears that the pain of hearing Hennessey's words created. "So that's what all those seminars were, huh? Trips back to Ohio to be with your husband and son?"

Dollar couldn't believe it. All the women he'd done wrong, and the one he'd planned on doing right did him wrong. Karma was a bitch indeed. This wasn't how things were supposed to go down. This wasn't what was supposed to happen. Hennessey was going to be that woman who turned Dollar into an honest man, that woman who kept him honest. A woman like his mother.

"But, I got good news for you, Dareese. Your investments, they shot through the roof.

"You have enough money to live at the Waldorf-Astoria every day for the rest of your life damn near. That's what I needed to tell you last night," Hennessey said, as her infamous smile spread across her face.

Dollar wasn't smiling. He was paralyzed by a feeling of betrayal.

"See, once again, I was looking out for you," Hennessey said. "You think that money was really supposed to be getting invested? Hell no. That was me. I had the bank investor do it. He was none the wiser, but I went against protocol,

for you. I put my job on the line . . . for you."
She then got serious again. "I tried to tell you
about the money last night, but you wouldn't
listen. I could tell something was up just by the
way you were acting on the call last night." She
shook her head, once again wishing she'd been
wrong about Dollar. But the fact that the two
were standing face-to-face with guns pointed
was just another sign that he'd proven her wrong
yet again . . . and for what could be the last time.

"So please, don't do this," Hennessey pleaded."
Put the gun down. You're only at an attempted
armed robbery charge. You can walk out of here
with as little as five years. After that, you can
take all of your money and settle down, find a
nice girl."

"Five years." Dollar laughed, interrupting
Hennessey's lie. "I'm a fuckin' ex-felon who
was in for life who got out on a wild card. Do
you think all I'm gon' get is five years? Hell they
wanted my black ass back in the joint from the
moment they let me out. They never had any real
intention on ever letting me live my life did they?
They've been expecting me to fuck up. You're
proof of that. And when I did, I was going right
back to jail, huh? Well fuck that, and fuck you,
bitch. I ain't going back to jail." Dollar cocked
his gun.

"We can work this out. I'll help you. I've looked out for you thus far," Hennessey said, still overlooking the fact that this was strictly business and that her relationship with Dollar was for hire. Hennessey had tried so hard not to look deep enough within him to find the good. But she knew underneath his hard exterior was a young man with dreams from the ghetto who got caught up in reality's nightmare.

"You'll help me, huh?" Dollar said doubtful.

"I'm helping you now!" Hennessey lowered her tone. "Why the fuck you think the cops haven't already busted through those doors and blown your head off? Because I didn't call for backup. That's why. But if you don't think one of them broads behind the counter hasn't already alerted the police somehow, you're kidding yourself. And what do you think is going to happen when they see you aiming a gun at one of their own?"

Dollar paused before speaking. "They're gonna do what you ultimately set out to do. See me dead. Because if it comes down to it, you'll put a bullet right through my head, won't you?"

Hennessey swallowed hard but didn't speak.

"Say somethin' goddamn it!" Dollar said as he jerked the gun, scaring the security guard and forcing Hennessey to cock her weapon. "Oh, it's like that?" Dollar said to her.

"Please, Dareese," Hennessey pleaded.

"Stop fucking calling me that. My name is Dollar, Dollar Bill, muthafuckas. Y'all hear that?" Dollar said to the people in the bank as he removed the knit hat from over his face. "Dollar, Dollar Bill, y'all!"

"Okay, Dollar," Hennessey said in an apologetic tone. "Just think, when you get out, you'll be a rich man. You'll have something to look forward to."

At this point Hennessey's words created an internal inferno in Dollar's body. His eyes bulged with tears as he gripped the gun tighter. He didn't know how much longer he could go on with this alone. He had never expected to be broken down like this. He needed his backup.

Where the fuck are my boys? was all Dollar could think. The three of them could have handled this shit. It didn't have to be so fucked up. Dollar gazed over at the door hoping to see Tommy and Ral coming through it.

Catching Dollar off guard, fearing for her life and the life of the security guard, Hennessey used her quick and better judgment and began to fire multiple shots at Dollar.

All of a sudden one of the bank customers jumped up from off of the floor and began to fire a gun. The customer appeared to be a man who was dressed in a tan jogging suit with a matching ball cap. Dark sunglasses covered his eyes. The customer fired a shot to the security guard's leg that hunched him over and away from Dollar. He then fired another fatal gunshot to the security guard's head. Quickly, trained and skilled, the customer put one in Hennessey's chest, which took her down, but not to her grave.

The customer then walked over to Dollar and placed his head on Dollar's bloody chest. Dollar had taken bullets to the chest, stomach, and leg. Dollar's heart was beating fast and hard.

It was as if his heart was going to jump right out of his chest. Dollar was paralyzed. He couldn't move. His bucked eyes stared straight up as his heart beat like African drums.

"It burns," Dollar said. "Shit, it burns."

"I'm so sorry I was late," Tommy said as she removed the dark sunglasses from her face. "Fuckin' around with that Ral. Went to get him this morning. Son of a bitch overdosed. I couldn't save him this time, D. I went to a pay phone and called 911 then tried to get here as fast as I could. I see I wasn't in time to save you either."

Tommy raised her head and looked at Dollar who couldn't respond. He looked deep into Tommy's eyes, recognizing her, he tried to speak, but no words came out. He wanted to tell her how the bullets felt like heated pokers spearing through his body. He wanted to tell her thank you for showing up and that it was okay that she was late. He wanted to tell her that he loved her too. Right now, with his life flashing before his eyes, he had no pride. Dollar had no ego or persona to hide behind. He loved her. He loved Tommy and he wanted so badly to be able to let her know, but Dollar couldn't speak.

A single tear made its way out of each of Dollar's eyes. Tommy kissed Dollar on his lips that were seeping with blood. It took every ounce of strength in her not to let the tears fall from her eyes. She then grabbed the gym bag full of money that was lying beside Dollar, placed the sunglasses back on her face, and exited the bank.

As Tommy walked to her car she could hear sirens approaching. Police cars whizzed by her as she put the key into the ignition and drove off. Everything had turned out as planned after all. Tommy knew that the anonymous tip she had called in to Hennessey from inside the bank lobby only seconds before Dollar entered would give her plenty of time to work out her plan before the cops arrived. Hennessey was a pig who had been trailing Dollar. Tommy had smelled her from the first time she'd met her. She anticipated Hennessey not being far behind. Tommy had also noticed that look in Hennessey's eyes when it came to Dollar. Ultimately Hennessey would have a hard time choosing between business and Dollar. Tommy'd had that problem as well once upon a time.

Dollar had taught Tommy to let other muthafuckas hustle and then catch them slippin'. He had trained her well. He just never imagined that he would one day be one of those muthafuckas that she would catch slippin'.

Like the song says, love will make you do right. Love will make you do wrong. Tommy's love for Dollar over the years was proof of that cliché. But in the end, she had to make a choice.

As Tommy drove away from the scene of the crime she removed the baseball cap and let her long hair flow in the wind.

Tommy then glanced down at the bag full of money and was sure over $500,000 was stuffed inside of it. That meant that after paying Storm and Thunder for the M&M she had ordered on Ral, she would have plenty left over to pack up her nieces, move to the East Coast, perhaps, and open up her bookstore.

Looking at herself in the rearview mirror, Tommy wondered if she would be able to live with the decision she had made against her comrades. She picked up a stack of the money from the gym bag. She ran it underneath her nose and inhaled deeply. After taking in the scent, that aphrodisiac to muthafuckas from the streets, Tommy exhaled. A smile found its way to her mouth. It was a smile that was a cross between a seductive grin and a mischievous smirk. It was an "I'm that bitch" smile. Yeah, she could live with the decision she had made. She could live with it just fine.

Inside the bank Dollar lay on the lobby floor barely holding on to his life. It was true what they say about one's life flashing before their eyes. Dollar thought about his brother and all of the times they had shared, the times they hadn't shared, and the times they would now never get to share. "Which of the dead men pictured on currency wasn't a president?" was a question that popped into Dollar's head. It was a question that he could have asked his little brother.

Ironically enough, Dollar even thought about his father. He thought about Romeo's last-ditch effort to make things right by him and his family. He gave his life for Dollar, to give Dollar back to his family, back to the streets. He wanted Dollar to be able to do for them what he hadn't done himself. Dollar had been too bitter and selfish to appreciate the sacrifice. But now, now that it no longer mattered, Dollar understood.

All of the dirt Dollar had done paraded through his mind as he lay near death. Dollar even thought back to his days of being locked up. Jail was hell and life was hell, but now, with all the fucked-up shit Dollar had done, he would truly experience hell. No way would the doors of heaven be open for this gangsta, or would they?

Dollar thought of Crissy's words back when he was in the jail infirmary: "God forgives us all." As Dollar took his last breath, he hoped that Crissy was right.

About the Author

Joy, a native of Columbus, Ohio, now writes under the name BLESSEDselling Author E. N. Joy. In the year 2000 she formed her own publishing company, END OF THE RAINBOW projects. Her sole purpose with END OF THE RAINBOW was to introduce in all those she encountered the quality of sharing her grandmother had instilled in her. This domino reaction would incite those with a passion in life to envision and manifest it, and for those unaware of their passion, to unearth it. Joy shares what she has learned in the literary industry by instructing writing and publishing workshops.

In 2004 Joy branched off into the business of literary consulting, in which she provides one-on-one consulting and literary services, such as editing, ghost writing, professional read-throughs, write behinds, etc. Her clients consist of *New York Times* bestselling authors, first-time authors, national bestselling authors, and entertainers. The end result of a couple of her clients' projects resulted in Joy being able to present their manuscripts to a publisher and land book deals for them.

Joy has come a long way since the debut of her first title, *Please Tell Me If the Grass Is Greener*. Since then she has published two diaries of poems titled *World On My Shoulders* and *Flower In My Hair*, she has collaborated on the publication of an erotica anthology titled *Twilight Moods* in which her contribution is titled "Daydreaming at Night," and she was also featured in *The Game: Short Stories about the Life*, in which her contribution is titled "Popped Cherry." Joy has also written a children's story titled *The Secret Olivia Told Me* that received an American Library Association Coretta Scott King Honor. The book club rights were acquired by Scholastic Books and it has sold almost 100,000 copies.

Joy self-published her first full-length novel titled *The Root of All Evil*. It was eventually picked up by a major publishing house and rereleased. In addition, they signed Joy to two other novels: her *Essence* magazine bestseller, *If I Ruled the World* (the prequel to *Mama I'm In Love with a Gangsta*), and *When Souls Mate* (the sequel to *The Root of All Evil*). They also signed Joy to a novella deal titled *An All-Night*

Man, in which Joy's contribution is titled "Just Wanna Love Ya." Joy's triumphant street novel titled *Dollar Bill* is also an *Essence* magazine bestseller. Needless to say, Joy will no longer be penning street lit, erotica, or secular fiction. Joy completed a Christian fiction novel titled *Me, Myself, and Him* (March 2008). In this novel, a woman struggles in her walk with Christ. Of course, this novel pushes the envelope of Christian fiction, but it wouldn't be Joy's true literary style if she didn't. "I have matured both as a writer and spiritually. My walk in life has changed, therefore my writing has changed. I just hope that the dedicated following of readers I've been so blessed to have earned will decide to take this spiritual journey in the written word with me, as I shift to pen what God has called me to do."

Joy continued by saying, "When God called me, I had to be obedient and say 'Yes, Lord.' My intent is not to switch up to a different audience. Hopefully I won't lose the readers I already have, but gain the readers I don't have. I know I might have to give up a few, but my soul still says YES!"

You can visit JOY at:

www.JoylynnJossel.com
www.enjoywrites.com

ORDER FORM
URBAN BOOKS, LLC
97 N18th Street
Wyandanch, NY 11798

Name (please print):_____

Address:_____

City/State:_____

Zip:_____

QTY	TITLES	PRICE

Shipping and handling: add $3.50 for 1st book, then $1.75 for each additional book. Please send a check payable to:

Urban Books, LLC

Please allow 4-6 weeks for delivery.